WRONG FOR ME

The Motor City Royals Series by Jackie Ashenden

Dirty for Me

Wrong for Me

Published by Kensington Publishing Corporation

WRONG FOR ME

FOR ME

Jackie Ashenden

KENSINGTON BOOKS
www.kensingtonbooks.com

KENSINGTON BOOKS are published by

Kensington Publishing Corp.
119 West 40th Street
New York, NY 10018

All Kensington titles, imprints, and distributed lines are available at special quantity discounts for bulk purchases for sales promotion, premiums, fund-raising, educational, or institutional use.

Special book excerpts or customized printings can also be created to fit specific needs. For details, write or phone the office of the Kensington Sales Manager: Kensington Publishing Corp., 119 West 40th Street, New York, NY 10018. Attn. Sales Department. Phone: 1-800-221-2647.

Kensington and the K logo Reg. U.S. Pat. & TM Off.

eISBN-13: 978-1-4967-0393-4
eISBN-10: 1-4967-0393-6
First Kensington Electronic Edition: December 2016

ISBN-13: 978-1-4967-0392-7
ISBN-10: 1-4967-0392-8
First Kensington Trade Paperback Printing: December 2016

10 9 8 7 6 5 4 3 2 1

Printed in the United States of America

To my little bro. Thinking of you. Always.

Chapter 1

Rachel Hamilton came to a stop outside the battered metal roller door that was the entrance to Black's Vintage Repair and Restoration, the motorcycle repair shop owned by her friend Gideon Black. She took a breath.

The acid eating a hole in her gut wasn't from fear.

It didn't have anything to do with the fact that Levi was back.

It was only because she hadn't felt like breakfast that morning and hadn't eaten anything. Perfectly understandable and explainable. Nothing whatsoever to do with how sick she'd felt, how her stomach kept turning over and over like a gymnast doing a complicated floor routine whenever she thought about Levi getting out of jail.

Nope. Nothing whatsoever to do with that.

Her palms were damp, but that was because it was hot. Same with her dry mouth. She should have had some water or something.

But you didn't because you would have thrown it up.

Rachel closed her eyes.

No fear. None. That's what had gotten her through life so far, and that's what would get her through this. She just had to pull her armor on, pretend she gave no fucks whatsoever. It was the only way to protect herself. It was the only way to deal with the man who'd been inside for eight years.

The man she'd put there herself.

Her former best friend.

Oh Jesus. She was shaking.

Okay, so perhaps she shouldn't think about that. She should think about how many fucks she gave instead. Which was none at all.

But naturally all the pep talks in the entire universe weren't going to help, and, when she opened her eyes, the nausea was still sitting right there and she was still shaking like a leaf.

Get. Yourself. The. Hell. Together.

Mentally she put herself in her usual snarky, sarcastic armor, the one specially designed to keep the world at bay, as she dug her nails into the palms of her hands. Her nails were nice and long these days, so they hurt biting into her skin. But that was good, and she welcomed the pain. It helped her focus, helped her center herself.

Taking another breath, she pushed open the small metal door inset into the big roller one, and stepped into Gideon's garage.

For a second she paused, trying to normalize her breathing, letting the familiarity of the garage settle her. It had always been a safe place for her, somewhere to go when she needed company, a good friend, a sympathetic ear. Gideon had gathered together a small group of kids from the Royal Road Outreach Center years ago, kids who were alone in the world, and even now, a decade later, they remained close friends. Gideon, Zoe, Zee and Levi. They were still there for one another, still looked out for one another.

Except you didn't. You weren't there when Levi needed you most.

Rachel swallowed, ignoring the thought. She couldn't afford to be thinking that kind of shit, not now. Not when she was barely holding it together as it was.

The smell of engine grease and oil filled her lungs. It was a comforting smell. There was a big metal shelf and a classic Cadillac up on a hoist blocking her vision, but she could hear the sound of voices. Gideon's, deep and rough, and Zoe's lighter tones. And then someone else's . . .

Rachel stilled, the sound going through her, painful as a sliver of glass pushed beneath her skin.

A masculine voice. One that used to be deep and rich, full of laughter and bright with optimism. A warm, encouraging, friendly voice. One that used to make her heart feel lighter whenever she heard it. But now . . . now it sounded dark, with a roughness that hadn't been there before. Like the voice of someone unused to speaking aloud.

Levi.

A shiver ran the entire length of her body.

He was here, only a few feet away. After eight years.

Come on. You have to do this. Stop being such a fucking coward.

She forced herself to move forward, past the metal shelf, heading down toward the end of the garage where a long workshop counter was positioned against the wall beneath a massive row of grimy windows, some with different colored panes of glass.

The summer sun was shining through those windows, illuminating Zoe, small and slender, her black hair pulled back in a ponytail, sitting on the counter with her legs dangling. Beside her was Gideon in his blue overalls, all shaggy black hair and heavily muscled shoulders, leaning back with his arms folded.

Another man stood with his back to her. He was as tall as Gideon, which was pretty goddamn tall at nearly six four, and built just as massively. The cotton of his black T-shirt stretched over shoulders that would have done a gladiator proud, while his jeans hung low on his lean hips. The combination of sun through the dirty windows and harsh fluorescent lighting of the garage drew out shades of tawny and deep gold in his shaggy dark hair.

Her heart twisted painfully hard.

She remembered those shoulders, that lean waist, that dark hair turning gold in some lights. Except he'd been . . . not quite as built back then. He'd been thinner, more greyhound than Rottweiler, and his hair had been cut short.

He's changed.

Well, of course he had. No one went to prison for eight years and came out the same person.

Perhaps if you'd even gone to see him once in all that time . . .

She blinked hard, digging her nails deeper, using the pain to focus once more.

And maybe she'd made a sound of some kind, an inadvertent gasp or the soles of her platform motorcycle boots scraping on the rough concrete floor, because suddenly, the man standing there with his back to her swung around.

She stopped dead, as if that sliver of glass had finally reached her heart.

Levi looked the same. Exactly the same. Still shockingly handsome with the strong line of his jaw, now rough with deep gold stubble, and high, sculpted cheekbones. Straight nose and long, deeply sensual mouth. Silver-blue eyes that . . .

Her breath caught, glass cutting straight through her heart and out the other side.

No. She was wrong. He didn't look the same. Not at all. There were lines around his mouth and eyes, lines that hadn't been there before, and that wasn't due to age. That was something more. There was a ring piercing one straight, dark eyebrow, and beneath that it looked like his eye had turned completely black, his pupil huge, a thin ring of silver blue circling it.

She couldn't stop looking, couldn't stop staring, the shock of seeing him hitting her like a wrecking ball. And then there were more shocks, more blows, as the differences in him began to filter through her consciousness.

The piercing. That one dark eye. The width of his shoulders and the way his T-shirt molded over a chest and stomach ridged with hard muscle. And his arms . . . Jesus, his tattoos. Around each powerful arm was a series of black bands, each one decreasing in width until the bands around his wrists were merely black lines. They were simple, beautiful, highlighting the strength of biceps, forearms, and wrists, and the deep, dark gold of his skin.

When the hell had he gotten those? Levi had never wanted tattoos, no matter how much she'd told him they'd suit him. She'd even teased him about being afraid of the pain, though she had known that wasn't the reason. Levi hadn't wanted the tattoos because he hadn't wanted anything to get in the way of his dreams of escape.

Escape from their shitty Royal Road neighborhood. Escape from Detroit.

He'd planned to get money enough to leave, get a good job in a high-flying company. Have an apartment that didn't have dealers lurking on the stairs and drunks on the sidewalk out front. Build a life that was about more than mere subsistence and struggle. A life that didn't include tattoos.

Looked like he didn't give a shit about that now.

You can't get a high-flying job with tattoos on your arms. You can't get one with a record either.

The acid in her gut roiled, and she had no idea what to say.

Levi didn't break the heavy, impossible silence, and he didn't smile. He just stared at her as if she were an insect he'd found crushed under the heel of his boot.

Say something, you idiot.

But her voice seemed to have deserted her entirely. All she could do was stare back at him, this man who'd once been her best friend. Whose dreams used to help her believe that there was more to life than existing on her grandma's Social Security checks and hiding from the child protection agencies that wanted to take her away and put her in a foster home. More to hope for than a crummy job in the local diner or behind the counter at the 7-Eleven.

But that friend had once been Levi Rush.

She didn't know who this man was, with his pierced eyebrow, tattoos, and aura of leashed violence and menace. A man like all the other thugs who seemed to infest Royal Road.

And then, as suddenly as he'd swung around to stare at her, the quality of his strangely asymmetrical stare changed. Became focused, intensifying on her the way a sniper locks onto a target.

It was unnerving. Frightening. And Levi had *never* frightened her before.

He looked even less like her friend than ever before. More like a general about to conquer a city. With her being the city.

Her protective mechanisms, ones she'd built up over a lifetime of being on her own, kicked in with a vengeance, and she'd lifted her chin almost before she'd had a chance to think about whether being prickly really was the best way to handle this.

Eight years ago she would have launched herself into his arms for a hug.

But it wasn't eight years ago. It was now. And she'd made so many mistakes already, what was one more?

"Hey, Levi," she said, her voice sounding pathetic and scratchy in the echoing space of the garage. "Long time no see."

Levi had waited a long time for this moment. Eight years to be exact. And it was happening just as he'd predicted.

He'd thought she'd stand there with her chin lifted, that guarded, fuck-you expression on her lovely face. Staring at him like he was a stranger, holding him at a distance the way she did with people she didn't know and didn't trust.

And sure enough, she was.

But even though he'd braced himself, the sight of her again after all these years emptied his lungs and killed his voice anyway. He should have known. She'd always had that effect on him, even back when she'd been fifteen and still in school, and he'd been eighteen and feeling like a dirty pervert for wanting her so badly. Even when she'd been his best friend, the person he was closest to, and being near her had been such a goddamn torture.

But now he wasn't her friend any longer, and he'd spent almost a decade in jail.

Maybe that was why he felt like he'd been hit over the head with an iron bar. He had just been deprived of female company.

But no, it wasn't that. Because on the drive back from St. Louis to Detroit with Gideon there had been plenty of women all over the goddamn place. And then there had been the warm hug Zoe had given him. Yet none of that had inspired this kind of feeling in him. Only Rachel did. Only Rachel *ever* had.

She stood there now, not far away from him, with her long hair loose down her back and dyed a brilliant, electric blue. She wore a tiny, tight-fitting tank top that plastered over her full breasts like plastic wrap, a little black denim miniskirt that barely grazed the tops of her thighs, fishnet tights, and black platform boots that made her long legs look even longer.

Jesus, she was so beautiful. Snow White, he'd once thought, back when he'd been that dumb fucking teenager and in love with her. Back when her hair had been black and her dark eyes had looked at him with warmth and trust and friendship.

No warmth in those dark eyes now though. Or sweetness in that full, sulky mouth of hers. Her lovely face was hard, her expression as tightly closed as the door to the cell that had been his home for so long.

Anger, the simmering rage that had become so much a part

of the fabric of his life that he almost didn't notice it anymore, tightened inside him.

He ignored it. There was plenty of time for that. Plenty of time for everything now.

Levi almost smiled. Because that expression on her face wasn't going to last long if he had anything to do with it. And he was most certainly going to have something to do with it.

After eight years inside he had some justice to claim.

And he was going to claim it from her.

Levi straightened and folded his arms. Stared at her. He could feel his dick begin to get hard, reacting to all the honey-colored skin revealed by her fishnet tights and the luscious curve of her breasts beneath her tank top. But he'd had a long time to learn how to control his bodily responses, and so he controlled them now. Effortlessly.

Something in her gaze flickered briefly, but he knew what it was. He'd become very adept at looking for fear in people, and he could see it in her right now.

She was afraid of him, and it didn't cause him any regret at all. Because she should be.

Rachel shifted on her feet, betraying her nervousness, which was hugely satisfying. "So, not even a hello?" Her husky, sexy voice was edged with a familiar sarcasm, yet even so, he heard the fear running underneath the sarcasm like a cold current in a hot spring.

Satisfaction turned over inside him, settling right down in his gut like a sleepy animal.

Nervous and afraid. Just the way he wanted her.

Slowly, he began to walk toward her.

Rachel's eyes widened, but she held her ground.

He didn't stop.

And when it became clear that he wasn't going to, her eyes widened even further, a momentary flare of fear lighting up the darkness in them. She took a couple of steps back.

He didn't stop, moving inexorably forward.

She cursed and began to back up faster, stumbling a little as his longer stride brought him closer, until she was walking backwards quickly, her breathing getting faster. "Levi, what the fuck are you—" Her words were cut off as she backed straight into the door to the garage.

And he kept coming, closer and closer, right up to her, putting out his hands at the last minute and placing them with great care on either side of her head, caging her against the door with his body.

She shrank back against the metal, obviously trying to pull away from him, but there was nowhere for her to go.

And this time, he did smile.

Because finally she was exactly where he'd pictured her for so many lonely fucking years. So many *angry* fucking years.

At his mercy.

"Hello, Rachel," he said softly, clearly.

She stared back at him for a second, the fear large and black in those wide, dark eyes. And then the actual fact of her nearness began to penetrate his consciousness.

They weren't touching, but he could feel her heat, smell the scent of her skin—sweet, like she was something good to eat, and yet not too sweet. Vanilla maybe or some kind of flower smell; he wasn't sure which. He didn't remember her smelling like that before, but underneath that there was a slight hint of feminine musk that was all Rachel, so achingly familiar.

Someone behind him was shouting at him, but he ignored it, as desire, want, need, rose up inside him, hungry and raw, desperate to claim her. Because she was so close, so fucking close, and it had been so fucking *long*, and he'd promised himself . . .

But right at that moment the fear vanished from her eyes like a light turning off, and anger flared instead. "What the hell is wrong with you?" Her hands came up, and she shoved at his chest. "Get the fuck away from me!"

She was surprisingly strong, but he'd had eight years of resisting people who'd tried to push him in various different ways, and, if he didn't want to be pushed, he wouldn't be. Then again, he'd made his point, so he let her shove him back a couple of steps, putting some distance between them.

He heard his name being called again—probably Gideon getting pissed with him—but again Levi ignored it, his focus entirely on the woman in front of him.

Her cheeks had an angry flush to them, her chest rising and falling fast in time with her breathing. Anger glittered in her eyes and filled the space between the two of them, tight, hot, and dense as a neutron star.

Then she stepped forward, and this time it was her turn to get right up close, to get in his face the way he'd gotten into hers. "What kind of hello is that, Levi?"

As if she were the one who was justified in getting angry. As if she had the right to demand things from him.

His own anger, already simmering away, boiled over.

He reached for her, sliding his arm around her waist and hauling her against him, eight years of rage dying to be let loose. He had so much he wanted to say to her, and yet, when it came down to it, only one thing mattered.

She had to pay. She had to pay for what she'd done to him.

Their gazes clashed, both of them furious. Her hands were flat against the plane of his chest, pushing at him hard, her body rigid. Yet despite all that, she felt so good against him. Warm and soft, everything a woman should be . . .

"Hey!" Gideon shouted from behind him. "What the fuck is going on? Let her go, Levi."

Yeah, Jesus. Get a hold of yourself. This is not the way it's supposed to go.

Fuck. His control was usually way better than this. He had to stick with the plan, not let her make him crazy like she always used to, damn her.

He gave a low, slightly feral-sounding laugh and released her, raising his hands in surrender and stepping back. "Nothing's going on. Just saying hi."

Rachel's chin was lifted, fury glittering in her eyes. Her arms were at her sides, hands curled into fists like she was ready to throw a punch. Spots of color glowed on her cheeks, and she was looking at him like he was the devil himself.

Fair enough. As far as she was concerned, he was.

Gideon had come up beside them, giving Rachel a look before glancing back at Levi. "I don't want this shit in my garage; I already told you that. I know you two have issues, but—"

"Issues?" Levi interrupted, unable to help himself. "What issues? Oh, right, you mean the fact that she never visited me in the whole eight years I was inside? Not once? Or even how she fucked off when it was time to deliver her statement to the police and—"

"*Enough.*"

It had been a long time since Levi had obeyed anyone who wasn't a guard, and he wasn't about to start now, especially since he was free. But years of respect and trust had ensured Gideon a certain amount of loyalty, so Levi made himself stop and shut the fuck up. Probably a good thing anyway since clearly he needed to get himself back under control again.

Rachel had said nothing, but as he watched, he could see a fine tremble shaking her, almost imperceptible, like a subtle earthquake.

Anger. Definitely anger.

Gideon looked at her. "You okay?"

Levi fought down the instinctive burst of irritation that went through him. Christ, as if he'd ever hurt her. Put the fear of God into her, sure, and maybe scare her. Make her suffer in a very specific way, definitely. But no, he'd never hurt her, and Gideon should know that.

Then again, Gideon knew how angry Levi was. Levi used to

ask him where Rachel was every time Gideon came to visit. And Gideon knew how bitter the answer "she decided not to come" had been, especially when Zee and Zoe had also made the effort.

But not Rachel. Never Rachel.

She would pay for that too.

Rachel gave a stiff nod, glancing away from Levi at last. One hand lifted to rub her arm, a familiar, nervous gesture from years ago.

He found his gaze following the movement of her fingers, noticing for the first time her tattoos, a full-length sleeve of deep red roses and other flowers amid dark leaves spilling down over her skin. The drooping head of a rose hung over her shoulder too, scattering a fall of red petals like drops of blood over her chest.

It was a beautiful design. Beautiful work. And familiar. She'd used to draw stuff like that in the notebooks she had constantly lugged around with her. Was it one of her designs?

Gideon cursed under his breath. "Look, I get that this is difficult. But if you two can't be in the same room without wanting to kill each other, maybe it would be better if Rachel went home."

"It's fine, Gideon," Levi said.

"Is it?" The other man's dark eyes were sharp. "Because it sure as hell doesn't look fine to me."

Levi crushed his anger flat. Made himself hard and cold, the way he'd been for the past eight years. The only way he'd managed to survive. "I appreciate your coming for me, Gideon. I appreciate everything you've offered me since I got back. But what's between Rachel and me is none of your fucking business."

"What's between us?" Rachel's voice was hoarse and a little thick. "There's *nothing* between us. Nothing at all."

Levi shifted his gaze back to her. He didn't speak, just held her dark eyes with his, because they both knew exactly how much bullshit that was.

Her mouth set in a hard line, and he remembered that, her stubborn will. Like him, she hated backing down. On anything.

Well, this week she would. He'd make her.

Gideon sighed. "Okay, fine. Rip each other to shreds; see if I care. But don't do it here, okay? Blood is very difficult to get out of concrete."

Rachel said nothing, staring at Levi for one angry second.

Then abruptly she turned on her heel and strode out of the garage.

Oh, shit no. She wasn't leaving that easily, not when he hadn't said what he wanted to say.

Levi stepped forward after her, only to find Gideon's large, powerful hand gripping his shoulder, stopping him.

"Levi," Gideon said in a low voice. "Let her go."

Levi stiffened.

No. This is Gideon, remember? Not Mace or any of his hench-assholes. Or one of the guards. So maybe relax and not break his fucking arm.

Levi let out a long, silent breath, making his muscles loosen. Then he glanced at his friend.

In the car on the long drive from the Central Michigan Correctional Facility in St. Louis back to Detroit, Gideon hadn't mentioned Rachel, keeping the conversation firmly about what was happening with Zoe and Zee, and the garage. Filling Levi in on how Zee had been revealed to be big, bad Joshua Chase's long-lost son and on his engagement to the daughter of one of Detroit's most wealthy families. And then Gideon had told Levi that Levi had a job he could come back to and could crash on Gideon's sofa until he found himself a place to live.

It was all typical Gideon, generous to a fault. But the guy was operating on the assumption that Levi was the same man who'd gone to prison on manslaughter charges eight years earlier.

And he wasn't.

The Levi who'd gone into prison had been a boy compared to the man he was now. A much harder man. A man who knew what he wanted and had put into motion meticulous plans on how to get it.

After all, he'd had a lot of time to think about it.

Levi smiled at his friend and gently pulled Gideon's hand off his shoulder.

Then he strode straight out the door after Rachel.

Chapter 2

Rachel walked swiftly along the sidewalk, her heart beating fast and her palms damp, rage bubbling inside her like a vat of boiling oil. And she didn't even know whom she was angrier at: Levi or herself.

Levi for coming at her like a speeding train. Or herself for standing there and taking it.

Of course, what was even worse was the fact that getting angry with him was wrong, especially when he had every right to be pissed at her, every right to feel furious.

Every right to push you up against that door?

Her mind shied away from that while her heartbeat accelerated and her mouth dried.

She should never have stood there like a fucking idiot and let him come at her. She should have stood her ground and faced him down like she did with everyone other asshole who tried to get in her face.

But you didn't. Because you're afraid of him.

The summer sun was hot on her shoulders, but inside she felt cold. Like she'd been cold for weeks, months . . . years . . .

"You mean the fact that she never visited me in the whole eight years I was inside? Or even how she fucked off when it was time to deliver her statement to the police?"

She swallowed down the hard lump in her throat.

She'd known he would be angry with her, but she hadn't been prepared for quite how *furious* he actually was. A small part of her had hoped that he'd understand why she hadn't come, why she'd run away when the police came to take her statement all those years ago. That maybe he'd have thought about it and realized how impossible it had been for her.

But clearly he hadn't. And really, she didn't know why she'd expected he would, because she sure as hell wouldn't have thought about it if she had been in his shoes.

The lump in her throat refused to go down.

She should never have gone to say hello the day he'd returned to Royal. She should have waited a few days. Shit, maybe even gone out of town. But she'd wanted to not be a coward, just this once.

You still are.

Rachel bit her lip. Yeah, she was. No point in denying it. She'd fucked up big time already, and now she was fucking up even more by running away. Fleeing like a scared little girl or a kicked puppy with her tail between her legs.

God, she was pathetic.

Making a cursory check for traffic, she crossed the road, heading toward the only other place in her life that she felt safe—Sugar Ink, the tattoo studio she'd set up a couple of years earlier in an old, abandoned factory building down the street from Gideon's.

There would be time to think about Levi later. Right now, she had some clients due and her other pet project to think about— getting enough money together to actually buy the building from whoever owned it.

It had been abandoned for years before she'd moved in, another casualty of the collapse of the auto industry and Detroit's huge population decline. She'd claimed it for her tattoo studio, and since then, she'd started encouraging local artists to use it as an impromptu art gallery. The idea had taken off, and now the once boarded-up, abandoned wreck had taken on a new lease on life. A former tattoo client had set up a café in one of the rooms, turning out the best coffee outside of downtown, and at night, one of her artist friends served drinks behind a makeshift bar. All of this was illegal of course, but the cops turned a blind eye, because hell, Royal Road needed something good and positive in the neighborhood.

It needed fewer abandoned buildings and more people going about the business of living.

Her little operation was going well, but she knew that if she wanted to keep it going on a permanent basis, she was going to have to find some way of buying the building itself. Already there were developers poking around in Royal, looking for bargains, wanting a slice of the gentrification projects that were sweeping the city.

Rachel was all for improvements, but gentrification smacked of money, and no one in Royal had money. The last thing the neighborhood needed was a whole lot of shops and apartments that no one could afford to buy or live in.

She slowed her pace as her building loomed into view, then came to a stop, hauling her keys out of the pocket of her denim mini.

The building was brick, the outside liberally coated in graffiti, which she'd left since much of it was bright and colorful and perfect for a tattoo studio. But she'd replaced all the massive windows and gutted half the interior of the ground floor, leaving a huge, airy, industrial-feeling space that was her studio.

It had taken her a long time to get it done, even with Zee and

Gideon's help, but it had been worth all the time and effort. She'd given them both tattoos to say thank you, and had paid Gideon back every last cent he'd loaned her.

It was all hers now, completely. All except the building itself.

Unlocking the big glass door of the studio, she pushed it open and went in, pausing to switch on the pink neon Sugar Ink sign she'd stuck in one of the tall, narrow windows.

Then she crossed over to the big metal counter near the door that Gideon had made for her and switched on the computer sitting on it, wanting to check her client list for the day. Xavier, the other tattoo artist who worked with her, would be starting in an hour or so, but her first client was due in about ten minutes.

She placed her hands on the counter and felt the cool metal against her palms. Then she breathed slowly in and slowly out, trying to calm herself down, because no one wanted a stressed and angry tattoo artist working on them.

The studio door opened abruptly, then banged shut.

Dammit. Was her first client here already? Clearly they were nervous if they were here this early.

Rachel sighed, plastering on a smile and looking up.

Only to meet one silver-blue eye and one dark, both staring at her with such intensity all the air in her lungs vanished for the second time that day.

Fucking Levi had followed her.

She swallowed, then straightened up. "What the hell are you doing here?"

He didn't answer immediately. Instead he shifted his glance from her, doing a slow survey of her studio as if he owned it himself and was cataloging every piece of it. The bank of tattoo chairs and workbenches that ran down one wall, the worn but comfortable velvet couch that sat opposite the metal counter and served as a waiting area. The jewelry cases that showcased local artists' work and the small collection of clothes racks where she sold a limited number of pieces by more local designers. The worn, exposed brick of the walls, the battered wood floor. Then, finally, his gaze settled on the big mural that adorned the wall opposite the chairs.

It was one she'd painted herself as her first claim on the building. The head of a woman with flowing black hair and sugar-skull imagery overlaid on her face—big dark eyes and roses and birds flying around her head with more roses and other flowers behind her. Like the roses on Rachel's arm, it was a gritty reminder that there was beauty even in the middle of all the dirt and violence that was life.

His gaze lingered on the image for a long moment, and stupidly she could feel a flush rising in her cheeks.

Crazy. Why the hell would she blush at his looking at that mural? She wasn't embarrassed about it. Shit, every client who came in here saw it. What did she care what he thought about it? What did she care if he even looked at it?

Because you've always cared what he thinks. And you still do.

Rachel forced the thought away. She'd been on her own for years. She didn't need anyone's approval, and she didn't need his either.

Levi shifted, tilting his head as he studied the picture, and she found her gaze roving over him in return, following the way the black cotton of his T-shirt pulled tight across his broad chest and around the swell of his biceps. How it molded to the taut, ridged plane of his stomach and highlighted his lean waist.

So much power. So much strength. She'd felt it when he'd backed her up against that door in the garage. He'd come at her like an avalanche, unstoppable, inexorable, and . . . Christ, she didn't even know why she'd backed away from him considering she never backed away from anything.

Maybe it had been the anger in his eyes, because there had

been so much of it and it was so very obvious. He'd been burning with it, and something inside her had just . . . been scared. Not that he would hurt her physically, because he'd never been that kind of guy, but that he'd hurt her in other ways. Emotional ways.

You deserve the hurt. You deserve the pain.

Her jaw tightened. Jesus, she'd paid enough, hadn't she? Anyway, it hadn't been pain she'd felt when he'd caged her against the metal of the door. There had been something else there, an undercurrent of heat beneath the fear. A kind of breathless excitement she hadn't felt since . . .

You were sixteen.

Oh, fuck.

Rachel tore her gaze from him, staring down at the metal counter instead, her heartbeat racing. God, she'd thought she'd put that hideous mess behind her years ago. Apparently not.

Levi had lived with his alcoholic dad in the apartment next to the one she had shared with her grandma, and they'd gotten to know each other as neighbors. He'd been older than her and kind and funny and made her laugh when nothing else much did. He helped her out when she needed help. Her grandma's dementia had gotten to the stage where she couldn't do a lot of things herself and needed to be watched, and even though Rachel preferred looking after her grandma herself and hated to ask anyone for help in case it drew the wrong sort of attention, she had let him help. And of course, she'd fallen into the throes of a hopeless crush on him because he was also tall and unbearably good-looking, and basically the only other person in the world with whom she'd had any sort of connection.

He'd been the one who'd dragged her out to the Royal Road Outreach Center, where she'd met Gideon and Zee and Zoe. He'd been the one to make her a part of that little surrogate family.

But he'd never shown any interest in her in *that* way whatsoever, a fact that had caused her much heartache at the time. So she'd told herself to forget about it, to just see him as a friend. And eventually the heartache had disappeared and so had her crush.

It had been hard and painful at the time though, and she did *not* want to go there again. Especially not considering the mess she'd made of their former friendship—emphasis definitely on the "former."

"This place is yours, right?" The deep rumble of Levi's voice was almost a shock after the silence.

Steadying herself, she lifted her head and found his gaze on hers, the silver blue of one eye in stark contrast to the lightless dark of the other. And she had to force herself to hold his gaze, to act as if the intensity of it didn't scare her. "Yes. Didn't Gideon tell you?"

"He might have mentioned it. On one of his visits."

She caught the implication, the slight emphasis on the words "his visits," making the guilt shift inside her. She ignored it. "Answer the damn question, Levi. What are you doing here?"

"I want to talk to you."

"I can't right now," she said flatly. "I have a client coming in ten minutes."

"Cancel it."

"What? No. I'm not canceling it. Look, what about you come back later and we'll figure out a time to—"

"No." The word cut across hers like the blade of a guillotine coming down across a sheet of paper. Or someone's neck.

She blinked. "What the hell do you mean 'no'?"

"I mean no, I'm not fucking coming back later. We're having this conversation, Rachel, and we're having it now."

An unnamed fear curled in her heart, tangling with the shock of seeing him again and the guilt she'd buried so far down she had almost forgotten it was there. But she felt the guilt now. Oh yeah, she *really* felt it now.

It made her angry.

You always knew you'd have to face him one day. That you'd have to explain.

Well, sure. She owed him an explanation; that was true. But she couldn't let him come in here and start ordering her around like he owned the place. Because he didn't. This was *her* place. This was *her* studio. In here she had the power, not him.

"You can wait an hour, can't you?" She threw her shoulders back, gripping the metal of the counter for strength. "I have a business to run, and coming in here demanding I cancel my appointments, just because you want to talk to me, is pretty douchey behavior, Levi."

He tilted his head, studying her for a long minute. Then he came toward her slow and easy, like a hunter stalking prey, his boots making heavy sounds on the wooden floor. And she felt herself wanting to take a step back the way she had in the garage, run away before he caught her.

But no. She was not going to run. Not this time.

Rachel took a silent breath and waited, still holding on to the counter, proud of herself that she didn't look away or flinch as he came closer and closer, until he stopped right in front of her and there was only the counter between them.

She'd forgotten how he towered over her. And now that he was much broader through the chest and shoulders, his presence felt like a mountain looming over her.

A mountain that would fall on her and crush her if she wasn't careful.

"Cancel the appointment, Rachel," he ordered, not taking his gaze from hers. "Or I'll do it for you."

A helpless tremble shook her, which was infuriating. God, she really had to get herself together. Showing weakness of any kind was a mistake, as she'd learned to her cost.

"You do that, and I'll call the cops." At least her voice sounded level, thank God. "I'll have you arrested for trespassing."

An expression flickered through those fascinating eyes of his, and she thought it looked like satisfaction. "You can try. But it won't be me they'll be taking away."

She frowned. "What?"

This time there was no mistaking it as one corner of his mouth turned up. Definitely satisfaction. "I can't be trespassing on my own property," he said slowly, as if to a child.

"What do you mean 'your own property'? This building is owned—"

"By me."

Shock held her rigid. That couldn't be true. This building had been abandoned for years, and she'd been trying to track down the owners of it for a while now and hadn't been able to find them. Anyway, how could he have bought it? He'd been in jail. Buildings cost money, and he didn't have any.

"Don't be stupid," she said. "You don't own this building."

His eyes glittered. "Oh, but I do. In fact, I bought it a couple of years back." His smile deepened, as white and savage as a tiger's. "Which means that I'm not the one trespassing. You are."

Rachel paled, and, in another life, if he hadn't become the man he was and she had still been the girl he remembered, he might have felt sorry for her. But neither of those two things was true, and so he didn't.

Instead he watched the color drain from her skin with almost clinical interest. He'd thought a lot about this moment too, when he finally told her that she and her precious studio were illegally trespassing in the building he owned, revealing at last the leverage he was going to use against her.

He'd imagined her face, imagined her going white just as she was doing now. Or maybe flushing with anger instead, her dark eyes glittering.

It didn't matter though, what she felt. Her emotions were irrelevant.

He wanted what he wanted, and he was going to get it.

He was fucking *owed*.

"No." Rachel started shaking her head. "No, that's ridiculous. You can't own my building. You just can't."

"I can, and I do."

Her forehead creased. "But . . . you've been in *jail*."

"So?"

"So?" she repeated. "How can you have bought it if you've been in jail?"

"I had contacts who bought it on my behalf." He watched her, savagely pleased at the bewilderment that crossed her face. "What? You think I did nothing with my life all those years? That I just sat there with my thumb up my ass?"

"No . . . But I . . ." She stopped, her tank pulling tight as she took in another quick breath, long, silky black lashes veiling her gaze. "Okay, so I know you want to talk, and I'm good with that. But could we please do it at another, more appropriate time? Like when I haven't got a full client list?"

Of course. Because it was all about her.

Levi put his palms down on the metal counter in front of him and leaned on it. She was looking down, refusing to meet his eyes, the little coward.

"I don't give a fuck about your client list," he said quietly and with finality. "You're going to listen to what I have to say. So you'd better get comfortable, because this could take a while."

As if on cue, the door to the studio opened and there was the sound of tentative footsteps coming closer.

Levi pushed himself away from the counter and turned to find some skinny little shit of a guy looking nervously around. Obviously the client Rachel had been talking about.

"Fuck off," Levi ordered curtly.

"Hey," Rachel protested from behind him. "You can't talk to my—"

Levi turned and silenced her with a look, before turning back to the client again.

The man was staring at him wide-eyed, looking like he might wet himself.

"What did I say?" Levi said.

Not needing to be told twice, the man took off out the door without a word.

There was a sudden, dense silence.

Levi swung around, meeting Rachel's furious gaze head on.

She'd gone pale with anger. "You asshole." Her voice was low. "You fucking asshole."

Like he gave a crap what she thought of him. For two years the fact that she never came to visit, that she never contacted him had haunted him, had eaten away at him. Then his father had died, and Levi had been beaten within an inch of his life for getting on the wrong side of one of the prison gangs, and after that, he'd stopped giving two fucks about anyone or anything.

Nothing except the icy rage that had made a home for itself inside his chest. And the justice he would claim for himself once he got out.

So she could get all angry with him for being rude to one of her clients; he didn't care.

The only thing that mattered was getting the explanation he was owed.

"Sit down," he ordered, inclining his head toward the velvet sofa opposite the metal shop counter.

She straightened, her hands curled into fists again, like she was going to take a punch at him, her expression full of cool defiance. "No."

Stubborn little bitch. Well, two could play at that game. "Sit. The fuck. Down."

"I'm not going to—"

"Or else I'll come around that counter, pick you up, and sit you down there myself."

Her mouth went flat, twin flames of anger burning in her eyes. Then with a short, sharp movement, she pulled open a drawer under the counter and took something out. A Colt nine millimeter. "Pull another stunt like you did at Gideon's, and you might find yourself without some valuable part of your anatomy." She wrapped her fingers around the weapon, holding it in her small hand. "Understand?"

The Levi of years ago would have been horrified at the thought that she'd need to defend herself like this from him.

The man he was now only lifted an eyebrow. "Sure you know how to use that?"

"I don't know." Her dark eyes promised retribution. "Want to find out?"

But he was tired of arguing with her. "Go sit down."

She went this time without protest, holding the gun in her hand as she rounded the counter and went past him, sauntering as if she had all the time in the world, swinging her hips so his gaze was helplessly drawn to the bounce of her blue ponytail and the sway of her ass.

His dick liked that. His dick liked that a lot. Because it really hadn't seen anything as good for far too fucking long. Unfortunately though, it was going to have to wait.

Before he'd been inside, he'd never had trouble getting laid. He knew the power of his own looks, knew the power of a smile too, and the combo had gotten him as much pussy as he could handle.

All except the one woman he couldn't have. Her.

He'd never turned his attention on her, no matter how badly he'd wanted her. She'd been too young and her home life too fucked up for him to mess with her like that. So they'd stayed just friends.

But he'd always harbored dreams about how it would be if they weren't living in Royal. If they could somehow make it out together. If he were as rich and powerful as the guys in suits downtown. He'd take her away then, take her away where life was better, where they could be happy.

Unfortunately, that plan had been ruined by eight years in jail.

Fortunately, in that time he had gotten together a better one.

Rachel sat down, leaning back against the couch cushions, the gun in her lap. Her hair gleamed deep blue against the red velvet, making her skin seem even paler, especially in contrast to her black fishnets and miniskirt.

Black and red and blue. Vivid, intense colors for a vivid, intense woman.

She looked up at him, her chin proud and stubborn, her eyes guarded. "Talk then. Say what you've got to say, and get the hell out of here."

No prizes for guessing why she was so defensive. She knew what she'd done and that it had been wrong.

He took a few steps over to the couch, then stopped, folding his arms and staring down at her. "Two things. First, eight years and you never came to see me. Not once."

The hard line of her mouth flattened even further. "Yeah, look, I'm—"

"Shut the fuck up. I haven't finished."

She fell silent, her gaze falling to the gun in her lap.

"I'm up here, coward." How dare she not even look at him?

Slowly, her lashes lifted, and her gaze met his. And all he could see was that defensive rage. But he knew where that was coming from: she felt guilty. Which was good, because she should.

"Second, you never came to give that statement to the police after it happened. It might not have ended up making any difference to my sentence, but you still never came and gave it."

He remembered that night vividly. Following Rachel down the alley at the back of Gino's because he'd been worried about her, his heart sinking with every step. Then seeing the shady figure of a well-known dealer, the guy pulling at her clothing, and her pale, terrified face. Levi hadn't thought; he'd only moved fast, jerking the asshole off her and punching him in the face. The guy had fallen and had hit his head on the pavement. There was the sickening crack of bone hitting concrete, and then all the blood . . .

Rachel said nothing, her dark gaze flickering as if she wanted to look away, but was forcing herself not to.

Good. Because he wasn't going to make this any fucking easier for her.

"I went to jail for years," he said, making his voice flat and cold. "All because I wanted to help you. Which makes it your turn now."

Her throat moved in a convulsive swallow. "What do you mean, it's my 'turn' now? I wouldn't have thought you'd want my help."

"I don't want your help. But you owe me, and so I've come to collect."

Another flicker in her dark eyes. "Collect what?"

He didn't smile this time, because there was nothing to smile about. This was as serious as it got. "You, Rachel. I've come to collect you."

She frowned. "I don't get it."

Of course she wouldn't get it. He'd never told her how he felt. He had guarded and protected her, made sure she never caught a glimpse of what he really wanted from her. Because he'd been her friend, and she'd needed a friend more than she needed anything else.

Well, now that friendship was dead and gone, and he could do whatever the fuck he liked.

"It's very simple," he said. "There's a thing I want. A thing I want from you."

Maybe she knew; maybe she sensed it, because she suddenly went very still. "What thing? If you want to know why I didn't come, I didn't because—"

"Don't give me your fucking excuses." He locked her gaze with his, leaving her in no doubt that he meant every word of what he was going to say next. "I know why you didn't come, believe me. In fact, I've had nothing but time to think about what I'd done that would make you leave me to rot in that fucking jail cell. And you know what conclusion I came to?"

"No." Her voice was hoarse, barely audible.

"I came to the conclusion that you didn't give a shit."

Her jaw went tight, and she blinked. But she stayed silent, lines of tension bracketing her lovely, sulky mouth.

"What? No protest? Well, I guess that's just going to make what I say next pretty fucking easy." He dropped his arms and stalked over to her, closing the remaining distance so he was standing right in front of her. Then he leaned forward and placed his hands on the back of the couch on either side of her head, so there was no chance of retreat, no chance of escape. Because the time had come for her to stop avoiding him once and for all.

"So don't worry. You don't have to give me your excuses," he said softly. "The thing I want is you. In every way there is."

She blinked. "You mean . . . ?"

"I mean, I've wanted you a long time, Rachel Hamilton. So now I'm going to have you."

He could see the shock cross her face and bloom in the depths of her eyes, all her muscles stiffening. "I see." Each word was so precise it could have been etched in glass. "And do I get a choice about this?"

He leaned in a little further so his mouth was near her ear, inhaling the sweet scent of her, letting it go straight to his head like the kick of a good bourbon. "Of course you do. But if you say no, I'm throwing you and your goddamn studio out of this building and knocking it the fuck down."

Chapter 3

Rachel stared straight ahead; all her muscles locked and stiff with shock.

It was like a pair of hands was squeezing her ribcage, compressing her lungs so that all the air rushed out of them and prevented her from taking another breath.

Her brain wouldn't work. It kept stumbling over the phrase *I've wanted you a long time, Rachel Hamilton,* then picking itself up, only to stumble again over *So now I'm going to have you.*

He couldn't mean what she thought he meant. He couldn't. Could he?

It was difficult to think with him leaning over her like that. In fact, it was next to impossible. Because not only did she have to contend with the shock of what he'd said, she also had to contend with the fact that he was pretty fucking close. And that she could feel the heat from his body for the second time that day, and it was pouring off him, hot as a goddamn furnace.

She could smell him too, an unfamiliar, woody, smoky scent that seemed to ignite something inside her. She didn't remember him smelling like that before and it was . . . God, so good. Because under that smoky scent was a smell she *did* remember. Masculine and warm. The one that reminded her of friendship, easy smiles, and easier laughter. Levi.

She blinked. His muscular arms were on either side of her, the fascinating black rings of those tattoos banding them, and she had the almost uncontrollable urge to touch the tattoos, trace them. And then maybe to touch the soft cotton of his T-shirt, follow the ridges of his abs, see whether they felt as hard and as hot as they looked . . .

What the hell are you doing?

Good question. Because she sure as hell had no idea. She'd wanted him once before, but that had been before she'd really understood what it was that men and women did together. And then she'd found out, and then . . .

No. She wouldn't think of that. Anyway, looking at him like that was the last thing she should be doing, especially considering the other thing he'd said. About kicking her out of her building.

His building now.

The thought was an electric shock, making a shudder go right through her and breaking the weird physical paralysis that was gripping her.

She turned her head, meeting his ferocious gaze head on.

No, she wasn't going to talk about his threat to throw her out of this beautiful building and destroy the business she'd built with so much blood, sweat, and tears. Or about the fact that he'd wanted her for years, something she'd used to dream about when she'd been younger and far more innocent. Her mind simply shied away from that, and she just couldn't deal with it.

Instead she stared at him, ignoring everything he'd just told her, focusing on his handsome face instead. "What happened to your eye?" she asked bluntly.

He didn't even blink at the question. "I had the shit beaten out of me. One of my pupils is permanently dilated."

Her insides twisted. Oh Jesus. He'd been beaten hard enough he'd sustained a permanent injury?

What? Jail's not exactly a party; you know that. Just like you also know who put him in that jail to start with.

She forced that thought away too, because that was another minefield she didn't want to enter. "What about the eyebrow ring? I thought you didn't like piercings."

"I don't. I keep it as a reminder."

"A reminder of what?"

He moved his hands on the back of the couch, shifting back a little. "Of what happens when people fuck with me."

She shouldn't have asked her next question; she really shouldn't. But she couldn't help herself. It just came out. "And what happens when people fuck with you?"

He smiled, and it was terrifying. And a completely separate part of her could only watch in confusion because it was so very unlike the Levi she knew. That Levi had never looked dangerous. Oh, he'd always been very certain about what he wanted, very sure. He'd possessed a kind of confidence in himself that had bordered on arrogant, but it had never bothered her. In fact, she'd found it oddly reassuring. With her own life full of uncertainty, Levi's lack of uncertainty had been comforting.

Still, he'd never had this . . . edge to him. This aura of contained violence and barely leashed menace. A wildness that thrilled something inside her right down to her most basic level.

Maybe that was why it was so terrifying. Because wildness was the last thing she wanted, and certainly not now, not when she'd finally gotten some stability in her life.

"What happens?" Levi lifted one hand from the back of the couch, and, before she could move, he took her chin in his hand, holding her tightly. She stiffened, trying to pull away because for some reason his fingers felt like they were burning her. But he only firmed his grip. "What happens is this," he said, and leaned forward.

And covered her mouth with his.

She froze, unable to believe what was happening.

Levi was kissing her. *Levi* was fucking kissing her.

Adrenalin surged like the tide, and she sat there absolutely rigid, because it had been twelve years since anyone had kissed her, and she still remembered what that had been like. Wet. Uncomfortable. Unpleasant and wrong.

Because the last person to kiss her had been Evan.

So it was a shock to find that there was nothing unpleasant about this. Nothing uncomfortable or wrong. Levi's mouth was firm, decisive and yet soft, warm.

It was so unexpected she couldn't breathe. Couldn't move.

He ran his tongue along the seam of her lips, then pushed inside, and all of a sudden, a prickling wave of heat swept over her skin, leaving her almost shaking.

God, what was happening to her? Because this was Levi, her friend. And she'd kissed him a thousand times before, chaste kisses on the cheek or the forehead. But nothing like *this* . . . Slow and lazy and achingly hot.

This is what a kiss should be. . . .

Something inside her rebelled, at the same time as something else surrendered, and she shuddered, her mouth opening under his as he began to explore her more deeply, holding tight to her chin. And it felt like his fingertips were imprinting themselves on her skin, as if every whorl and ridge would be marked there when he let her go.

He tasted like peppermints, but with a dark, alcoholic flavor underneath, like bourbon or maybe rum, and it was so . . . good. She could feel her body begin to belatedly wake to life, her skin getting tight, an ache between her thighs.

Evan made you feel good too, sometimes.

An old, half-forgotten instinct kicked in, and suddenly she was ripping her chin from his grip, knocking away one of his arms, and propelling herself up, the gun slipping sideways off her lap and onto the cushions as she got off the couch.

He let her go, saying nothing as she took a few unsteady steps, putting some distance between them, her back to him. Her heartbeat was hammering in her ears, and her mouth felt weird, all full and swollen. She couldn't seem to get enough air in her lungs.

"Get out." A faint huskiness edged her voice, the frayed edge of a fear she thought she'd long put behind her. "Just get the hell away from me."

"I want an answer, Rachel." His voice behind her was as cold and as flat as it had been before. As if he hadn't just punched a hole clean through the armor she wore every day. "I'll let you have the day to think about it, but tonight I'm coming back here, and I'm staying. Which means you're either going to be in bed with me or you're going to be out on the street. Your call."

She curled her fingers into her palms, driving the nails deep again, trying to settle herself. Using the pain to put that armor back in place. She was desperate to turn around, to tell him what he could do with his goddamn ultimatum. Such as go to hell and never come back.

"I'll think about it," she lied.

But she wasn't going to think about it. She already knew her answer would be no way in hell. Which meant that she was now going to have to find some way to keep Levi off her back before he returned tonight.

"You do that," he said. "I'll be back, baby. Don't forget."

"I'm not your fucking baby."

"No." And this time his voice held a note of something she didn't quite understand. "You used to be my sunshine."

Rachel closed her eyes, the word spearing straight through her chest.

Sunshine. That's what he'd used to call her back when their friendship had been brand-new. Sunshine for the brightness of her smile, he'd said. She'd told him that was pretty fucking corny, and he'd laughed, agreeing with her.

But whenever he'd called her that, or sometimes "Sunny" for short, she'd never protested or complained. Secretly she'd loved having a pet name, hoarding it like a dragon with a piece of treasure, glowing whenever he used it. Making her feel like she was something good, something bright, and not just the sad little girl who everyone left. The father who hadn't wanted anything to do with her. The mother who'd loved drugs more than she'd loved her daughter. The grandmother who'd struggled to look after her, only to succumb to dementia.

Yet Rachel didn't feel like anyone's sunshine now. Now, the name just made her feel like a fraud.

"Not anymore," she said.

"No," he agreed. "Not anymore."

There was a silence behind her.

She turned around, but he had gone.

Why had he said that? Why *the fuck* had he said that?

You used to be my sunshine.

She had, but that had been years ago. In another life, when he'd been a different man. He wasn't that man now, not even close. Prison changed a person, sometimes beyond recognition.

Levi stood on the sidewalk outside the building, one of a number he'd managed to acquire, and closed his eyes. Inhaled. The smell of the city filled his nostrils: trash and engine exhaust, hot asphalt, the rich scent of freshly ground coffee from the café next to the tattoo studio.

Royal Road had changed since he'd gone away. He couldn't believe how much. Oh, Gideon had said as much during his visits, and Levi's current plans all hinged on that very gentrification.

But it was one thing to hear about it; quite another to see it.

Opening his eyes, he took a glance up and down the street.

The signs of regrowth were there in the industrial-looking café, a vintage clothing store, and some kind of design shop with funky-looking bits of crap in the window. Housewares or "rich-people shit" as Rachel had liked to call it. A previously abandoned warehouse with the word *Anonymous* spray-painted on the exposed brick wall. It looked too artfully done to be a random bit of graffiti, and the door set into the wall beside it looked too clean and new for an abandoned building. Which meant that maybe the building housed some kind of club or bar or something.

Yet for all the new stores that had popped up, there were still traces of the Royal he remembered. The convenience store with its dusty windows and the cracked glass door. The sleazy sex shop with its lurid pink lighting and mannequins wearing naughty nurse outfits and rubber fetish gear. Gino's, the run-down, seedy bar they'd all used to try not to get carded in.

Jesus, this place. He'd hated it back then. Felt suffocated by the smallness of it. The narrowness of the world all the inhabitants lived in and the poverty of their lives. He'd dreamt of getting out, going somewhere clean and bright, where there weren't drug dealers hanging out on street corners and spent needles in the gutters. Where you weren't in danger of getting knifed if you had to go out after the sun had gone down.

Those days of dreams were gone.

After two years of silence from Rachel, Levi's father had died. Then Mace and his gang had caught Levi alone in the prison library and beat him half to death. And when he'd woken up in the infirmary, in agony, his dreams of escape in ruins, he'd seen those dreams suddenly for what they were. Childish. Futile. Fragile.

In that moment he'd known. Dreams were for children, and he wasn't a child any longer. Only action mattered. Only action was hard and concrete and certain.

So he'd taken the money he'd earned while working for Gideon, plus a nice fat and very unexpected life insurance payout from an old policy his dad had taken out years before, and through some third parties Levi had started investing it.

Then he'd earned himself a business degree.

Then he'd started investigating Royal Road, studying the neighborhood, looking at all the businesses currently operating there and buying up as many of the abandoned buildings as he could afford.

Escape was for cowards and dreamers, and he was neither.

He didn't need to find a better place. He'd *make* one. Starting with Royal. All it would take was money and determination, and he had both of those things in abundance.

He was going to make his dreams a fucking reality.

And that included Rachel.

He let out a breath, resisting the urge to take a glance at the building behind him, the one with the neon Sugar Ink sign in the window.

Gideon had told him all about her tattoo studio, and when Levi had realized the building housing it had been abandoned, he'd bought it just in case he needed the leverage.

Fuck, he could still taste her, still feel the imprint of her lips on his. It made the blood pound in his veins and his cock get hard. Made him feel like he was half drunk. Softness and heat and woman . . . everything he'd been missing for so long. God, he was so hungry.

Maybe that had been a mistake, to kiss her, but he'd wanted

to test himself—test her too. She'd been all rigid at first, and then her mouth had opened under his as if she'd been as desperate for him as he was for her. . . .

He shook himself, pushed the thoughts away. Then he turned and started heading back toward Gideon's, putting distance between himself and her because otherwise he'd be going back into that studio and bending her over the metal counter before either of them had a chance to breathe. And there was no way he was going to do that.

Finally he had some power, which meant all of this was going to happen *exactly* when and *exactly* how he wanted. He'd been at other people's mercy for most of the last decade. The last thing he wanted to be was at the mercy of his own damn body.

Back in the garage, he found Gideon under the Cadillac that had been up on a hoist, doing something to the car's exhaust, judging by the crunching metal sounds coming from beneath it.

Levi didn't say anything, just waited until Gideon finally rolled out from under the car. He was holding a wrench in one oil-stained hand, and there was a pissed look on his face.

Levi knew why Gideon was pissed. Pity Levi didn't give a fuck. "It's between Rachel and me, like I told you," he said before Gideon could utter a word. "I wanted to get a few things straight."

Gideon put the wrench on the ground and got to his feet, leaning back against the Caddy, his arms folded. He was silent a long moment, his gaze unreadable. "You okay?" he asked finally.

It wasn't what Levi was expecting. "Why? Do I not look okay?"

"You look . . . different."

"What do you expect? I only just got out of jail."

Gideon frowned. "That's not what I mean, and you know it."

Yeah, Levi did know it. Gideon had been a friend for a long time, ever since Levi had met him in the Royal Road Outreach Center one night after Levi's father had fallen off the wagon yet again. Levi had needed to get out, just get away, and there hadn't been many places a teenager could go except the center. Gideon had been there playing pool, a silent figure seemingly much older. He hadn't said a word to Levi, had just handed him a pool cue, and they'd gone from there. He'd even let Levi hustle twenty bucks out of him.

Levi pushed his hands into the pockets of his jeans. It was still weird to be wearing normal clothes and not a prison jumpsuit. "Yes, I'm okay," he said flatly, because Gideon was a friend and the guy had stayed loyal all these years since. They all had.

Except Rachel.

Yeah, except for her.

Gideon shifted against the metal of the car. "I know you're going to need some time to adjust and—"

"I don't need any time to adjust," Levi cut him off, an unexpected and unwelcome discomfort sitting in his gut. He hadn't told Gideon about his development plan for the neighborhood, mainly because Levi knew how protective of Royal Gideon was. The guy was deeply distrustful of the gentrification process and didn't want anyone messing with "his" neighborhood.

Sure, Gideon had wanted to get the lowlifes out of Royal just as much as Levi did, but Gideon's vision was limited. He didn't seem to understand how important it was to make the neighborhood grow and thrive. Safer was good, but now Royal needed to attract more people. People with money to spend. And the businesses where those people could spend that money.

Gideon was content with the rundown neighborhood the

way it was, but Levi wasn't. He was going to make things happen; he was going to make things change. Gideon wouldn't be happy about that, but too bad.

Gideon's expression darkened at the interruption, his gaze narrowing. "What's up, Levi? You got something you want to say?"

He should tell his friend, especially about his arrangement with the Ryan Group, the investment company his lawyer had hooked him up with. Jason Ryan would be meeting with Levi and looking over Levi's plans. Levi was going to take him on a tour around the neighborhood and show him the area's potential. By the time Levi had finished, he was going to have the guy showering him in cash.

Oh yeah, Gideon's going to be super fucking impressed with you.

As in not. But Gideon was just going to have to suck it up.

"A few things." Levi held the other man's gaze. "I should have told you earlier, but I don't need a place to stay, and I don't need a job."

Surprise flickered over Gideon's rough, blunt features. "What? But I thought that was a done deal. You were going to help me here in the garage and stay on the couch until you got yourself a new place."

Yeah, he really should have told Gideon earlier. But he hadn't. Mostly because Gideon had been so pleased to help him out, and Levi hadn't wanted to seem ungrateful. "Thanks for the offer," he said. "But I've already got that shit sorted out."

Gideon stared at him. "Such as?"

Levi debated a moment on what to tell him. Not the whole plan quite yet, since he was still sorting out the details himself and needed to get the final agreement from Ryan, but he could tell Gideon a little.

"I have a place in a building a couple of blocks away. Got it while I was inside." As in he'd bought the entire building, had the top floor gutted and remodeled into an apartment, with plans for more apartments in the rest of the building.

Gideon shifted against the car. "Uh huh. What about a job?"

"I've got a few contacts looking into opportunities for me." It was the closest he could come to the truth without actually telling Gideon. "And until I get an answer, I have some money I had stashed away before I got locked up."

Gideon raised a brow. "Opportunities, huh? And what opportunities are these, Levi?"

Irritation twisted in Levi's gut at the implications in the other man's tone. "What do you mean by that? They're all entirely legal, Gideon. If that's what you mean."

There was a silent tension gathering between them.

Then abruptly, Gideon sighed. "I'm not implying anything. If that's what you want to do, by all means do it. I was just hoping you'd stay here a while and help out in the garage. I need another mechanic."

Levi's irritation eased. Christ, he really needed to not be such a touchy bastard. It was hard though, to remember how to trust people. Especially after so long being among people you couldn't. Where you couldn't afford to be weak, not even for a moment.

He tried to relax the tense muscles of his shoulders, rolling them surreptitiously. "What about Zee? Wasn't he working with you?"

Something in Gideon's face changed, a wry amusement flickering in his eyes. "Zee's been expanding his gym and working with the outreach center. He hasn't got time these days, and certainly not now that Tamara's moved in."

"Oh? That society chick?"

"Yeah." Gideon pushed himself away from the car. "You can meet her tonight. We've got a little welcome home party planned."

A flicker of regret shot through Levi. It would have been good to catch up with everyone, but he'd already decided what he was going to do tonight, and it didn't include a party. "Sorry. I've already got plans."

Annoyance crossed Gideon's face. "What plans?"

Levi shifted on his feet. He didn't want to disappoint Gideon, but Levi had waited a long time for this, and he wasn't going to wait anymore. And he certainly wasn't going to give the other guy an in-depth explanation as to what exactly those plans involved.

Still, if Levi was going to blow off a party his friends had organized in his honor, he needed at least a plausible excuse.

"Been a long time since I got laid," he said. "You know what I'm saying?"

Something Levi couldn't read flickered through the other man's gaze, then Gideon's expression relaxed. "Yeah, that I can understand. What about we make the party earlier then? It was Zoe's idea, and she'll be really disappointed if it doesn't happen, plus Zee and Tamara were looking forward to catching up with you."

Well, Levi hated to disappoint Zoe. And it would be good to talk to the others, to socialize like a normal person for a change. If he could still remember how.

"In that case, sure," Levi said. "Sounds great." He could delay his reckoning with Rachel for a party. Especially if it made his friends happy.

"Damn straight." Gideon bent to pick up the wrench. "Don't forget we look out for one another, man. Always have; always will. We're family."

Once Levi had found that reassuring, especially as a boy whose only family had been a broken-down, alcoholic father, a man who, after he'd been made redundant from his job, had discovered he loved a whisky bottle more than his own son.

But things were different now.

Levi had learned a few things while he'd been in jail. Mainly that family was all very well, but when it all turned to shit, the only person you could count on was you.

He didn't need anyone to look out for him. He was better off on his own.

Always had been. Always would be.

Chapter 4

Rachel was sitting on the couch in Sugar Ink's waiting area, leafing angrily through a magazine, when Xavier dumped the espresso he'd gotten from Mike's, the café next door, onto the low table in front of her.

"Here," he said. "Now, are you going to tell me what the fuck is wrong with you?"

Reaching for the coffee, she held it in her hands, letting the heat seep into her palms. Not that she needed any more heat because God knew she felt like she was burning up with anger already.

"Nothing I want to talk about," she said curtly.

"Rachel." Xavier sounded irritated. "You've been snapping at clients all day, and I bought you a fucking coffee. Come on, out with it."

Xavier was the other tattoo artist she worked with, and he was a great guy—except when it came to asking her what the matter was when she didn't want to tell him. He could be a persistent bastard too when he wanted to be.

She sighed and leaned back on the couch, taking a sip of the coffee.

Xavier, pierced and tattooed, and wearing a tight black tank, low-slung jeans, and a pair of dirty red Chucks, was standing on the other side of the table opposite her, his arms folded. He had red, orange, and yellow flames licking up each of his forearms, the colors standing out beautifully against his dark skin.

Not as simple or as clean as Levi's rings.

The thought irritated her, and she found herself scowling.

What the hell was she going to tell Xavier? Because if Levi ended up kicking her out of the building, then that was going to affect her friend too. And it would be a damn disaster since neither of them could afford new premises. It would pretty much mean the end of Sugar Ink.

Her stomach lurched.

She'd worked hard for her studio in the years since Levi had been gone, and she couldn't let it go just like that. Then again, keeping it meant she was going to have to give Levi what he wanted—unless she could think of an alternative to offer him. An alternative to herself.

Rachel took another sip of her espresso, caffeine buzzing in her veins, the hot liquid burning her mouth.

"Levi's back," she said, keeping her gaze on her magazine. "I saw him this morning." Xavier hadn't met Levi, and he didn't know how difficult things were between them now, but Xavier did know that they'd once been friends.

"Holy shit," Xavier muttered.

"Yeah, you could say that." Rachel hesitated, then looked over at him. "He told me he owns this building."

"Okay." Xavier lifted an eyebrow. "Is that a problem?"

It wouldn't be if Levi weren't using the building in question as leverage for a twisted kind of payback. Or punishment. Or whatever it was he was trying to get from her.

I want you, Rachel Hamilton. . . .

Rachel looked away again, her stomach lurching even more. Which was crazy and weird. It was only sex, after all.

And it's not the first time you've used it to save yourself.

Unease twisted in her gut, a long and deliberately forgotten fear. She pushed it aside. God, what had happened with Evan had been years ago, and she'd long gotten over it. So maybe her odd feelings about Levi's demand now were due to the fact that he'd once been her friend, and so it was strange to think of him as a lover. Plus the fact that she hadn't had sex in a while. Years even.

But that was only because she wasn't into casual hookups, and, as for relationships, well, she was happy being on her own, relying on no one but herself. She didn't want some other person to have power over her, to own her.

Maybe one day, when her business was doing well and things were more stable, she'd be ready, but not until then.

And certainly not with Levi.

"It's not a problem, no," she finally said.

But she couldn't have sounded very convincing because Xavier frowned at her. "Fucking liar, Hamilton. I'm not going to get you coffee again if you're not going to be straight up with me."

Rachel cursed silently. Xavier was a good guy, loyal and generous, not to mention a great artist. He had a dedicated client list, people who couldn't get enough of his designs, plus contacts throughout the rest of Detroit who brought yet more clients from all over the city and beyond. He was a vital part of her business, which meant she probably needed to tell him the truth.

Bracing herself, Rachel drained the rest of her espresso and put the cup back on the table with a click. "Okay," she said, glancing up into Xavier's deep brown eyes. "Here's the deal. Levi wants me to do something for him, and he basically told me that if I don't do it, he'll kick us out of the building."

Xavier's frown deepened into a scowl. "What the actual fuck? Where is he? I'll get a friend of mine to—"

"It's not like that," Rachel interrupted. "I . . . fucked up." She let out a short breath. "I'm kind of the reason he's been in jail all this time, and he's really pissed about it."

Usually Xavier was pretty chill, calming clients' nerves with a laugh or a wicked grin. But now his strong features were set in grim lines, his expression forbidding. "What is this 'thing' he wants you to do?"

Oh, great, she *definitely* didn't want to tell him that. "You don't need to know."

"I fuckin' do."

"He won't hurt me, if that's what you're worried about." At least he wouldn't hurt her physically, that much she knew for certain.

Xavier's expression darkened even further. "That's not the issue. He's blackmailing you."

Well, it *was* blackmail, no point prettying it up. "Doesn't matter what it is," she said tautly. "If I don't do it, Sugar Ink won't have a home."

Xavier moved, the chains on his belt jingling. "Fuck that. I know some people. I can get him to change his mind."

She knew what Xavier meant. The "people" he knew were linked to various underground crime organizations for whom intimidation was a specialty. They came to Xavier for his designs, and sometimes they didn't pay, promising certain "favors" instead. Rachel never knew if Xavier ever took them up on those favors, but the fact that he trotted his connections out now made her wonder.

But Rachel wouldn't use Xavier's shadowy contacts against Levi. Sure, her ex-friend was being the world's biggest asshole, but there was no way she was going to screw up a second time and get him hurt.

"No." She said the word with as much certainty as she could muster. "That's not the answer."

"Seriously? If he's blackmailing you, then—"

"He's got a right to it, Xavier."

"A right?" The other artist scowled. "What the fuck do you mean by that?"

Rachel sighed, trying to find the right words to explain and failing. Mainly because it wasn't something she could even explain to herself. "I only meant that he's got a right to be angry with me. I wasn't much of a friend to him when he needed me to be, so . . ." She lifted a shoulder. "I know why he's angry, and, if I were him, I'd probably do the same thing."

Except she wouldn't make it about sex the way he had.

Are you sure about that?

The stud in Xavier's eyebrow glittered in the summer sun coming through the windows, reminding her uncomfortably of Levi's own eyebrow ring. *A reminder of what happens when people fuck with me.* Then his mouth on hers, burning hot . . .

Heat prickled over her skin, and she had to look away, back down at her phone that was sitting beside her empty espresso cup on the table, checking the time blankly.

Jesus, these feelings . . . Wherever they were coming from and why, she didn't want them.

"So what?" Xavier demanded. "You're just going to let him do whatever it is he's going to do?"

I want you. In every way there is . . .

A shiver went through her, bone-deep, but she didn't want to acknowledge that either. What she wanted was for this to be over, one way or another. But the simple fact was, there *were* no alternatives to what Levi wanted, not when what he wanted was her.

In that case, you know what to do, don't you?

She supposed she did. And hell, why not? If he wanted a couple of rounds in bed, it wasn't a big deal. She'd get over the weirdness of banging her friend, and he'd get whatever it was out of his system, and then they could both move on with their lives, no harm, no foul.

Certainly better than her business going down the damn toilet.

She stared at her phone for a long moment, letting the decision settle down inside her, and, strangely, along with it came a certain kind of relief.

Yeah, it was time to stop avoiding Levi. It was time to face him. Time to pay whatever it was she owed him. And if that meant sex, it wasn't like she hadn't had demands placed on her like that before. It wasn't as if this would be different.

Different than Evan?

No, Jesus. She really needed to stop thinking of Evan.

"I'll talk to him," she said carefully. Telling Xavier that she was going to do whatever Levi demanded was probably not the best idea. Xavier was very protective of her and Sugar Ink, and she didn't want him getting into any confrontations with Levi, especially given how different Levi was now.

She had a horrible feeling that it wouldn't be Levi who'd end up getting hurt.

At that moment the door opened, and a small, slender woman in black jeans and an oversized black T-shirt came in, her thick, curly hair neatly tied back in a ponytail at her nape.

Xavier's grim expression eased. "Hey, pretty," he said.

Zoe pushed her glasses back up her nose. "What's up, Xavier?"

"The sky. Clouds. And the sun. Usually." Xavier always did like to tease her.

Zoe frowned and wrinkled her nose. "Dick."

He laughed. "What? I was trying to be funny."

"And failing." With a dismissive sniff, Zoe glanced at Rachel. "This party tonight. Gideon's having it early because apparently Levi has some 'stuff' to do."

Ah, yes, the homecoming party for Levi. Gideon had texted her earlier about it.

"Yeah, okay," Rachel said. "I told Gideon I'd be there." The "stuff" Levi had to do was probably going to be her.

Zoe wandered over to the couch and sat down beside Rachel, her hands on her thighs, large golden eyes owlish behind the lenses of her glasses. "How are you doing?"

Rachel sighed inwardly. Of course Zoe would be worried for her. Zoe worried about everyone. Conscious of Xavier's gaze, Rachel gave the younger woman a smile. "I'm okay. Honestly, Zoe."

Zoe's forehead creased. She opened her mouth to say something, and then, obviously realizing that Xavier was still there, gave him an annoyed glance. "A little privacy please?"

He grinned. "Oh, come on, chick conversations are the best kind."

Their banter was familiar, usual, and Rachel was tempted to stay silent and listen to them to get her world back and revolving on its axis again. Not to mention that she wouldn't have to answer any of Zoe's well-meaning but likely highly irritating questions.

But then one of Xavier's clients turned up, and Xavier was soon deep in conversation with the guy about some design or other. And there was no away to avoid Zoe's questioning look, at least not without being a complete bitch.

There were plenty of people she had no trouble being a bitch to, but Zoe wasn't one of them.

"It's really okay," Rachel said after a moment. "Levi actually came after me earlier, and we talked it out." Which was kind of the truth.

The worry on Zoe's face eased. "That's good. I don't mean to pry. I know you don't want to talk about it. I just like to know you're okay."

Rachel gave the other woman a smile. Zoe was shy, but she had a fiercely protective streak—much like Gideon. It was endearing, if irritating, at times. "Well, I am, so stop worrying, okay?"

Zoe looked down at her hands, now clasped in her lap, and Rachel got the distinct impression that it actually wasn't all that okay. "Levi's different," Zoe said quietly. "He scares me."

Unfortunately, Rachel knew exactly what the other woman meant. "You can't expect him to be the same guy after all that time in prison, Zoe."

"Yeah, I know. I don't mean I think he'd hurt me, it's just . . . he seems so much harder. Like he's lost something."

Rachel wanted to close her eyes, because she knew what Zoe meant by that too. "He'll get it back," she said, trying to sound like she believed it. "We just need to give him some time to adjust."

"That's what Gideon said. But I think he was lying."

Rachel gave Zoe a look. "What do you mean he was lying?"

"I mean I don't think he believed it himself." Zoe paused. "I think Levi worries Gideon too."

It went without saying that if Gideon was worried, then Zoe was worried for Gideon. Mainly because the younger woman had a painful case of hero worship that didn't seemed to have waned over the years Rachel had known her. A worship that Gideon appeared to be utterly oblivious to.

"It's kind of understandable," Rachel said, trying to be soothing, which didn't come naturally to her. "Levi went through a lot in prison; Gideon knows that. But I'm sure it'll get better over time." Empty words. Pity she didn't believe them.

Zoe's expression was measuring. "You're scared of him too." It wasn't a question.

"Not like that. I know he won't physically hurt me either."

"But that's not why you're afraid, is it?"

Rachel had to look away. Zoe was a good friend, but even so, Rachel didn't want anyone to see the truth of what Levi made her feel. Didn't want to have to explain it, especially when she didn't quite have the words for it herself. "No, it's not," she said merely. "But I'm sure that'll get better too."

Another thing she didn't believe.

"He's so angry." Zoe's voice was quiet. "Is it because you never went to see him?"

Rachel's throat felt suddenly tight. None of the others had ever asked her for the reasons why, and she'd never offered them, because after all, no one liked admitting to cowardice. She didn't particularly want to admit it now either. So all she said was, "Among other things."

"But you'll sort it all out, won't you? I mean you and Levi. You'll get back to being friends again soon."

There was such hope in the words that it made Rachel's chest ache. "I'm sure we will, Zoe."

But Rachel didn't believe that either. Because whatever friendship Levi and she had once had was dead and long gone.

And it was never coming back.

Levi sat on one of the battered metal chairs in Gideon's garage, a beer in one hand, trying to relax and not keep staring at the door at the garage's entrance, waiting for the moment when Rachel would arrive.

She hadn't turned up yet, which was fucking typical.

Maybe she won't even come. That would also be fucking typical.

His jaw tightened, and he took a swig of beer, focusing his attention on Zee and the cool blonde sitting in his lap instead.

It had been good to catch up with his friend and meet his lovely Tamara too. Also to talk about the past that Zee had kept hidden all these years. Levi had met a few associates of Zee's crime-boss father in jail. Zee had been happy to hear it, knowing those assholes were going to be in prison for a long time.

In fact, the guy seemed revoltingly satisfied all round, which wasn't any wonder given the woman he was with. Levi had never seen Zee smile so much. Clearly Tamara was good for him, which was great and all, but that kind of shit never lasted. And Levi should know since he'd had the same hopes back when he'd been young and dumb and still pining after Rachel.

Before reality had ground those hopes into dust.

But no, his hopes weren't going to be dust for too much longer. He was back, and soon Rachel would be here, and all those hopes would then become reality. He'd make sure of it.

He lifted his beer, took a sip, smiling at something Zee had said, but the smile felt pasted on. Like Levi had lost the habit somewhere along the line. Like in jail. No one smiled much inside, because there was fuck all to smile about.

It didn't help either that impatience was making his muscles tense. He kept staring at that goddamned door. And he knew the others had noticed because he saw the glances that flowed between Gideon, Zoe, and Zee.

Hell. They were only worried, he knew that, but what the fuck did they expect? That he'd come back and everything would be the same as it had been? That nothing would have changed in all the time he'd been away? That he would still be the same guy?

The anger he tried to keep locked down simmered inside him, mixing with the impatience, making him feel restless, like he wanted to go do something violently physical.

You will. Tonight. With Rachel.

Yeah, *fuck* yeah. There would be a reckoning tonight. And Jesus Christ, he couldn't wait. He was going to make her want him. He was going to make her burn. . . .

Unless of course, she pulled her avoidance crap and didn't turn up.

That would be a pity. He'd meant what he'd said when he'd told her he'd kick her the hell out of his building. He always kept his word about shit like that. And he wouldn't regret it, not even a shred.

He'd been lying in the bed she'd made for him for the past eight years; now it was her turn to try it out.

Tamara turned her head and whispered something in Zee's ear, making him laugh. Levi found the sound vaguely shocking. Laughter was another thing he hadn't heard much of lately.

But then he stopped thinking about that, because at that moment the door of the garage opened, and Rachel stepped inside.

He went completely still, staring at her, his brain momentarily short-circuiting, all the breath leaving his body.

She was wearing some kind of loose, flowy black top that was utterly see-through, with nothing underneath but a black lace bra. A black leather miniskirt wrapped around her hips, and her long legs were bare. On her feet were a pair of platform sandals with an intricate network of silver straps that coiled around her calves like vines.

The blue was gone from her hair. Now her hair fell over her shoulders, black and glossy, just the way he remembered it, like a pool of ink spilled fresh from the bottle. Her eyes were very dark, ringed with black eyeliner, her lids dusted with some kind of sparkly silver shadow. Her mouth was painted a deep, dark red and promised all kinds of sin.

She met his gaze head-on, her chin slightly lifted, and he felt the impact of it like a punch right to his solar plexus.

Finally, *finally,* she was here. And she was so fucking beautiful.

He could feel himself getting hard, his body kicking into high gear, scenarios about what exactly he was going to do to her running through his head. Because he knew what this was; he could see it in her eyes. Her outfit and the calm expression on her face said it all.

She was going to accept his ultimatum.

Not that you gave her a choice.

Something uncomfortable shifted inside him, a lighted match to the petrol of his anger. No, that was fucking bullshit. He'd given her a choice—it wasn't a good one, no, but, hell, that was life, wasn't it? She didn't have to accept it.

That studio means something to her.

She'd been born an artist, always drawing or doodling, and he'd always thought she was going to go to art school or something. At least, that's what they'd discussed when they talked about their plans for the future. He'd encouraged her to aim high, because she had the talent and she had it in spades.

But clearly the art college thing hadn't happened, and instead she had a tattoo business. A business that given the cool, eclectic look of her studio, she'd obviously put a lot of work and time into.

A business she clearly wasn't going to give up easily.

If the past hadn't happened the way the way it had, he would have been proud of her. But it had, and it wasn't pride he felt. Right now, all that mattered to him was the leverage that studio was going to give him.

Leverage to get her to do what he wanted.

As if she'd read his thoughts, Rachel looked away from him, coming over to where the others were sitting by the workbenches, smiling as they greeted her.

Levi watched her as she moved, unable to take his gaze off her. The fabric of her gauzy top shifted with her movements, and, beneath it, he could see the tattoos marked into her skin, the material covering them like a veil that revealed tantalizing glimpses.

Roses and vines and thorns. The roses were a reminder of beauty amid death, she'd told him years ago, when he'd watched her draw them in her notebooks. There were a lot of them on her arm now, and the one drooping across her shoulder, casting petals across her chest, dying . . .

Levi lifted his gaze from the tattoo to her face, studying the fine lines of her: determined jaw, slightly turned-up nose, the straight, black slashes of her brows. A strong, beautiful face, but so very guarded.

What did that dying rose mean? Why had she put it there? Because it *did* mean something. Rachel had always been very particular about her tattoos.

The anger inside him shifted and coiled like a restless beast. So many changes, so much that was different. He'd told her he didn't want an explanation from her about why she'd ignored him for so long, but actually, maybe he did.

Maybe he wanted to know everything. Every single fucking thing.

Draining his beer, he put the bottle down on the floor before shoving his chair back, the legs making harsh scraping noises on the concrete as he stood up.

Everyone turned toward the sound, staring at him.

He ignored them, staring at Rachel, the tension in the garage abruptly skyrocketing. He ignored that too. "Upstairs." He kept his voice curt, lifting his chin in the direction of the metal stairs that led to the office.

A hard, echoing silence fell.

"Levi," Zee said, his silver eyes narrowing. "What the fuck, man?"

Levi gave his friend a cold glance. This had nothing to do with Zee. It had nothing to do with any of them. This was between Rachel and himself.

"It's okay, Zee." Rachel said unexpectedly, her tone calm. "Levi and I need to have a chat."

Zee frowned, looking from Rachel to Levi and back again.

Levi said nothing. He wasn't going to justify himself, not to anyone. Yeah, he was probably coming across as a major tool, but he didn't give a fuck. He was a different man now, and the sooner they accepted that, the better.

Gideon, leaning against the workbench, was looking at him too, his gaze unreadable. Beside him was Zoe, sitting on the bench with her legs dangling. Her expression, unlike Gideon's was an open book, worry gleaming in her golden eyes.

They're all afraid for Rachel. Because you're being an asshole.

Levi shrugged the thought away, making for the metal stairs without another word. They could think what they liked. He wasn't going to hurt Rachel; he only wanted what they could have had if things hadn't all gone to shit. If she'd been the friend she was supposed to have been, and not the woman who'd left him to rot in the dark.

He climbed the stairs, feeling the silence behind them press against his back like a giant hand. He didn't turn around, stopping at the top where the door to the office was and pushing it open. Only then did he turn, holding the door open for Rachel as she came up behind him.

She didn't look at him as she stepped past him into the office.

It was a little space, with a rundown couch shoved up against the wall and a large battered wooden desk opposite. An office chair was pushed into the desk, a surprisingly sleek and expensive-looking computer sitting on the desktop. Nearby was a bank of metal shelves full of filing boxes, folders, and other office supplies.

Above the computer monitor was a *Sports Illustrated* swimsuit issue pic of some blond chick he didn't recognize. Next to it, almost like a companion picture, was photo of a dark-haired guy wearing nothing but low-slung jeans, carrying a tire and smoldering at the camera. Given that Gideon probably wouldn't have put the guy picture up, that was no doubt Zoe trying to prove a point.

Eight years ago he would have smiled. Now, he ignored the pictures, staring at Rachel as she walked over to the couch, coming to a stop, then turning around.

Levi shut the door after them, then locked it.

Her gaze flickered at the sound of the lock, but all she said was, "You don't want to maybe wait until after the party?"

"No."

She eyed him. "Too impatient for your answer?"

He folded his arms, leaned back against the door. "You don't need to tell me. I know you're going to say yes."

Temper glowed briefly in her eyes, then it was gone. "Of course I'm going to say yes. Not that you gave me much choice about it."

"I gave you a choice. You didn't have to agree."

"Like I was going to say 'Sure, kick me out. Ruin the business I've spent the past five years building. What do I care?' "

An uncomfortable sensation inside him shifted because there was a note in her voice he didn't like. It ran beneath the anger, a raw kind of tone that sounded like . . . hurt. Which did nothing for his temper.

"You could get a new building," he said carelessly. "It's not a big deal."

A muscle flicked at the side of her jaw. "I can't get a new building. I can't afford it."

"Why not? I would have thought after a few years, you'd be doing well enough to afford rent at least."

Her mouth had gone flat. "Times are tough. If you hadn't noticed."

"Hadn't noticed?" He dropped his arms, pushed himself away from the door, prowling closer to her. She stiffened, but held her ground. " 'Course I fucking noticed. Or is it all about you, Rachel? Since everything always is."

Her throat moved. This time it was her turn to fold her arms, a defensive posture, one designed to keep him at a distance.

Fuck that. He'd been kept at a distance for too long, and the time for it was past. He didn't want closed, defensive Rachel, the armored front she showed the rest of the world. He wanted to pull apart that front, destroy the barriers and walls she'd put up over the years, smash them into pieces, and leave her with no defenses at all. He wanted her lost and vulnerable and needing him the way she once had. The way he'd needed her.

Levi came to a stop right in front of her, staring down into her dark eyes. The shadow on her lids glittered, and, beneath the thick fan of her lashes, her gaze seemed to flicker, as if she couldn't hold the pressure of his gaze for long.

The heat of her body was so close, and he could smell her, that vanilla sweet scent that had always made him want to lick her skin to see if she tasted as good as she smelled. Well, now he could. Now he could do everything—*everything*—he'd ever fucking wanted.

At the base of her throat, her pulse beat fast, as if she knew what he wanted and was afraid.

She never used to be afraid of you.

The uncomfortable sensation twisted again. Conscience, regret, or longing. One of the stupid soft emotions he'd gotten rid of while in jail, the emotions that made him weak. Emotions he couldn't afford. Whichever one it was, he ignored it.

She lifted her chin, challenging him in spite of her fear. "For what it's worth, I'm sorry."

Sorry. The emptiest of all empty words.

He bared his teeth in a smile that had nothing to do with amusement. "What for? For running away and not making that statement? For leaving me in a cell for years without even a visit? Or even a fucking letter?"

That challenging, direct look didn't waver. "For all of it."

He almost laughed. "You think all I want is a fucking apology? That a 'sorry' will make it all better?"

"No." Her jaw had gone tight. "I just wanted you to know that I was, that I still am."

His anger snarled, wanting out. He forced it down, keeping it leashed. "Save it. It's not an apology I want, *Sunny*."

A brief, bright flicker of hurt flashed in her eyes at the sound of his old pet name for her. But then it was gone, all her barriers back up, her gaze guarded. "Okay, well, so tell me whatever the fuck it is you do want. If it's sex, fine. Let's just do it, and then we can both put this behind us and move on."

So she was thinking a quick blow job, a quick screw on the desk, and he'd consider it good. That everything would be forgiven. That they could go back to the way it had been between them.

She was so fucking wrong. She'd forgotten what they'd been to each other. What she'd been to him. She'd forgotten everything.

Now it was time to make her remember.

He'd loved her once a long time ago. Loved her as a friend and more than that, far more than that. Yet he'd kept his distance to protect her, waiting until the day he'd have more to offer than the regular shitty life they already had.

He had more now, and the time for waiting was over.

It was time to forget all those stupid fucking dreams he'd once had. Time to make them a reality.

It was time to finally take what he wanted.

Chapter 5

Rachel's heartbeat was so loud in her head it was amazing she could hear anything at all.

Levi was standing right in front of her and so damn close. All tall, broad, furious heat and tightly leashed power. One silver-blue eye glittered as his gaze burned into hers, while the other was full of darkness. But in both a deep, hot anger glowed, along with a kind of raw hunger that made all her insides draw tight.

He didn't touch her, his arms hanging loose at his sides, and she was so agonizingly aware of him she couldn't seem to catch a breath. Aware of the golden skin and hard muscle of his arms, striped by those incredible black tattoos. Of the stretch of black cotton over his powerful chest and flat stomach. Of the woody, smoky scent of his body, the unfamiliar one that made her want to turn her face into his neck and just inhale.

She'd been building herself up to this for the past hour, and she had thought she was fine with it. That she was ready to give him the quick fuck, or whatever it was he wanted from her. Get it over and done with.

But the reality of him so close, the aura of leashed rage burning off him, made everything . . . different. Rage poured off him in waves, the force of it like a hot wind straight out of a furnace, almost physical in its intensity.

Maybe apologizing had been wrong, but she'd suddenly felt that she needed to. She'd wanted him to know straight out that she knew she'd fucked up and she was taking responsibility for it.

It wasn't going to fix anything. She knew that too.

But here she was, ready to give him what he wanted, make whatever payment he thought he was owed. Then she could go back to her business, and he could go back to . . . whatever it was he had planned now that he was out of prison.

Upstairs at his welcome-home party was not what she'd been expecting, but then, he'd always been an impatient kind of guy.

She swallowed, trying to moisten her dry mouth and ignore the deeply unsettled, nervous, scared feeling in her gut.

He was looking at her, as if he wanted to take her apart, eat her alive. And it made some deep, forgotten part of her quiver and wake up.

Which *so* didn't make any sense. Evan had looked at her that way, and she'd hated it, loathed it. But the way Levi was looking at her . . . somehow it felt different, and she didn't know why.

Bullshit. You know why. Because it's Levi.

Yeah, and? She'd put the crush she'd once had on him—that stupid, innocent, teenage crush—behind her. He shouldn't affect her in that way anymore.

But somehow he did. Somehow that intense, terrible gaze of his was making all kinds of emotions knot and tangle inside her. Fear. Nervousness. And beneath it all, bizarrely, a kind of excitement she didn't want to name.

He was silent a long time, unmoving, and then, when he did finally move, raising one hand to her hair, she almost flinched, every nerve ending drawn tight with anticipation.

An expression she couldn't decipher flickered over his handsome features, then was gone. His fingers touched one lock of her hair, pushing it behind her ear, his fingertips grazing her ear, leaving a trail of sparks in their wake.

She shivered helplessly, that deep unease shifting inside her. *It's just sex. Remember? Calm the hell down.*

"What did you do to your hair?" he asked, his voice deep and rough.

She blinked. "What?"

Levi took one strand between his thumb and forefinger, rubbing it like it was a fine piece of silk. "It was blue before."

Why the hell was he asking her about her hair? She'd been expecting him to give her some kind of order, like get on her knees and suck him off or something.

"It was just a temporary color," she said, her own voice gone thick.

"Why?"

"Why what?"

"Why did you change it?" There was something ferocious in his eyes, something demanding. "Was it for me?"

She debated lying. Telling him it had nothing to do with him, but that wasn't quite the truth. "You said you wanted me so . . . You have me." The Rachel she'd once been, not the Rachel she was now.

Slowly, he wound the black strand around his finger, never taking his gaze from hers, a faint pressure against her scalp as he pulled it tight. God, he was so close, and he smelled so good. Why did she like that so much?

"Tell me what you're expecting from this, Rachel."

She let out a silent, shaky breath, trying to keep inside all those stupid, tangled feelings. "A night? A couple of nights? I mean, I'm assuming you're going to want me to suck your cock now or something."

The expression on his face was impenetrable, but she found herself looking at it all the same, studying his face as if it were some kind of oracle and could tell her the future.

He was so hot. Almost ridiculously handsome in many ways. She remembered from school how he'd used to get teased for his looks, how he'd get called "pretty boy" and all kinds of other, worse names. But now he'd grown into those looks and was even hotter, if that was possible. The ring in his eyebrow and the dilated pupil of one eye were imperfections that made his features harder, more masculine somehow. There was also a scar that projected out from his eye socket, a white line that curved up to his temple, making him look nearly piratical.

Yet that mouth of his, so beautifully shaped, was the same, and she had the same feelings about it now as she had back when she'd been crushing on him so bad so she couldn't even look at him without blushing. Like she wanted to trace his lower lip with her finger, with her tongue. . . .

"Wrong," Levi said, pulling on the strand of hair he had wrapped around his finger, sending a small prickle of pain over her scalp.

She blinked, fighting not to give him any reaction to the small pain, or to the fact that she was, apparently, wrong. "You mean you don't want a blow job then?"

"Oh, I want one, all right. But only when I say so." He tugged a little harder. "And I haven't said so yet."

She swallowed, confused and trying not to show it. She'd been hoping that a night would be all he'd want, that all she'd need to do was give him that and it would all be over, her debt discharged.

But clearly he had other ideas.

"What? That not to your liking?" He gave her hair another tug, and for some reason she felt the pull of it like a current of electricity going straight down the middle of her body. "Unfortunately, that's not up to you."

"Well, all right then." She tried to concentrate on what he was saying and not on the tugging on her hair. "Perhaps you should tell me what *you* want then. The suspense is kind of killing me."

"I don't give a fuck. I'll tell you when I'm good and ready." He rubbed his thumb back and forth along the strand of hair coiled around his finger, as if he was caressing it. "Why didn't you talk to the police that night, Rachel?"

Her mouth was dry. "I thought you didn't want any explanations. I thought you didn't give a shit."

"Maybe I changed my mind." His gaze was a sword, pinning her in place while his thumb moved on her hair. "Call it curiosity."

A deeply buried anguish curled up inside her, and she wanted suddenly to get away, to get out of this room where he took up all the space and all the air, where she couldn't breathe. Get out and away from him.

But she couldn't.

You owe him this.

She took another deep, silent breath. The truth was going to sound so pathetic, and there was no way to make it any less so. She was ashamed of it. She was ashamed of herself. "I was afraid," she said baldly, attempting to keep her voice at least a little bit steady. "The police would have wanted to know why I was in that alley, and they would have investigated. They would have taken me away from Gran, and I couldn't leave her. You know I couldn't. She had no one else to look after her but me."

Again she couldn't read the expression in his eyes; they were cold, hard. "And the next eight fucking years of complete silence? No phone calls. No letters. Not even an e-mail. Do I get any explanation for that?"

She swallowed again, because her mouth was so damn dry, and her heartbeat felt like it was about to burst through her chest. "I thought you wouldn't want to see me. I kept meaning to come, I swear. In fact, about six months after you went inside, I took a bus to St. Louis, and then . . ." She faltered, remembering the wave of fear that had gone through her at the halfway point of her trip, so bad she'd almost thrown up. The thought of seeing him in that place, looking at her with such hate. And even at that time she'd known he would hate her—after all, she was the reason he was there in the first place.

"Then you chickened out," he finished for her. There was no emotion in his tone, no hurt or betrayal. Just a flat stating of the facts that made her behavior sound somehow even worse than it already was.

Her eyes felt sore, dry and prickling. But she hadn't cried for years, and she wasn't going to start now. Tears solved nothing. "I thought you'd hate me. I thought I'd be the last person in the world you'd want to see." And the thought of seeing that hate in the eyes of the best friend she had in all the world . . . It had been too much.

"How did you know that?" Levi asked in that same flat, cold tone. "You never even made the effort to find out."

What else could she say? She hadn't. "No, you're right." There was a crack in her voice. "I didn't."

"You were my best friend in the whole fucking world, and you left me to rot in jail."

The facts were like knives, cutting her. And all she could do was stand there and take it. "Yes."

"My father died while I was in jail. I never even got to go to his funeral." He paused. "Because of you."

She wanted to close her eyes, protect herself somehow, pull on her angry, sarcastic armor. But she didn't. She made herself look into his familiar and once-beloved face, made herself see the changes prison had made to him, bear the anger in his gaze. See the hate in it.

Everything she'd feared was true. She'd lost him.

Like that's a shock. You lost him years ago.

Grief turned over in her heart, but she shoved it away. She wasn't going to let him see her hurt. She wasn't going to be weak. "If it helps, I went for you." Going to the funeral in his stead had been a pathetic attempt to make some kind of amends. But it wasn't enough, and she had always known it wouldn't be.

The expression on his face didn't alter. "If you think that changes things, you're wrong." He gave one final tug on her hair, then released it. "Raise your arms."

Swallowing her instinctive refusal at being told what to do, she did what he asked, slowly raising them above her head.

Levi stepped forward, so close now they were almost touching, the scent of him swamping her, and her breath caught.

Then he gripped the hem of her top and lifted it, pulling it up and over her head. Warm air slid over her bare skin, raising goose bumps along her arms and across her shoulders.

She shivered as Levi tugged her top off and let it drop negligently onto the floor, leaving her wearing nothing but her bra. The way he looked at her made her feel like she was wearing nothing at all.

He took a step back, his head tilting to one side, studying her as if she were a statue or a work of art and he couldn't decide whether he liked it or not.

The unease that had been swirling around in her gut deepened, and she couldn't understand it. She'd been naked in front of a guy before, and, sure, it had been humiliating, but that had been years ago. So long she could barely even remember it.

Yeah. Right.

She ignored the snide thought. Made herself look back at Levi as if it didn't matter that he was looking at her with all the intensity of a hunting tiger.

"I used to imagine you naked a lot," he murmured, his gaze running down over her body, a raw, hungry look glittering in his eyes. "In fact, that's what kept me going all this time. Thinking about you naked and the things I'd like to do to you."

Her breathing accelerated, though she tried to calm it, her heart racing. She didn't know how to feel about the things he was saying, didn't know how to deal with them. She'd had no clue he felt that way about her, not one.

"You never said anything." A completely inane comment, but it was the only thing she could think of to say.

"No, I didn't. Because you weren't there to say it to, obviously." His attention rose once more to her face. "I used to imagine those things before I went inside too."

Shock went through her. "What do you mean before?"

The lines of his face were so hard, the laughter that used to live in his eyes totally extinguished. "I wanted you when I shouldn't have. When you were younger. You were so fucking beautiful. I used to dream about you at nights, used to get hard thinking of you. But I made sure you never knew."

She couldn't seem to get a breath, her lungs encased in concrete. Jesus. If she'd known—

If you'd known what? You wouldn't have done what you did with Evan?

Ah, but she'd had to do that. She hadn't had any other option. "W-why? Why didn't you say anything?"

His gaze held hers, direct, inescapable. "You were too young and too vulnerable. I wanted to take you away and give you the kind of life you deserved, not be living hand-to-mouth in some shitty apartment in Royal."

She felt like he'd hit her over the head and her ears were still ringing from the blow. "But you . . . But . . ."

"I didn't want to tell you, not until I had enough money for us both. Enough money to look after your gran and my dad, to get us a better life somewhere else." The words were so cold, all the emotion stripped away. "But then you had to go to that alley behind Gino's, try to do that deal, and it all went to shit." He paused, and his attention dropped once more to the lace bra she wore. "Didn't mean I stopped thinking about you though. Didn't mean I stopped wanting you. Didn't mean I stopped waiting for you."

She had to look away then, because it hurt. It just fucking hurt. Once she would have cut out her heart for the chance to be wanted by him, but then she'd made the first of her terrible mistakes, and, after that, she'd buried the want so deep she'd never felt it again.

But with him so close now, she knew it burned there still. It had never gone away.

Levi moved closer again, his heat a wave of warmth over her skin. And he reached out, sliding one finger under the strap of her bra where it rested on her shoulder. She went still, his touch searing all the remaining air from her lungs.

He'd touched her before, many times. Hugs and kisses. An arm around her shoulders. A comforting pat here and there. But nothing like this.

It felt like he was slowly running a flame over her skin.

She trembled as he ran his finger back and forth, light and slow, his gaze fixed to her face, studying her reaction.

"Has anyone touched you like this since I've been away, Rachel?" he asked softly.

At least that was one truth she could give him. "N-No."

His finger slid around and over her collarbone, and she couldn't understand why she was trembling. Those other touches he'd once given her hadn't made her feel like this, as if her skin had gotten so tight she might burst out of it.

"No one at all?"

She couldn't speak this time. What the hell was wrong with her? Why the hell was she feeling like this? It was only a touch, nothing more.

"Why not?" His fingertip moved to the hollow of her throat and paused, resting there lightly.

You know why not.

Strange how difficult it was to think with his finger resting right there on her skin. With the heat of his body so close and that maddening, tantalizing smoky scent wrapping around her senses. It disturbed her, especially the ache that was beginning to form, right down low inside her. An ache she'd only ever felt when—

She stopped the thought dead.

"Because I don't have time for that kind of thing," she forced out. "I'm too busy."

"That's not the reason." He moved his finger back and forth, a light, tantalizing caress, and the ache inside her deepened. "I want to know, Rachel. I want to know who you've been seeing."

"Why?" She almost choked. "Why is that so important to you?"

"You don't get to ask the questions." His stroking finger paused, pressing lightly against her pulse. "Only I do. Now tell me."

You can't tell him the real reason. You can't tell anyone.

"I just didn't meet anyone I wanted, okay?"

Levi's finger pressed a little harder. "What about me?"

Her throat closed up, the ferocity of his gaze almost unbearable.

"The truth." His voice was a low growl, an order. "You owe me, Sunshine."

Sunshine.

Bastard. How dare he use that name, knowing what it meant to her. What it meant to them both.

Anger twisted through her, and she met his stare with something of her old challenge. "Does it matter? You're going to take what you want from me anyway."

The light was behind him, glossing the deep, dark gold of his hair and shadowing his face. One eye was in darkness, the other bright and fierce, but something flickered through them, a shadow, a cloud passing over the sun.

"Oh, it matters," he murmured. "Because, no, I'm not going to take. I'm going to make you want to give it to me. I'm going to make you beg for it. I'm going to make it so you can't think of anything else but me touching you." He slid his finger up the column of her neck, trailing it lightly over her skin before taking her chin between his forefinger and thumb, holding her steady. "I'm going to make you so fucking desperate. Exactly the way you made me so fucking desperate." The shadow had gone from his gaze now, only hunger and fierce determination glittering there.

And she shivered again, deep in her soul. Frightened. Yet it was a fear that was intertwined with something else, a dark, intense thrill.

Why the hell are you getting off on this? Or do you only like it when sex is a transaction?

A long forgotten feeling swept through her, joining the confusing tangle already knotting in her gut. Shame. It burned like acid, corroding her insides.

She pushed it savagely away. No, fuck, she wasn't feeling that anymore, just like she wasn't going to feel desire. She was done with both of those. So he wanted to make her want him? Well, she could do that. All she had to do was pretend, and she could pretend with the best of them. He'd never know the difference. After all, Evan hadn't.

His expression betrayed nothing, and, since her voice had gone missing, she remained silent. He released her chin. "Turn around."

She obeyed without protest, only to have every muscle lock as she felt his hands settle on the catch of her bra, undoing it. The straps slid off her shoulders, warm air moving over her bare skin as the fabric fell away, her breasts freed.

Pretend. That's all she had to do. Protect herself and pretend.

He discarded her bra onto the floor.

She stared at the office wall straight in front of her, every single atom of her awareness focused on the man behind her. He had to be standing close because she could feel his heat at her back.

And then he touched her, that maddening finger resting on the nape of her neck before trailing lightly down the column of her spine, sending out little shockwaves of sensation, like ripples from a stone thrown into a quiet pond.

She steeled herself against them, biting down on the shaky sound that threatened to escape as his finger came to rest on the small of her back. And it was only then that she remembered what she'd had Xavier tattoo there. It made her want to turn around, grab for something—anything—to protect herself with.

But it was too late.

"What's this?" His finger moved on her skin, tracing the tattoo, the outline of a small sun with stylized rays extending from it.

A black sun. A dark sun.

"Is that what I think it is?" Levi murmured, his touch circling it, around and around.

She'd had it done six months after he'd gone away for good. Black because she couldn't bear color in it, and right down low on her spine so she'd always have it at her back. A private reminder that would mean nothing to anyone but herself.

And Levi.

Her jaw was tight, and she remained silent, not saying a word. She didn't need to reply; he knew what it was and what it meant.

He was quiet, his touch falling away, and there was a moment when the silence was so deafening it was like the aftermath of an explosion.

Then voices came from downstairs, Gideon's deep laugh and Zoe's lighter one. Tamara saying something and Zee's husky tones replying. The sounds of friendship and acceptance, of safety. Of family.

It felt wrong to be up here, half-naked and trembling, while life went on downstairs. Wrong to let Levi touch her when the others were so close. What did they think was happening up here?

Don't think of that. You're going to do this, give him what he wants to save your business, and then you're going to move on. Like you did before.

Levi's hands were at the catch of her leather mini, and he was undoing it, pulling down the zipper, sliding the leather down her thighs, pulling the skirt down to her ankles and making her step out of it. Leaving her in nothing but her black lace panties and silver platform sandals.

And as she had when he'd touched her back, she made sure she was steel. Ignoring the shivers that chased through her as she felt him come close again, as his hands pulled at the side of her panties, fabric tearing and falling away from her body so that she was naked except for her sandals.

There was another dense, heavy, impossible silence.

The heat behind her receded, and she heard him take a couple of steps back. But she didn't make the mistake of thinking he was leaving, not when she could feel the weight of his gaze resting on her.

This was nothing. She'd done this before. And then she'd imagined that she was on a beach, lying in the sun. It hadn't touched her then. It wouldn't touch her now.

"I thought about you like this a lot," Levi said, after what felt like years. "Standing naked in front of me. Ready to give me whatever I asked for."

Her heartbeat was loud in her head, and her palms felt damp.

No, she was on the beach, and the sun was hot. That's why she was hot. It was the sun, nothing else.

The heat at her back returned, Levi coming close, and she stiffened despite everything. Then one of his hands came down on her hip, and the feel of his palm against her naked flesh nearly made her cry out. It burned her, seared her, left a scar on every sense she had.

Calm the hell down. This is easy, remember?

Yeah, she remembered. She was *not* here with Levi. She was at the fucking beach. There was sand underneath her, and she had a drink in her hand. And no one was touching her. No one at all.

But he was, one arm sliding around her waist and pulling her up against him, so that the hard heat of his body was pressed to her spine. Keeping one hand on her hip, he rested the other flat on her stomach, his fingers pointing down, almost but not quite brushing the soft curls between her thighs.

All the breath left her lungs in an explosive rush, her body going absolutely rigid with shock. She felt suddenly dizzy, overcome by sensation. The rough denim of his jeans against her butt. The hard wall of his chest at her back. The incredible heat of his palm against her stomach. And the smoky scent of him all around her . . .

She couldn't move. Couldn't even think.

Warm breath feathered the back of her neck and then beneath her ear, and it didn't matter how much she tried to think of the beach, of tropical sun and sand, she remained firmly right here, every nerve ending she had tight with awareness.

"I dreamt of this too." His voice was soft, the rich timbre of it roughened with heat. "Of holding you like this." His hips shifted, and she could feel the hardness of his cock against her butt. "Of bending you over and getting inside that tight little pussy. And I will, Rachel, make no mistake, I will. But you know what I want right now."

She stared at the wall, trying to moderate her breathing, trying to control the wild beat of her heart and the terrible, empty ache between her thighs. The one she didn't want, the one she was trying to distance herself from however she could. "What's that?" she forced out.

His hand on her stomach stretched out lazily while the other pressed hard into the flesh at her hip. Then she nearly gasped as she felt the brush of his mouth against her ear, his voice a rough murmur against her skin. "You know, sweetheart. I told you. I want you desperate. I want you to suffer like I did."

He left her no time at all to process that, the hand on her stomach pushing down, sliding into her damp curls, finding the hard bud of her clit with unerring accuracy and applying firm pressure.

Rachel jerked in his arms, a lightning strike of sensation spearing her, punching right through the steel she thought she'd encased herself with, ripping a helpless, choked sound from her.

"You like that?" Another dark, rough velvet murmur.

You're supposed to pretend.

Yes, yes. Pretend to him that she wanted him. Pretend to herself that she didn't feel anything, that she was on the goddamn beach.

"Yes." Her own voice sounded so husky. "Yes, I love it."

Instantly his hand moved away, and she almost sagged in his arms in relief, her thighs trembling. Yet he didn't release her, keeping the hard wall of his body at her back, his hand pressed against her stomach. "You don't sound convinced. Perhaps I need to try something else?"

"No," she wanted to say. "No, don't try anything else," but this wasn't supposed to matter. This wasn't supposed to affect her, so she stayed silent as his hand slid down again, but this time slowly, so achingly slowly. His fingers brushed through the damp curls between her thighs, tangling in the soft damp hair, before closing into a fist and tugging gently.

A gentle pain, a sharp jolt of sensation.

She let out a harsh breath and closed her eyes, trying to visualize her beach again, the sun, the sound of the water. The cool feel of the drink in her hand.

"Is that better?" His mouth brushed the side of her neck again, lower this time. "Or perhaps this?" There were teeth against her skin and pressure as he bit gently down on the sensitive cords of her neck.

Pretend. Pretend.

But it wasn't happening. The beach image shattered behind her eyes, and she made some kind of sobbing sound in her throat as the hand between her thighs released her, then achingly slowly began to part the soft folds of her pussy. The combination of his bite and the movement of his hand made her vision blur, made her forget what she was supposed to be doing.

She was supposed to be distancing herself. She was supposed to be pretending.

But then the other hand at her hip was moving down too, and he was holding her open, spreading her with one hand while the other stroked down the center of her sex in one light, long movement. And she couldn't hold back the groan that escaped her. Couldn't stop the jerk of her hips or prevent the tremble of her thighs.

Then he did it again. And again. Long, slow strokes of his finger, sliding down, pausing at the entrance to her body and circling around, pressing gently, almost pushing in but not quite, then sliding back up again.

She hadn't been touched like this before. Never ever. She hadn't even touched herself like this. It was . . . maddening.

A wave of heat broke out all over her skin, scorching her as a pleasure she didn't want to admit to began to gather in a tight, hard knot.

Think of the beach.

Yes, God, she had to. It was the only way to keep herself distant, protect herself.

"You're desperate now, aren't you?" He flexed his hips, the hard ridge of his cock pressing against her butt, his finger stroking up and down. "You want me, Rachel?"

She was shivering, and she couldn't stop. "Yes . . ." It was supposed to be a lie. At least, it had to be a lie, didn't it? Because she couldn't actually want him. Couldn't actually want this, not really.

"You don't sound sure." That maddening, stroking finger moved away, and she felt him grab one of her wrists. Instinctively she resisted, but he drew her hand with inexorable strength between her thighs, guiding it. "Here, I'll show you."

She couldn't stop him, her jaw tight and aching as her own fingers slid over her sex, feeling her own slick flesh, the evidence of her own desire wet on her fingertips.

"See?" The rough purr of his voice was like a touch. "You like this, Rachel. You want this."

There was a voice in her head, a different voice, telling her the same thing, and she tried to block it out. Because she didn't want this; she never had. The words she had said were only pretend.

But her body, the traitorous bitch, wasn't pretending, and when he guided her finger higher, to her clit, sliding her fingertip over and around it, transmitting tiny electric shocks of sensation down each nerve ending, she couldn't tell herself it wasn't pleasure she felt.

It *was* pleasure. So much of it, like a fire building inside her. *You can't feel this. You're not allowed.*

And just like that, the dark, insidious sense of shame was swamping her, choking her.

Hardly even aware of what she was doing, Rachel jerked herself out of his arms and away from him, stumbling forward a few steps, reaching out blindly to the desk in front of her to stop herself from falling.

Her breath was coming hard and fast, and everything ached. And that shame, that terrible sense of humiliation, seemed to pervade her every pore.

"Point proved, wouldn't you say?" Levi's hard voice was roughened, the cold edge blunted by the heat running through it. "I think we both know you want me."

She leaned against the desk, forcing herself to stop shaking, willing away the toxic combination of unfulfilled desire and shame that burned in her blood. What could she say to that? Nothing. He had, indeed, proved his point.

"What you feel now?" he went on, relentless. "That's what I've been feeling for eight years. Every fucking night. So now you're going to suffer through it just like I did."

A belated anger stirred inside her. Anger at him for doing this to her, for tearing her armor apart like it was made of tissue. Anger at her own weakness, because, Jesus, she should have been able to withstand Levi.

She pushed herself away from the desk and turned around, suddenly not giving a shit that she was naked. She met his disturbing, uneven gaze. Wanted to face him, show him that she was stronger than he seemed to think she was.

He was standing so close and obviously not expecting her to turn, because when she did, he took a step back, his eyes flaring in shock. Then the shock faded, replaced by a naked hunger, a burning need that slammed into her with the force of a blow.

Levi didn't move, and yet his whole body was rigid, a muscle flicking in his jaw. And she had the impression that it was only his own titanic will that was stopping him from closing the distance between them.

For some reason that made her feel better, made her feel as if she had some of her power back, which was weird considering she was naked and he wasn't. She straightened, putting her shoulders back and watching as his gaze dropped down her body. Like he couldn't help himself.

"What?" She raised an eyebrow. "No blow job? No screw on the desk? That's not what you promised, Levi."

He turned sharply away, his hands jammed into the pockets of his jeans. "I'll come for you tomorrow," he said, rough, curt. "Be ready."

"What do you mean tomorrow?"

He was still a moment. Then his gaze came to hers, the echoes of that need and hunger lingering in his eyes. "If you think this is all I want, you're wrong."

Foreboding turned over inside her. "But I—"

"Tomorrow, Rachel." He gave her one last intent look, then he turned and headed toward the door, unlocking it, pushing it open and letting it slam shut after him.

Tomorrow. Jesus Christ.

The wood of the desk was hard and cold against her bare skin, making her aware of her nakedness. Making her aware too of the heat between her thighs and the slow throb of desire that hadn't gone away, that hadn't faded one iota.

More voices floated up from downstairs, calling out good-byes from the sounds of it. Probably because Levi was leaving.

So much for a homecoming.

Rachel passed a shaking hand across her forehead, shoving away the unfulfilled ache, pretending she didn't feel a goddamn thing. Then slowly she bent to pick up her clothes from the ground and began to dress. Unfortunately she couldn't do anything with her ripped panties, so she had to stuff them into the wastebasket and hope like hell no one would know she had nothing on underneath her skirt, and that no one would go looking through the trash later.

Hope that they wouldn't have heard her cry out and wouldn't

guess what had happened upstairs. Because she didn't think she could stand it if they did.

Smoothing down her skirt, she crossed to the door and put her hand out to open it, pausing a moment to take a breath and make sure her armor was in place.

Then she pushed the door open and went downstairs, as if nothing had happened.

Chapter 6

Levi stepped out of the ice-cold shower the next morning and grabbed the lone towel on the rail, drying himself off roughly. He'd hoped the cold water would ease the fire burning in his blood from the night before, but it hadn't made the slightest bit of difference.

He was still hard. And he still ached.

He could still feel the heat of Rachel's soft, slick pussy against his fingers and smell the musky scent of her arousal. Could still hear the sound of her cry as he'd run his fingers around and around her clit, making her shake in his arms.

And he could still see her leaning against Gideon's desk, completely naked, all lush curves and golden skin. Full breasts and silken curls between her thighs. The sight was burned into his brain as indelibly as the ink of his tattoos into his skin.

He was never going to get that out. Never.

Little bitch. She'd turned to face him deliberately; he was sure of it. Making sure he got a good look at her nakedness. And it had only been sheer force of will that had held him back from screwing them both into oblivion on Gideon's desk.

Thank Christ, he'd managed to hold onto his control, because a quick end to this was not what he'd been planning. She had to suffer first, like he'd suffered. Be left aching and wanting, with no relief in sight.

Now dry, Levi put the damp towel back on the rail and stalked out of the bathroom and into his bedroom.

It was mainly empty, apart from the air bed in the middle of the room.

He stopped and stared at the bed, frowning. That was going to have to go, especially if Rachel was going to be here. Which she would, because that was all part of his plan too.

She was going to live with him, just like he'd always dreamed. In a nice apartment, where there weren't drug deals going on in the hallway and lowlifes gathering in the stairwells. Or whores next door taking clients and loud, drunken parties at all hours. Where she didn't have to worry about anything or be afraid of anyone.

Anyone except you, right?

He shoved that thought away, dressing quickly then turning to go through the set of double doors that led from the bedroom into another large space, where there were windows set in the ceiling, flooding the area with light. The space had been painted white, just like rest of the apartment, and he could already see it, Rachel standing here in front of the massive canvas propped up against one wall, brush in her hand.

Her very own studio. Where she could create the art she loved.

Levi leaned against the white painted brick, mentally measuring up the space. He hadn't wanted to stock the studio since he knew fuck all about painting, had been planning to take Rachel shopping at an art store so she could get the supplies she wanted in fact, but he had a couple of things already in mind to put in here. A sweet architectural light fitting he'd seen in a home magazine in the prison library a while back. A long chaise lounge since that was the kind of shit artists put in studios. Except this one would be upholstered in soft black leather because Rachel was edgy like that, and when he came in here to see her after she'd spent an afternoon painting, he'd push her down onto it, get inside her, make her scream. . . .

His breath caught. His jeans were suddenly way too fucking tight.

No more goddamn fantasies. Time to make this shit a reality. Now.

Pushing himself away from the wall, he stalked back through the apartment, grabbing his keys from the counter in the kitchen before letting himself out.

He walked to Rachel's tattoo studio, observing the neighborhood with a business eye as he went. Running over the plans he already had in place. A massive space in the old building by the sex shop that should hopefully attract a few big-box stores. And then in the building down the street a ways, some more apartments, not too high-end, but nice enough to get a few more people with money in the area.

Rounding a corner, he came to a halt, staring at the building across the street.

Rachel's building.

This would be his jewel in the crown. He'd gut the whole thing, get some fucking fancy architect to redesign it while keeping the industrial feeling that rich people liked. Then he'd put all the really high-end décor shit into it. Make it exclusive and expensive, and maybe put a café in the basement, or one of those specialized supermarkets that sold gourmet food.

Man, he'd have those rich folks looking for a cheaper alternative to downtown lining up with their checkbooks at the ready.

He smiled, feeling better than he had in weeks. Satisfied finally to be making progress on all those plans that had been stuck in his head for way too long.

Levi crossed the street and approached the building, pulling open the door to Sugar Ink and stepping inside.

Music vibrated through the space, a hard, house bass line that had him grimacing since he wasn't into that kind of crap. Resisting the urge to tell them to turn that shit down, he scanned around the studio instead, spotting Rachel sitting next to one of the tattoo chairs, in the process of inking a client.

Her black hair had been pulled back into a neat ponytail, the look on her lovely face pure concentration. He recognized that look, the one she got whenever she was drawing in her notebooks, with her brows pulled down and her tongue between her teeth, her hand moving as delicately and precisely as that of a bomb disposal expert defusing a bomb.

For a moment he stood there staring at her, watching her hand move across her client's skin, creating beauty as she went, oblivious to the fact that he was standing there, oblivious to everything but what she was doing. And something heavy and painful caught in his chest.

He remembered this. Remembered watching her like this. Wishing she would look at him with that same concentration. Touch him with that same focused delicacy. And he remembered, too, the ache of knowing she never would.

But not now. Now, she's yours.

Yeah, she fucking was.

Yet for reasons he couldn't explain, irritation coiled inside him as he turned away and went to sit down on the battered velvet couch in the studio's waiting area. He didn't know what the hell was wrong with him. Probably impatience. But he could wait while she finished what she was doing. It would give him a moment to take a closer look around the space in greater detail anyway.

He'd seen it the day before of course, but then his head had been too full of her to really appreciate it. Now, he sat back and looked around at the exposed brick of the walls, the industrial lights, the jewelry displays in what looked to be old hospital medicine cabinets, and the collection of clothes on a battered iron rail.

The whole place looked cool and quirky, just the kind of place hipsters would come looking for bird tattoos, and yet with a grim, semi-seedy edge that would appeal to old-school-style clients.

His gaze shifted to the massive piece of graffiti art on the wall opposite the tattoo chairs. A beautiful woman's face with a sugar-skull overlay. A crown of roses circled her head, an explosion of flowers and birds and vines erupting from behind her and climbing up the walls. Definitely Rachel's work; he'd recognize it anywhere.

It was beautiful and yet disturbing at the same time with the image of death over the woman's face. Which made it kind of perfect for a place like this.

Christ, she had so much talent. And it was cool to see how she'd managed to make her dreams a reality in the form of this studio. Except she could have aimed higher. So much fucking higher. She'd once wanted a gallery in New York, or to study in Paris, and she certainly had the talent.

Why the hell had she settled for a goddamn tattoo parlor?

The door banged open, and a man walked in, chains jingling from his belt, flames inked onto his arms. He paused, then pulled a face. "Jesus, Hamilton, not this shit music again."

She didn't look up from her work, merely extending one hand and showing him a middle finger.

The man laughed, then sauntered over to the metal counter where the register was, going behind it and bending to fiddle with something. Instantly the house beat was gone, replaced by something quieter and folkie.

Which was kind of weird for a tattoo studio, but then this guy obviously worked here, so who knew?

The guy straightened, then, spotting Levi sitting there, he

came around the counter and approached the couch, a friendly smile on his face. "Hey, can I help you?"

Not in the mood to chat, Levi didn't smile back. "No."

The man's eyes narrowed, his gaze dropping to the black bands around Levi's arms. "Nice blackwork. Who did it?"

An artist in prison. With staples and stolen ink. The tattoos had taken forever, hurt like fuck, and cost him a shitload. But the pain had been a kind of meditation, a way to pass the time. And the rings, well . . .

"No one you know," Levi said.

The man stared at him a long moment. "You're Levi, aren't you? Rachel's friend."

There was something about the look in the guy's dark eyes that Levi didn't like. "What's it to you?"

The friendly manner had dropped from the other man entirely. He put his hands in the pockets of his low-slung, ripped jeans, giving Levi an unfriendly look. "I'm Xavier," he said. "I work here with Rachel. And I hear you're blackmailing her."

Levi almost laughed. "Is that what she told you?"

"I don't give a shit if you've just come out of jail or what." Xavier's stance was all aggression, the look on his face grim. "She's my friend, and, if you hurt her, I'll fucking hurt you back. That's all I'm saying."

For a minute Levi just sat there and stared at the other man, debating whether or not to drag him outside and beat the shit out of him. Because he could. He'd gained himself quite a reputation inside for being able to take care of himself and deal with anyone else who fucked with him, and although this guy looked strong, Levi was pretty confident he could take him down if necessary.

But then that would probably violate the terms of his parole quite significantly, and Levi wouldn't risk going back inside just for the pleasure of putting his fist in this asshole's face.

Fuck's sake, not everyone is a threat. You've been inside way too long.

Yeah, Christ, he had. Time to chill the hell out.

He lifted his shoulder. "Rachel can take care of herself. She's a grown woman."

Xavier glowered at him, clearly spoiling for a fight. "If you want to talk to her, she's busy with a client."

"I can see that. I'm not fucking blind."

The other man's expression darkened even further. Without taking his gaze off Levi, he said, "Yo, Hamilton. You got someone here to see you."

At that, Rachel finally looked up from her work, glancing over to where Levi sat, her eyes meeting his. And he felt desire hit him like a brick to the head, a kind of shuddering impact that he felt right down to his bones.

Yet her face remained expressionless, and, after a moment, she glanced back down at the arm she was in the process of inking, as if she didn't give a shit Levi was sitting there waiting for her. As if he were just another client waiting for her artistry.

"I'll be another ten minutes," she said, and raised her tattoo gun again.

Whatever, he wasn't going anywhere. He could sit here all day if necessary.

Xavier eventually left Levi alone as another client came in, and Levi just sat there, leafing through various tattoo and hipster fashion magazines, waiting until Rachel finished up.

It wasn't ten minutes in the end but half an hour, and as her client went out the door and she finished cleaning up her station, Levi pushed himself to his feet and stood there, his arms folded, waiting.

She didn't look at him as she put her equipment in an autoclave and pulled off the disposable latex gloves she wore, throwing them into a wastebasket under the long counter that ran the length of the wall. Taking her own sweet fucking time.

Eventually though, she turned and came over to where he stood.

She wore a tight strapless top made out of some kind of silvery fabric and formfitting leggings of black leather. On her feet were a pair of black, platform boots with silver buckles. Black eyeliner ringed her eyes, along with more of that silvery shadow he recognized from the night before.

She looked tough and edgy and so goddamn sexy he had to drop his arms and put his hands in the pockets of his jeans to stop from reaching for her.

"Gideon is pretty pissed off about the way you left last night," she said after an awkward moment of silence.

Yeah, he knew that. He'd seen the texts his friend had left, and heard the annoyed voice mail message. And he did feel pretty bad about it.

But after what had happened between him and Rachel, Levi hadn't been able to face sitting back down with the others and drinking beer like everything was fine. Especially with a hardon the size of Texas in his jeans.

"I know," he replied. "I'll talk to him later. Right now, you and I need to have a conversation."

"Great." Her expression was shuttered. "Another conversation. Just what I need." She folded her arms. "Will I have to be naked for this one too? Because I don't think I want to have it here if that's the case."

Looked like Gideon wasn't the only one pissed with him, not that Levi was surprised given the way he'd left her. Good. That was what he'd intended.

He studied her, noting the dark circles beneath her eyes. "I told you I'd make you suffer."

A faint stain of color washed over her cheekbones. "I didn't suffer."

"Why not? Did you touch yourself, sweetheart?"

The color deepened until her cheeks were almost the same

red as the vivid red ink of the rose drooping over her bare shoulder and the scatter of petals falling over the smooth skin her chest.

Weird that someone who looked so edgy should be so goddamn prudish.

Abruptly she turned and glanced to where Xavier was, chatting with his client as he inked the guy's back. "Can we do this somewhere else?" she murmured. "I'm not talking to you about this here."

Damn straight they weren't. "I wasn't planning on talking to you here. I have something to show you."

Her brow creased. "What?"

Without thinking, he held out his hand to her. "Come on. You'll see."

Her gaze dropped to the hand he held out, but she made no move to take it, leaving him standing there like a tool with his hand extended.

Fuck that.

He reached forward and grabbed one of her hands, closing his fingers around it tightly. All the muscles in her arm went stiff, a gleam of anger in her eyes, and he could feel her resisting him.

He held on tighter. "I said, come on."

The anger glittered brighter, but the resistance in her arm faded. "Where are we going?"

"It's a surprise."

That didn't win him any points either—he could tell by the stubborn cast to her jaw—but she said nothing, merely calling out something to Xavier about going out for a bit, then letting him lead her out of the studio and back into the summer heat.

She remained quiet as they walked along the sidewalk, her hand unmoving in his. Maybe it had been a mistake to take her hand, because all it did was make him bitterly conscious of the softness of her skin against his, of the warmth of her.

He'd planned to show her the apartment, but he'd wanted at

least a bed in there before he actually screwed her. Somewhere to get comfortable, where they could both settle in, because this wasn't going to be fast and over before he knew it. He wanted to take his time.

Levi glanced down at the hand holding Rachel's. At the black letters he'd had inked into the backs of his knuckles as another reminder, the *PATI* that went with the *ENCE* on the other hand.

Patience.

Yeah, he had to remember that. He'd had to learn how to cultivate that patience through all the years inside, and it had been tough, but he'd learned. Just like he'd learned all about control.

Patience and control were the keys to power, to getting shit done. And that hadn't changed just because he was out.

Rachel said nothing as they walked. She didn't look at him. Her hand was relaxed in his, but he didn't make the mistake of thinking she was comfortable with it where it was. She was only doing this because he'd blackmailed her into it. Just like her letting him touch her upstairs in Gideon's office had been.

A heavy, uncomfortable sensation moved in his chest, and it felt like regret, which annoyed him. Because regret wasn't going to get him what he wanted. Only patience, only control. Only focusing on his goddamn goal.

Besides, she might only be doing this because of the blackmail, but she'd definitely wanted him. Hell, he'd felt the proof of that himself, in the wet heat of her pussy against his fingers, in the way she'd moved against his hand, wanting more.

She *did* want him. She just didn't like the fact that she did. Which was fine; he could work with that. In fact, it might just make everything that much sweeter.

Five minutes later, Levi unlocked the door to his apartment building and led her inside. There was a small foyer area with stairs circling up above their heads and an antique-looking cage elevator right in front of them.

He strode to the elevator, pulling aside the sliding metal screen that was its door and gesturing her into it. She went without a word, not looking at him as he pulled the metal screen shut and punched the top-floor button. The elevator jerked, then started going up.

It was a tiny space, and she was standing so very close to him. Her scent made his mouth go dry, and he couldn't stop looking at the way her silvery top molded to the luscious curves of her breasts. He wanted to push the fabric down, trace the scatter of rose petals with his tongue, free her tits, put his mouth on her skin, lick her up like honey. Suck on her nipples and make her scream . . .

Her gaze flicked to his, then away again, color creeping over her lovely skin, the space between them hot and thick with tension.

So, she knew what he was thinking? Good.

The elevator came to a jerking halt, and Rachel was reaching out for the metal handle, hauling the door of the cage aside as if she was desperate to get out. Desperate to get away from him.

He made no move to stop her, because again, he wasn't going to have her quick and dirty, and certainly not in a fucking elevator.

Patience and control. That's how it was going to be until he got what he wanted.

He was going to make her beg, and nothing was going to happen until she did.

Rachel was shivering, her heart thundering; she was desperate to breathe. She didn't know what he'd done to her, but the way he'd looked at her had brought back all those feelings from the night before. The desperate, unfulfilled ache. The tight, hard knot of pleasure. The choking shame. And all she could think about was getting out of the fucking elevator, getting away from him.

She stepped out of the little iron cage, putting some distance between them and walking quickly into the center of the small hallway the elevator opened out onto.

Then she stopped short, realizing there was nowhere else to go except down the stairs off to her right. Swallowing, she tried to get a grip on herself. Tried to ignore the way her breasts felt heavy and full, the fabric of her top rubbing against her sensitized nipples. It made her want to shiver.

Damn him.

"What the hell are we doing here?" she demanded, not looking at him and hunching her shoulders as he came up beside her.

She'd thought this building had been just another of the abandoned ones, and yet, when he'd unlocked the door and taken her inside, the place had been clean. There was no trash in the corners or graffiti on the walls. The windows all had glass in them, and there had even been lighting. Totally different from her tattoo building when she'd moved in, when it had taken her a week just to clean up the trash on the ground floor.

"You'll see." Levi continued past her and on down the hallway to where there was a door, his boots making scraping noises on the bare wooden floor. He stopped in front of the door, getting his keys out.

She stared at his tall, broad figure, the fascinating black bands around his arms highlighting the perfect muscularity of his biceps and forearms as he reached for the keys. He was in a blue T-shirt today, the color deepening the dark gold of his skin and hair, a pair of old and faded jeans sitting low on his hips. He bent his head as he fit the key into the lock, and she found herself staring at the strong column of his neck, the odd vulnerability of his nape. Her fingers itched, like she wanted to touch him there, stroke him, feel the silky soft curls of his hair against her skin.

A weird thing to think of doing. Especially when touching him anywhere was the last thing she wanted to do.

Sure you don't. You couldn't stop thinking about it last night. You can't stop thinking about it now.

Rachel stuffed her hands into her pockets and bit her lip. Well, it was true she hadn't been able to sleep very well the night before, but that wasn't because of Levi. Definitely not.

Liar.

She bit her lip. Hard.

When she'd finally gotten home from Gideon's, she'd thought she was okay, that she'd successfully packed away all those un-wanted physical feelings into a box in the corner of her mind somewhere, never to be opened again.

But after lying awake for hours, unable to sleep, she'd fi-nally been forced to admit to herself that far from being suc-cessfully packed away, those physical feelings were somehow leaking out, making her restless and hot and achy.

Her mind kept replaying the feel of his fingers on her, the heat of his body behind her, the way he'd held her, touched her, over and over again. Until she'd had to get up and have a very long, very cold shower just in order to get some sleep.

Even now she could still feel that ache, the slow, steady pulse of desire between her thighs.

And along with it, that horrible, dirty feeling, the way she'd always felt after Evan—

No. Think of the beach. Think of the goddamn beach.

Levi pushed open the door at last and turned, gesturing her inside. The look on his face was completely enigmatic.

"What's in there?" she asked, a weird foreboding tightening in her gut.

"You'll see."

"Levi . . ."

"Go in, Rachel."

Ridiculous. She was being ridiculous. There was no reason to be afraid to walk through that doorway. And since when had she ever given in to fear anyway?

Pulling herself together, she brushed past him and stepped through the doorway into another short hallway.

She walked down it, not bothering to see whether or not he'd followed her, coming to a big arched entranceway that led into the most stunning apartment she'd ever seen.

Stopping dead in the entranceway, she stared around her, eyes wide.

There was no furniture, but the brick walls looked to have been freshly painted white, while the wooden floorboards had been stripped back, polished, then varnished. Big windows let in lots of light, making the rich honey of the floorboards almost glow. The ceilings were high, giving the place an airy feel and making it seem huge.

She took a few steps into the empty room, the sounds of her footsteps echoing. The smells of fresh paint and varnish lingered in the air.

The room seemed familiar to her somehow, as if this was an apartment she'd once been in or seen a picture of somewhere. An apartment she'd once thought she'd love to live in. Because it was definitely the kind of place she'd always thought was really cool. Lots of space and full of light.

Nothing she could ever afford herself of course.

Levi's footsteps sounded behind her. "What do you think?"

She turned and met his intense blue and black stare. "What do you mean 'what do I think'? I don't know what this place is or why I'm here."

Levi walked over to the windows in a kind of long, loping stride that had her watching the way he moved, unable to take her eyes off the sheer athletic grace of him. He stopped, glancing out the window before looking back at her.

The sun coming through the glass picked up the gold in his dark tawny hair, catching the same glints in his ridiculously long eyelashes. It made his one dark eye seem even darker, the blue of the other lighter, and glinted off the eyebrow ring in his left eyebrow.

Her heart lurched stupidly. He was so hot he almost didn't seem real.

Another feeling she remembered: the horribly painful crush she'd once had on him. Now it was as if she were standing on the edge of that precipice again, teetering on the brink, part of her wanting to throw herself off it and fall.

She'd always thought it would hurt to land, that it would break her. But the falling . . . God, the falling would feel so good.

Are you insane? Now?

Yeah, things were different now. He had changed so much he was almost unrecognizable as the friend he'd once been. The boy whose smile used to brighten her whole day.

There were no smiles now, and as Levi braced one forearm on the window frame and leaned against it, his gaze was intense, compelling. "You're here because I wanted you to see what our apartment will look like," he said in that rich, rough voice of his.

She frowned, not understanding. "Our apartment?"

"This place. This is our apartment, Rachel. Yours and mine."

"What? What the hell are you talking about? I don't live with you. I've got my own place down on Park Street." It was her gran's cheap, crappy apartment that was even crappier but unfortunately no more cheap now.

He shifted against the window frame, the sun following the perfect lines of his face, catching a hint of gold stubble along his strong jaw. "Remember we talked about it once? We were having a conversation about our ideal places to live, and you told me you wanted an apartment that had lots of space and lots of windows."

Tension was knotting inside her. There was something about this place, something about the look on his face, in his eyes, that was making her feel . . . half afraid, half angry. "Yeah?" She couldn't keep the impatience out of her tone. "And?"

"And I wanted the same. I also wanted it to be on the top floor of a building so I could have a view. And I wanted it white because that was clean."

Oh, yeah, she remembered that conversation. The day she'd found out that he too was looking after someone. Except his father didn't have dementia; his father was just a drunk. She'd knocked on Levi's door needing something or other, she couldn't remember what, and he hadn't answered. But the door had been unlocked, and so she'd just walked in because he'd told her that she could. And she'd found him in a nasty, dingy bedroom, cleaning up vomit from the floor beside the bed, an older man fast asleep and snoring in the bed.

Levi hadn't been embarrassed about it, only matter-of-fact, but she'd seen the distress in his eyes, so she'd started telling him about her ideal apartment. They'd ended up having a big discussion about what each of them really wanted in a place to live and what made a home, a home.

White because he'd wanted it to be clean. Of course he did. . . .

Struggling both with the memory and with what he was saying now, she shook her head. "Yeah, yeah, I get that, but—"

"So I bought it for us, Rachel. This apartment, this building is mine. I had it cleaned up while I was inside, and I have some other plans for it. But this apartment right here"—he gestured around the room—"this is ours."

Shock was moving through her, making it difficult to think. "How did you . . . buy this building?"

"The same way I bought yours. With money I invested. Dad had an old life insurance policy that ended up paying out big when he died, and I had some money saved from working at Gideon's."

She took a breath, trying to get it all sorted out in her head. "Okay, but this isn't ours. I mean, like I said. I live in—"

"I want you to move in with me."

The words hung in the air, echoing in the empty space around them.

Rachel stared at him, conscious of how the shock was now spreading out inside her, freezing her in place. "Move in with you?" she repeated stupidly.

"Yeah. You can pack up your stuff, and I'll help you bring it here. Of course, there are a few things we're going to need, like furniture. A bed definitely."

She blinked as what he was saying finally pierced the shock clouding her head. "You're seriously asking me to live with you?"

Something glinted in his gaze. "I'm not asking."

Instantly she was bristling; she couldn't help it. "Jesus, Levi. I'm not—"

"I told you I wanted you in every way there was, and this is one of those ways." He said the words as if there were no room for argument, as if it was already a done deal and she'd already agreed. "And you're going to do it."

The shock was beginning to recede now, anger pushing it back. She had to take a breath to keep the anger under control, because seriously, was he insane? Was he really just expecting her to drop everything and move in with him, just because it was what he wanted?

"I thought you meant sex," she said flatly. "You didn't say anything about moving in with you."

He stared at her. "I never said I only wanted sex, Rachel."

He didn't. You assumed.

Fuck.

"No." It was the only word she could think of to say. "I'm not moving in with you, Levi. I'm just not."

He didn't reply immediately, studying her. Then he dropped his arm from the window frame, stepped away from the window, and began to come toward her.

Rachel stilled. No, she would not be intimated. No, she

would not be afraid of him. And as for that unexpected thrill of excitement, well . . . she was not going to be feeling that either.

The look on his face was cold. "Remember that night?" he asked softly, the edges of his voice icy with menace. "When you went looking for that dealer because you needed the money? Because you were too fucking proud and too fucking stubborn to come to me and ask for help?"

Her mouth dried, her hands curling into fists as she determinedly held her ground. Of course he'd bring that up. Of course.

"Yeah, you remember, don't you?" he went on, coming closer, implacable. "I saved you, Rachel. I killed a man for you. And because I did, because you were there where you shouldn't have been, every fucking dream of the future I had was destroyed. So now you're coming to live with me, and you're going to help me rebuild that future. Because you owe me. You *fucking* owe me." He towered over her, so big and powerful and full of so much fury, a cold, relentless fury like an avalanche.

She didn't want to back away, didn't want to give him any ground at all, but his anger . . . She felt battered by it, nearly flattened by the hurricane force of it. And no wonder. He'd had to nurse this anger for so long all by himself, with no outlet.

You do *owe him.*

God help her. Maybe she did. And yet knowing that didn't make any difference to her own anger. Or to the small, frightened thing inside her. The one who wanted to hide behind walls and doors, who didn't want to be found.

Her nails dug into her palms, the slight pain helping her stay her ground and not retreat from him, even though every part of her wanted to. "So, what? I have to pack up my stuff and come live with you, just like that?"

There was no softening in his face, no lightening of the intensity in his eyes. He was a wall of solid, muscular rage, barely held in check. "Yes."

"What if I don't want to?"

"I don't give a fuck if you don't want to."

"You don't care about my feelings at all?"

His beautiful, sensual mouth twisted. "No." The word was blunt and heavy, like a hammer blow. "You lost the right to have your feelings cared about each and every year you didn't give a shit about mine."

Okay. That was clear. That was absolutely crystal. "So if I say no, you're going to drag me kicking and screaming?"

"Yes." No hesitation at all.

That small, frightened thing in her gut curled up tight. "Jesus, Levi. You sound like a fucking stalker."

A muscle ticked in his jaw, the flames in his eyes flickering. "You know what'll happen if I don't get what I want. You and your business will go out on the street."

God, he was so hard. As if he were encased in armor far thicker than hers had ever been.

She stared at him, trying to find any hint of softness. Any hint of the friend who'd once meant everything to her, the lightness that used to be part of him. But there was none.

Her friend was gone.

A deep well of sadness suddenly opened up inside her, and she realized, with a kind of despair, that there was a part of her that had been hoping she could fix what she'd done, heal the rift between them, and get back to being friends again.

Yet looking at him now, she knew that wasn't going to happen. He'd changed so very much and was so very angry. Some wounds went too deep and what she'd done . . . It was fatal.

Nothing was going to make this better. Nothing.

The stone on her chest was crushing, and suddenly she was wildly, furiously angry with him. "Don't put this all on me! If you hadn't hit that guy, he wouldn't have fallen and cracked his head open, and none of this would have happened in the first place!"

The flames in his eyes leapt high, and suddenly he'd closed

what little distance there was between them, getting right in her face. "I didn't mean to kill him! I was trying to save *you!*" His whole posture was rigid, the force of his anger like a battering ram. "You shouldn't have even been there that night, so why the fuck were you? Why the *fuck* didn't you come to me first?" And she saw it then, behind the fury, that deep wound that had never healed and probably never would. The wound she'd caused. "You should have come to me, Sunny." His voice cracked terribly. "You should have fucking come to me!"

She felt dazed, as if a bomb had exploded between them and she'd been hit by the shrapnel, cutting her in a thousand places and all of them bleeding.

All she could do was stand there staring at him, unable to take her gaze away from the raw pain in his eyes, a hurt she'd never dreamed of.

You knew. Deep down, you knew how badly you hurt him. That's why he's so very angry with you now.

There was a horrible, crashing silence.

Then abruptly Levi brushed past her and stalked out of the room.

Rachel blinked, her eyes dry and prickling. He was right; she should have gone to him all those years ago, but there had been reasons she hadn't. Reasons she hadn't wanted to tell him then and she wanted to tell him even less now.

But you still did this. And now you have to fix it.

But it couldn't be fixed, could it? So what the hell was she supposed to do?

Without any real idea of what she was going to say to him, she followed Levi back into the hallway and down toward the back of the apartment, coming out into what was obviously a bedroom given the air bed in the middle of the space.

Beyond it was a set of double doors standing open.

Through them was another empty, airy room, with sun pouring through skylights in the roof. Levi was standing facing the wall, and, as she watched, all of a sudden he brought his fist back and slammed it hard into the brick.

She was moving almost before she was conscious of doing so, crossing the bedroom and heading through the double doors, approaching his tall figure.

"You fucking idiot," she said, barely knowing what the hell was coming out of her mouth. "You really looking to break your goddamn hand?"

He turned sharply, the fury stark in his eyes.

She ignored him, answering an impulse so deeply ingrained it was no longer conscious, reaching for the hand he'd punched the wall with and taking it in her own, looking down at his knuckles. They were skinned and bleeding. "Dammit, Levi. I'm always having to bandage you up."

His hand was heavy and hot in hers, long, blunt-tipped fingers motionless in her palm. There were letters inked onto the backs of his knuckles, the black outlines shaded with blood. *P. A. T. I.*

She stared at the letters, at his hand, suddenly realizing what she was doing: looking after him. Because she always had. Because way back then, she hadn't known how else to repay him for the help he'd given her and her gran. So she'd ended up putting Band-Aids on the cuts and ice on the bruises he often ended up with when his dad was on one of his binges. She couldn't cook to save her life, but she could boil an egg, and heat mac and cheese, so she did both for him, making sure he had something to eat in between his shift at Gideon's and his night job stocking shelves at the 7-Eleven. And when she'd had some spare change, she'd bought him that awful candy he liked, Pixy Stix, to cheer him up.

It hadn't been much, but it had been better than nothing.

Seemed that reflex was still there, a lingering memory of their friendship, the ghost of something that was long gone and yet, like water flowing down an old riverbed, somehow some of it remained.

Some instinct made her look up in that moment. Perhaps to see if he'd noticed her reaction to his wall-punch too and understood what it meant.

But there was only fire in his eyes.

And she knew it wasn't friendship he was thinking about.

Chapter 7

She was holding his hand. The way she'd used to, when he'd cut it while working at the garage or cleaning up the broken bottles his dad constantly left behind. And the look on her face was the same now as it had been back then, full of the annoyance she laid over the top of everything to cover how deeply she cared. But he'd always been able to see the care and the worry she tried to hide.

He saw a glimmer of it now. And maybe if he hadn't been so furious, both with her and himself, if he hadn't slammed his fucking hand into a fucking wall, he might have remembered what he'd intended and stuck to his plan.

But he was and he had, and the fury and the pain was a toxic mix in his gut. One that would explode at the slightest provocation.

And that provocation was the touch of her skin.

It was like a lit match set to bone-dry grass, igniting him. Setting fire to his patience and burning right through his control.

Levi pulled his hand from hers, grabbed her hips, and shoved her hard up against the wall. Burying one hand in the silky black mass of her hair, he jerked her head back and covered her mouth with his.

He could feel her shock in the way she went rigid, but he didn't care. He was too furious and too hungry, and both of those emotions were far easier to deal with than the pain that seemed to go all the way to his soul.

So he embraced them instead, pushing his tongue deep into the heat of her mouth, unleashing his anger and burying the pain. The taste of her was the sweetest thing he'd ever known, and he wanted more of it. So much more.

He kissed her deeper, harder, feeling the rigidity bleed out of her, her mouth beginning to move under his, kissing him back. It made everything burn hotter, become more desperate.

She'd lifted her hands to his hair, but he didn't want her touching him. It was too much, made him feel weak, and he wasn't going to be weak, not with her, not ever fucking again, so he released the hold he had on her hair, gripped her wrists and jerked them away.

He lifted her hands above her head, then crossed them at the wrist, pinning them against the wall. "You don't get to touch me," he hissed savagely in her ear. "You haven't earned the fucking right."

She was panting, her mouth full and red from the ferocity of his kiss, her cheeks stained with color. She stared at him, her dark chocolate eyes full of anger and what looked like grief. "It's over, isn't it?" Her voice sounded husky and thick. "Whatever we had between us is gone."

His anger twisted and knotted inside him, desperate for an outlet. "Yeah, it's gone. And you fucking killed it." Holding her pinned, he reached out and jerked down the silvery material of her top.

All thoughts of waiting had gone. He didn't want to anymore. He was tired of it. He didn't know what to do with his anger, with the terrible, desperate need that was clawing a hole inside him, and this was the only thing that made sense.

If you hadn't hit that guy . . . none of this would have happened in the first place!

Her voice echoing in his head, striking a nerve he hadn't known was exposed. He'd killed a man. It had been an accident, but she was right. He should never have punched that fucker, made him fall and hit the pavement. Yet Levi had. Because the guy had touched her, was going to rape her, and Levi had gotten so angry.

Patience. Control. There's a reason, remember?

But both of those things had somehow slipped out of his grasp, and now he was only conscious of his own need and the anger that demanded an outlet.

She flinched as her top came down, baring her breasts, but didn't protest as he bent his head and pressed his mouth to her throat, tasting the salty-sweet flavor of her skin, inhaling the vanilla and musk scent of her.

Christ, she tasted so good. Like he'd imagined except better, more intense than any of his stupid damn fantasies.

He licked a line from her throat down over the curve of one breast, pausing to taste those tantalizing rose petals tattooed onto her skin, licking each one, before finding the hard peak of her nipple, taking it into his mouth, and sucking hard.

She gasped and shuddered in response, her body arching into him, her wrists pulling against his hold.

Jesus Christ, he hadn't wanted her like this. He'd wanted to tease her, taunt her, have her suffer until she was on her knees begging him to fuck her.

Yet it had been too long. It had just been too fucking long, and now here she was, the woman he'd wanted for so many years, in his arms. Soft and warm and trembling, and he couldn't seem to make himself stop.

He couldn't help himself, licking that deep red nipple again, drawing another sound from her, before setting his teeth against her skin, biting her.

She cried out, but he didn't stop, pushing his other hand down between the two of them to the waistband of her leggings, pulling them down. Then he slid his fingers down into her panties, feeling slick heat and wetness against his fingertips.

She shivered, her hips jerking against his, and he didn't wait, sinking two fingers deep into that sweet little pussy, her body clenching tight around them.

He'd always wondered what she'd feel like, and now he knew. Hot. Tight. Perfect. And that helpless moan she made . . . The sound went straight to his dick.

He bit her again, then licked her nipple, fucking her slowly with his fingers as her trembling hips moved in time with his hand. As if she was hungry, wanting more.

"Good girl," he murmured, hardly knowing what he was saying, because the scent of her arousal was soaking the air around them, and he was so hard he couldn't think. "That's right, sweetheart. Ride my hand. Let me make you feel good."

He eased his fingers apart inside her, stretching her gently, feeling her shudder, her gasp hoarse in his ear. He was supposed to be getting her to do something, but he couldn't remember what it was. There was only the heat of her around his fingers, the musky scent of feminine desire and the salty-sweet taste of her skin.

Sunny. His Sunny. At last. At fucking last.

He tore his hands from her, reaching to jerk down his own zipper, getting out his painfully hard and aching dick. Then he got the wallet in the back pocket of his jeans out and extracted the condom he'd put in there only the day before, his movements clumsy.

Rachel didn't say a word, her eyes tightly closed, her breathing fast and hard, shivering against the wall.

Discarding the wallet on the floor, Levi ripped open the condom packet with his teeth and sheathed himself. Then he reached to pin her wrists again and looked down into her flushed face.

This was the moment he'd been fantasizing about for what felt like forever. The moment he'd wanted since the day she'd opened the door to his knock, the day he'd found her gran downstairs unable to remember which apartment she lived in, and so he'd gone to every apartment in the building trying to find out which one it was. And then Rachel had opened the door, her dark eyes and long black hair so beautiful. So wary. She'd looked at him, and he'd felt something deep inside him wake up.

He felt it now, even with the chasm between them. Even with all the barbed wire of their history. That thing inside him wanted her. It always had.

"Look at me," he ordered thickly. "Fucking look at me."

But her expression tightened in something like panic, and she gave a sharp shake of her head, turning her face away.

No. He wasn't having that; he just wasn't. So he took her chin in his hand, forcing her to turn back, then he leaned in close, their noses almost touching. "I want to see you, Sunny." His voice was a ragged whisper. "Look at me."

Slowly, her eyes opened, emotion dark in them, grief and anger and desire twisting like black currents in the depths of the ocean.

He tightened his grip on her wrists. "Tell me you want me."

A tremble went through her, and suddenly the emotion in her gaze drained away, and she seemed . . . oddly disconnected somehow. As if she weren't there.

The thought made him savage, fierce. "Give me the fucking words, Rachel."

Her lashes fell, thick and dark, veiling her gaze. "I want you,

Levi." Her voice was hoarse, and, again, there was something . . . not quite right about it.

This isn't the way it's supposed to be.

The thought sat there in his head, and he couldn't get rid of it. A sudden strand of doubt curled like hot wire through the ice of his anger and through the savagery, making him desperate to close the distance he could sense opening up between them. Close it in any way he could.

His hand was shaking with leashed desire as he urged her chin up, tipping her head back, gentle this time. She still didn't look at him, so he leaned in again, turning his face against her silky hair, inhaling the scent of it. "Please, Sunny," he murmured, barely conscious of how he was pleading. "Please. I need you to mean it."

She said nothing. But then he felt her pull against his restraining grip and, when he let one of her hands go, she brought it down. But not to push him away. Instead she pushed her fingers into his hair, then slid them around to the back of his head, coming to rest at his nape. Holding on.

"I want you, Levi," she whispered, and he heard it at last, the sound of certainty in her voice.

He was beyond being able to think then. He was beyond everything. All that mattered was being inside her. Now.

He reached for her leg, hauling it up around his waist, then he positioned himself, a feral sound escaping him as the wet heat of her pussy came into contact with the head of his cock. And then there was no more waiting as he thrust into her, deep and hard, slamming her up against the brick wall at her back.

She cried out, her pussy so fucking tight, squeezing him like a fist, like the way her fingers gripped the back of his neck. And there was a roaring in his head, his blood pounding in his ears. Pleasure uncurled like the lash of a whip, the heat of her almost blinding him.

Holy Christ.

He stood there for a moment, unable to move, buried deep inside her, the feel of her body around him a revelation. Tight, wet, and so fucking hot. So much better than he'd ever dreamed.

And then his body wanted to move and he let it, flexing his hips, thrusting harder, deeper, pleasure rushing in like the tide.

Her head had fallen back against the wall as she held tight to the back of his neck, her eyes closing again, but this time he didn't care. In fact he was glad, because he didn't want her looking at him. Didn't want her seeing how this was ripping him apart.

So he watched her instead as he thrust again. And again. Looking as she writhed against the wall, her bottom lip caught between her teeth, her breathing harsh and ragged. Watching as he turned her inside out.

He wanted to do that all day, watch all the ways he could take her apart, but the pleasure inside him was too demanding, the pressure insane. She was heat and sweetness, and some part of him hated her for what she'd done to him. For how she'd hurt him.

Hated her for how much he wanted her.

But this was his reward; this was his payment, so making sure her leg was wrapped up and around his hip, he let it go and reached for her jaw, gripping her hard while he covered her mouth, kissing her with all the anger and the savagery that burned in his blood.

Then he fucked her hard against the wall, slamming them both against it, taking her scream of release into his mouth as she came around his cock, muffling the sound of his own climax as it hit, far too soon and like a bolt of fucking lightning direct from the sky.

"Don't tell Gideon." Rachel pulled open the top drawer of her dresser and took out a whole pile of underwear. "I don't want him to know."

"Why not?" Zoe asked from behind her.

Dumping the underwear in the first bag she'd managed to pull out of the hall closet, Rachel reached for the next drawer. "Isn't it obvious? I don't want him getting all big brother on my butt about it."

"He won't," Zoe said, though they both knew what a complete lie that was. Gideon was the alpha of their particular pack, and any threat to one of them brought out the wolf in him.

God, Rachel *so* did not need Gideon in wolf mode making the situation with Levi even worse than it already was, no matter what Zoe thought.

The younger woman believed the sun shone out of Gideon's butt—no doubt a very muscular butt—so of course her default position was that people should tell him when they were in trouble.

But Rachel wasn't in trouble. She was a big girl, and she'd made her own decision. Sure, the choice Levi had given her was a crap one, but she'd made it anyway. She'd move in with him.

Levi had wanted that to happen as soon as possible, so here she was, in her shitty, rundown apartment, packing up her stuff like a good girl, exactly as he'd asked. While he . . . did whatever the hell it was he'd been doing for the past couple of days.

She'd purposefully not thought about what had happened between them in that apartment two days earlier, shoving feelings and the memories far to the back of her mind, purposely ignoring the ache between her thighs.

She wasn't ready to deal with that yet.

She wasn't ready to deal with Zoe yet either, but her friend had turned up wanting a full rundown on what had happened with Levi in the office at Gideon's welcome home party, and was annoyed she hadn't gotten it earlier. Not that Rachel wanted to tell Zoe anything. What was happening with Levi was too private, too painful. And Zoe wouldn't understand. Gideon wouldn't either.

Luckily the other woman had been distracted by the boxes strewn around the apartment. Boxes containing all of Rachel's stuff.

"That's exactly what he'd do, Zoe. And you know it." Rachel picked up another armful of clothes, not caring about what she was packing. She wasn't going to sit there for hours choosing what to bring, not when she didn't want to go anyway.

Zoe sighed. "Okay, okay. You have a point. But come on, moving in with Levi is a big deal. And Gideon will find out eventually anyway."

That all depended on how long Levi was planning for them to live together. Clearly he had some scheme that he hadn't shared fully with her. Still, she wasn't going to tell the rest of them until she knew for certain what was going on.

She should really have pushed the issue, asked for details, but part of her wanted distance, and so she'd let it lie.

Shoving the last drawer closed, Rachel got to her feet, then moved over to her closet, flinging open the door and pulling out more clothes, discarding the hangers on the floor. "I just want to wait," she said, dumping all the clothes in the bag that was sitting on her bed. "Until Levi and I have got things sorted out."

Zoe was sitting on the bed, frowning slightly. "Why are you moving in with him anyway?"

"For the same reasons most people move in together." Rachel turned away, back to the closet, not wanting to have this discussion right now, but unable to think of a polite way to end it. Zoe was a good friend, and Rachel hated being snarky to her. It was kind of like kicking a puppy.

"What? You guys are a couple now?" Zoe sounded shocked. "Since when did that happen?"

A couple. Yeah, not so much.

Actually, Zoe, he's blackmailing me into moving in with him because he's trying to recreate the life together that we never had. And I'm letting him because otherwise he's going to kick Sugar Ink out of its building.

Nope, she couldn't say that out loud. Rachel didn't want to worry Zoe, nor did she want Zoe to report back to Gideon. Gideon would take exception to the truth with Levi, and everything would blow up in their collective faces.

Like they all needed that to happen right now. Fuck knew, she didn't.

She took another armful of clothes. "Yeah, I guess you could say we are." Because what else could she say? "Roomies" just sounded ridiculous and wasn't true in any case. "And it happened a couple of days ago."

"What?" Zoe squawked. "Rachel! What the hell?"

Rachel turned and came over to the bed, depositing the clothes in the bag, pressing them all down before zipping it up. Then, bracing herself, she looked at the other woman.

Her friend's amber eyes were wide with surprise and the usual undercurrent of worry. Typical Zoe.

"Okay, so it's fast," Rachel said. "But he's been inside for eight years, and we decided, hey, why wait any longer?"

"Uh, *fast* is one word for it." Zoe pushed her glasses up her nose. "I thought you guys were just friends?"

Yeah, well, so had Rachel. "People change. You know."

Zoe frowned again. "Hope you don't mind my saying, Rach, but for a girl in a new relationship you don't seem all that happy about it."

"And what would you know about being in a new relationship?" The words were sharp, coming out before she could stop herself. And as soon as they did, Rachel felt terrible. Because Zoe wasn't the cause of her bad temper, and she shouldn't be taking it out on her.

Zoe looked away. "Yeah, okay. Fair enough."

Rachel cursed herself silently. "I'm sorry, Zoe," she said. "I didn't mean to say that."

The other woman glanced down at her hands, small and delicate and curled in her lap. "You're not wrong. I don't know anything about new relationships. I don't know anything about relationships at all."

Rachel sighed. "But you care. I get that."

Zoe looked at her. "I just don't want anything to happen, Rach. What we have here, with Gideon and Zee and Levi, it's good. It's a family. And now Levi's back, and after what happened with Zee and his dad . . . I don't want anything to happen that might, you know, break us all apart."

Something tightened in Rachel's chest. She didn't know Zoe's background—only what the other woman had told her, and that wasn't much. Zoe had been a foster kid who'd ended up at the same Chicago home Gideon was in. He'd looked after her until he'd aged out, coming back to visit regularly to see how she was doing.

Zoe had told Rachel that she'd begged Gideon to take her with him when he left, but he wouldn't because she was too young. And then finally, when she was twelve, he'd given in and taken her to Detroit.

Privately Rachel thought something must have happened in that particular foster family to make Gideon uproot Zoe before she was old enough to age out herself. But she'd never asked Zoe outright about it. She'd always gotten the sense that there were definitely some things that Zoe didn't want to talk about.

Which was fine. Rachel had plenty she didn't want to talk about herself.

But what Rachel did know was that Zoe's past hadn't been kind, so no wonder she was worried about what was happening with Levi. The little family they'd created with Gideon was probably the closest thing to stability Zoe had ever had.

"I know you don't," Rachel said quietly. "And it won't, okay? It's just this stuff with Levi and I . . . It's complicated."

Zoe grimaced. "Everything always is, isn't it?"

"Tell me about it."

The younger woman slipped off the bed. "So you don't want to talk about it, I understand. But if you ever want to . . ." She trailed off, sticking her hands into her back pockets and hunching her shoulders. "I'm here okay? I just don't want you to be unhappy. And I don't want that for Levi either."

Zoe's expression was so serious. It made Rachel's throat suddenly feel tight. There weren't many people in her life who'd stuck around, but Zoe was one of them. And the fact that she had made Zoe worth her weight in gold.

Leaving off fussing with the bag for a moment, Rachel came around the side of the bed and gave her friend a quick hug. "Thanks, Zoe. I appreciate it. And I'll talk to you about it, I promise. I just have to figure it out myself first, if that makes sense."

Zoe gave her a grin. "Yeah, it does."

At that moment there was loud knock on the front door of the apartment.

Rachel frowned. What the hell? She wasn't expecting anyone. "I better get that," she muttered, turning and going out into the tiny, dark hallway, making her way down to the front door.

She peered through the peephole first, since only an idiot wouldn't in this neighborhood. A couple of men in some kind of uniform stood outside.

Okay then. Probably weren't going to immediately knife her.

She pulled open the door, her tough-girl armor in place. The two men were tall and burly-looking, their shirts bearing the name of a moving company.

"Yeah? What do you want?" she asked belligerently.

"You Rachel Hamilton?" The guy was holding a phone and looking down at it.

"Who wants to know?"

He gave her a long-suffering look. "We're here to move your stuff."

For a second she could only blink at him. "What?"

"Mr. Rush ordered the apartment cleaned out and everything moved to this address." The guy held out the phone, and, sure enough, on the screen was the address of Levi's building.

That bastard. When he'd told her he wanted her to move in, she hadn't assumed she would give up her entire apartment. She'd assumed it would be a limited-time-only thing.

Clearly that wasn't what Levi intended.

Shock began to alchemize inside her, becoming hot, becoming anger.

The only contact she'd had with him for the past two days had been a text that morning telling her they'd talk more tonight about the details of their living arrangements. But he certainly hadn't mentioned wanting her to clean out her entire home.

That she hated the place made not the slightest bit of difference. It had once been her gran's apartment, and Rachel had lived here since she was five years old. She wasn't giving it up just on Levi's say-so.

God, she was doing what he wanted, wasn't she? Why did he keep asking for more?

She held up a finger to the two men. "Wait a minute."

Then she slammed the door and turned around, reaching into her back pocket for her own phone.

"What's happening?" Zoe had come into the hallway, one eyebrow raised. "Trouble?"

Rachel gave Zoe what she hoped wasn't a transparently fake smile. "No, everything's fine. Just some details I need to work out with Levi."

Zoe's gaze flickered to the front door, then back to Rachel

again. "Were those moving men I saw? Wow, this thing's for real, isn't it?"

It was. Too real.

Rachel gave Zoe another forced grin, then hit the button to call Levi. He answered on the first ring, which must have meant he was waiting for her to call.

"I have moving guys here," she said shortly. "They said you sent them."

"Hi to you too. And yeah, I did." The sound of his rich, rough voice, the first time she'd heard it in two days, made her want to shiver. Which only increased her annoyance.

"We haven't discussed this, Levi." Giving Zoe a meaningful look, she went through into the tiny living area of the apartment, because she didn't want to have this discussion with her friend right there. "When you said you wanted me to move in, I didn't know you meant move my entire goddamn life."

"Well, you should have," he said flatly. "Isn't that what most people do when they move in together?"

"I thought it was just going to be for . . . I don't know, a limited time. I didn't know you wanted me to give up my entire apartment!"

"It'll be for however long I want it to be." He said the words as if they were irrefutable facts, with no room for argument. "Look, there's no point paying rent when you're living with me. Besides, that place is a shithole. You've always hated it."

Rachel gripped the phone tightly, trying to get a hold on the tangle of rage and frustration inside her. "That's not the point."

"Then what is?"

"What am I going to do when this is over? Where the hell am I supposed to go?"

"We'll find you a new place. A better one."

That he didn't insist that it wouldn't be over only added more fuel to the fire of her temper, and for reasons she couldn't have articulated. "I don't want a better one, Levi. This is my home. This is where I lived with Gran, and you can't expect me to leave it just like that."

"Sure I can." There was an undercurrent of temper in his voice now, just like there was in her own. "I had to leave my home just like that. Why shouldn't you?"

It felt as if a hand had squeezed around her throat, making it difficult to swallow. "So this is revenge? I thought you wanted me to give you the future you never had."

"Call it both."

She took a ragged breath. "This is a punishment, isn't it?"

"Yes." No hesitation, none at all. "What did you think this was going to be, Rachel? Did you think it was real? That you and I could rekindle our beautiful friendship?"

Her throat felt as if it were full of barbed wire. "No." She had to force out the word. "I never thought that."

"Well, don't think it. Because our friendship is not what I want to rekindle with you."

Her phone vibrated in her hand, and, when she looked down, she saw he'd sent her a photo. It was of a bed, big and wide and set low to the ground. The frame looked like it had been carved from a single, massive, blocky piece of battered and worn wood, while the mattress, by contrast, looked like a cloud floating on top.

She stared at it, her emotions careering around wildly inside of her.

Slowly she raised the phone back to her ear. "Why are you showing me that?"

"Because we'll be putting it to good use tonight." There was no inflection in his voice. Just a statement of fact. "I wanted the frame to be strong enough for what I had in mind."

No, she wouldn't ask what he had in mind. Just like she wouldn't think about the empty, hollow ache between her thighs. The one she'd been trying not to think about ever since he'd had her up against the wall.

"It looks expensive." She couldn't quite keep the husky tone from her voice.

"It is. But I have money."

"Do you really need my opinion?"

"No. But I thought you might appreciate the fact that the wood comes from an old factory that was abandoned eight years ago." He paused. "Right about the time I went inside."

As if she needed another twist of the knife.

She took a silent breath, leaning against the wall near the grimy windows, looking at the dirty, rundown street outside. "Seems appropriate."

No, she wouldn't fight him, wouldn't protest. It would only make things worse. She had to stop thinking of him as if he were the Levi she remembered and start thinking of this like the transaction it was.

It was the only way she could deal with it.

"Very," he agreed. There was another pause, then his voice was quieter, deeper, softer. "I have plans tonight, Rachel. Big plans. Plans that involve a lot of pleasure for both of us, so don't count on getting any sleep."

She closed her eyes, unable to repress the shiver that whispered over her skin. *Don't tell yourself it's not anticipation.* "Don't worry, I won't."

"Because my fucking you against that wall . . . that was just the start." There was a promise in the words, a terrible promise. Terrible because it made her so conscious of that empty ache, of that need. Made her think about all the things she didn't want to think about.

Such as the feel of his cock, the beautiful stretch of him inside her. The pain of it, because he was big, and it had been such a long time for her, and he'd taken her so quickly. And how that didn't matter, not when she'd been so wet, not when the pleasure had so completely overwhelmed her.

She'd tried to distance herself from his desperation, tried keep herself separate, to disconnect. But when he'd begged for her to tell him she wanted him, his voice all ragged and cracked, the first hint of softness she'd seen in him, she hadn't been able to stop herself from giving him exactly what he wanted. The words. The hand in his hair. And then, no matter how hard she'd fought it, the orgasm that had come for her anyway, detonating inside her like a bomb. And afterward . . .

No. She wasn't going to think about what happened afterward. What always happened afterward. The creeping sense of shame . . .

"Do you want me to wear anything in particular tonight?" she asked, forcing the thoughts away.

"No. You won't be wearing it long, in any case."

Her heart gave a strange, fast thump in her ears. "Are you going to tell me what these big plans of yours are?"

"Of course not. But at least now we'll have a bed." Another pause. "Though maybe we won't need that either."

"Levi . . ."

"Tonight, Rachel. Be at the apartment by seven. And don't be late."

A vestige of her fighting spirit flared. "What if I am?"

"Try it." The roughness in his voice got even rougher. "You'll find out."

Then he disconnected the call, leaving silence buzzing loudly in her ear.

Slowly, she lowered her phone, putting it back in her pocket, her hand shaking.

Zoe must have let the movers in, because Rachel could hear her out in the hallway, talking to them.

And for a second Rachel didn't want to move. She just wanted to stand there in the tiny, dingy room that still smelled of the cigarettes her gran used to smoke. Surrounding herself with a past she'd always wanted to escape, and yet now, when it came down to it, she was afraid to step away from.

Because the moment those men came in and started taking away her furniture, everything would change. She knew it deep in her bones.

And nothing would ever be the same again.

Least of all herself.

Chapter 8

Levi pushed open the door to Gideon's garage and stepped inside. His friend had sent him a text earlier that day suggesting he stop by since Gideon had something he wanted to show him. Levi hadn't committed to anything since he'd had shit to do, but the meeting with Jason Ryan from Ryan Investments hadn't taken as long as Levi had thought and his little shopping trip had hit with success earlier than he'd expected. He'd told Rachel to be there at seven, so he had a bit of time.

Levi didn't know what it was Gideon wanted to show him, but he had a feeling his friend was after something more. Gideon probably wanted to have a heart-to-heart after Levi had stalked out of the welcoming party without a word.

Fuck, Levi really did not want to have that conversation right now. But then he couldn't avoid Gideon either, or the questions that Gideon would no doubt have for him. Questions about Rachel.

The garage was awash with light shining through the grimy windows and from the fluorescent bulbs on the ceiling. Gideon was bent over the same Cadillac he'd been working on the other day, fiddling with something under the hood.

He lifted his head as Levi approached and grinned, grabbing the rag draped over the fender and wiping his hands on it. "Been wondering if you were going to show."

Levi stopped and put his hands in the pockets of his jeans. "Yeah, I was going to text you back, but I had a lot of shit to do today."

Gideon dumped the rag on the fender again and leaned back against the car, the heels of his hands propped on the edge of the metal. His gaze was level. "Want to tell me why you walked out?"

Fuck. Of course. This was going to be another goddamn interrogation.

"No," Levi replied. "Not particularly."

"This shit with you and Rachel—"

"Is none of your fucking business."

"It is if she gets hurt." There was no accusation in Gideon's voice, just a flat statement of fact. "I've been looking out for her, Levi. The whole time you were away. She's part of this family of ours, and that makes her someone I need to protect." There was something very direct in Gideon's eyes. "Even if that means protecting her from you."

Anger coiled in Levi's gut, instinctive, defensive, his fingers curling into fists in his pockets.

What the fuck did you expect? You know Gideon. You know how he protects the people he thinks need protecting.

"You really think I'd hurt her?" Levi forced out, a part of him not wanting to know the answer.

Gideon didn't even hesitate. "Yeah, I do. I think that's exactly what you want. Not physically, but I think you want some payback all the same."

It was like the thin end of a blade sliding between his ribs. Made all the worse because of course it was true.

He didn't want to hurt her, but, yeah, he did want some payback.

Asshole. How could you do that her? You are *hurting her, and you know it.*

Yeah and so? An eye for an eye, etcetera. That's how it worked in jail, and Levi couldn't shake off all those years of prison justice just like that.

He was only taking back what should have been his.

Levi tried to get himself to relax because he hadn't come here for a fight, not with this man who'd given him so much, and yet words he hadn't meant to say spilled out of his mouth all the same. "Perhaps you should spend less time worrying about Rachel, and more time worrying about Zoe and the giant case of hero worship she's currently carrying around."

Gideon stiffened, every line on his face carved from granite. "What the fuck is that supposed to mean?" His deep voice was flat with authority.

Levi met him stare for stare. "Not so fucking pleasant when the boot is on the other foot, is it?"

The other man appeared to relax, but the look in his eyes was anything but relaxed. "We're not talking about Zoe. We're talking about Rachel. And you've changed, Levi. You're harder, colder. Put it this way—if you were me, wouldn't you be worried?"

Good question. And one Levi didn't want to know the answer to, especially when deep down he was afraid he already did.

Ignoring the pain that came with that knowledge, he lifted a shoulder. "Yeah, well. Prison can change a man."

Gideon stared at Levi for a long moment, then sighed, and the hard edge that had been there a moment before vanished. "I won't let you hurt Rachel, Levi. No matter how fucked up you are. No matter how much revenge you want. Because you're not the only one who's been through some shit in the past eight years."

They hit him weirdly, those words. And he didn't want them to have any impact, because obviously Gideon was talking about Rachel, and Levi was reluctant to think about what her life had been like since he'd been gone. What she'd been doing all this time. Obviously her gran had passed on—Gideon had mentioned this to Levi during one of his visits—and Rachel had managed to get her tattoo business off the ground, but apart from that . . . What kind of shit had she gone through, anyway?

"Right," Levi said, unable to help himself. "So I guess she had the shit beaten out of her too? And spent three months in solitary? Maybe she wasn't allowed to go outside without permission or even walk to her own bed without worrying who was going to stab her in the back?"

A shadow moved in Gideon's eyes, and Levi abruptly felt like a complete dickhead. He remembered Gideon's coming down to the station after he'd been arrested, arguing to get him out on bail, but the cops refusing, saying Levi was too much of a danger. Gideon had stayed there for hours, making a nuisance of himself, trying to get Levi out, until finally the cops had threatened to arrest Gideon too.

This wasn't only about Levi and Rachel. And she wasn't the only one Gideon had tried to protect.

But apologies were beyond Levi right now; he'd simply forgotten how to say the words, so he said nothing instead.

"I know you had it rough," Gideon said. "I'm not denying you did. I'm not denying that life dealt you a shitty hand. That's not what I'm saying. I'm just trying to point out that you're not the only one, okay?"

Fuck him. He was so fucking reasonable. And he always knew what to say to make you realize what a tool you'd been.

"She's moving in with me," Levi said, because if he didn't exactly agree with Gideon, then at least he owed the guy some kind of truth. "I had her pack up her apartment today."

Gideon's eyes widened. "What? How the fuck did you get her to do that? And why?"

"Where she lives is shitty and dangerous as hell. She shouldn't be there anyway."

Gideon pushed himself away from the car. "Levi, I swear to God if you've—"

"I want her with me." Levi didn't flinch away from the other man's gaze. "I want the life I thought I'd have with her. I'm not going to hurt her; I'm not going to do anything she doesn't want. I just want her with me for a while."

Gideon narrowed his eyes. "And what does she say about this?"

"She agreed."

"Like hell."

"She did." Levi took his phone out of his back pocket and held it out. "Call her if you think I'm lying."

Rachel might tell Gideon that the choice Levi had given her hadn't exactly been a good one, but if Gideon decided to talk to her about it, Levi was betting she wouldn't tell him the truth. What was between Rachel and himself was their business, not anyone else's. Not even Gideon's.

Gideon glanced at the phone, then back at Levi. He made no move to take it. "You didn't answer my question. Why?"

Okay, so at least there was some trust left.

Levi tucked the phone away. "I told you. I always wanted a life with her; you must know that. Or at least you must have guessed."

"I did wonder," Gideon admitted. "But you never made a move on her."

"I didn't want to until I'd made something of myself. Until I had money and could take her away from this shithole."

Gideon frowned. "Nice thing to call your old neighborhood."

A familiar impatience began to rise in Levi. They'd had this argument before, he and Gideon. "You know my feelings about Royal."

"Yeah, and it's changed a lot since you've been away."

Levi knew that. He'd seen the changes himself and approved. And soon, if he had his way and got the investment he needed, it would change again.

But now was not the time to have that discussion.

"I see that," Levi merely answered. "Anyway, I've got money now. And now I want to take her away. Away from that shitty apartment at least."

Gideon was silent, staring at him. Then he said, "And she was more than happy for you to swoop in and rescue her?"

Another good question. Rachel definitely wasn't a damsel in distress who required rescuing. Both he and Gideon knew that.

"She wants what I want." Technically not a lie, but only technically. Yet again, it was a complicated situation, and Gideon wouldn't understand it. Not Levi and Rachel's history or the emotional undercurrents.

Gideon wouldn't understand their chemistry either.

Gideon shook his head slowly. "She might, but moving into your apartment? I can't see her agreeing to that."

"Like I said, call her if you want. She'll tell you it's all good."

"And if it doesn't work out? What then? You just going to leave her with nothing?"

Something inside Levi, something he'd thought long dead, shifted. His conscience. "Of course I wouldn't leave her with nothing. If it doesn't work out, I'll find her somewhere else to live. Anyway, she's a grown woman. She can look after herself."

Gideon gave him a dubious look. "Someone's going to get hurt. You know that, don't you? And it's probably going to be her."

He's right. She's vulnerable, and you're being a complete ass-hole to her.

Levi shifted, grappling with his patience as he shoved the thought away. "You're not my fucking father, Gideon. And you're not my big brother. I don't have to answer to you."

There was a tense silence.

Gideon's unwavering stare made Levi restless, uncomfortable. Jesus Christ, the guy could give some of the other mother-fuckers in prison a lesson in menace.

"You're wrong," Gideon said at last. "A big brother is exactly what I am. And if you hurt Rachel in any way, I'll hurt you, understand?"

Yeah, he understood all right. That was something else he'd learned in jail; fuck with anyone's shit, and you were a dead man. Which meant he was walking a really thin line coming back here, wanting to do what he wanted to do. It would burn some bridges and then some. But he'd made his peace with that.

He didn't need any goddamn bridges, anyway. He'd build his own.

"I understand," Levi said flatly. "Was that what you wanted to show me? Or did you have some more fucking sermons to deliver?"

The expression in Gideon's eyes changed again, a fleeting look of frustration moving in them before vanishing. "Nope. Sounds like you got it all figured out."

"Yeah, I do."

"Well, okay then." Gideon inclined his head toward the door that led to the lot out back where they kept vehicles waiting to be worked on and those waiting to be picked up. "Come on. I've got something for you."

Levi followed him out into the summer heat, threading his

way through the parked cars, some of them gleaming, some of them battered and waiting their turn in the garage, until Gideon halted near the front of the lot, by the entrance guarded by a chain link fence.

A convertible sat up on blocks, its black paintwork cracked and peeling, rust eating into the metal. Levi ran a quick, professional eye over it, only half aware he was doing so. It needed a ton of work, which made it barely worth the effort. What the hell was Gideon doing wasting his time with it?

"I found this last week on Craigslist," Gideon said, putting his hand on the door. "Classic 1968 Firebird."

"I know what it is." Levi moved closer, examining the car. Okay, so maybe it wasn't as bad as it seemed. In fact, now that he'd gotten a better look, it was only surface rust. Probably wouldn't take that much to turn it into a pretty sweet ride.

He'd always liked Firebirds. Another thing he'd wanted to get for himself once he had the money.

"What do you think?" Gideon asked.

Levi shot him a glance. "It's pretty good. Why? You thinking about restoring it?"

Gideon's gaze dropped to the car, and he ran his hand along the cracked paintwork in an almost tender gesture. "No. I was thinking you might like to restore it."

"Me?" Levi stared at him in surprise.

"Yeah, you." One corner of Gideon's mouth curved. "Thought you might need a ride when you got out. And I thought you might want to familiarize yourself with engines again, have something to do." Slowly, he lifted his gaze from the car and looked back at Levi, his expression unreadable. "But I guess you've already got something to do. And you don't need to bother with engines anymore."

Levi's chest felt tight, making a part of him ache, a part he thought he'd cut out while he was inside, because it was less painful without it. And, Christ knew, he didn't need any more pain.

"You bought this for me?" His voice sounded as rusty as the fucking car.

Gideon nodded. "Yeah. Stupid, huh?"

He wanted to say, yes, it was stupid. That Gideon was right. Levi had something bigger and better to do than tinkering around with cars.

But he couldn't say it. That tight feeling in his chest wouldn't let him.

Instead, he looked away, back down to the Firebird, remembering the day Gideon had asked him if he wanted to help out in the garage.

Levi had been sixteen and had always liked fiddling with things—he'd had to fix a lot of stuff in the apartment because his father kept breaking things when he was drunk—so making the jump to messing around with engines wasn't a big deal. But the best part of it had been that Gideon was going to pay him.

Some of Levi's happiest moments had been spent with Gideon in that garage. Levi's mother had died when he was small, and he'd never had a proper father figure, never had a brother. But Gideon, even though he was only three years older than Levi, had been both of those things.

Gideon had taught Levi what it was to be a man. What family meant. And the safe space of the garage, with Gideon and his ready acceptance, had been Levi's savior on more than one occasion, just as much as Rachel had been.

Levi put a hand on the car, the metal warm under his hand.

It wasn't stupid. It was a typically generous Gideon gesture, and it mattered.

He didn't look at the other man. "What's the engine like?"

"Needs an overhaul. Probably take some time."

"Uh huh." He rubbed at a flake of paint. "You got room for this in the garage?"

"I'm sure I could find some," Gideon said.

Levi finally looked at him. "Do it. I'll come in tomorrow to take a look at what needs to be done."

Gideon didn't smile, but there was warmth in his eyes, and for some reason the uncomfortable, tight feeling in Levi's chest relaxed a little. "The door's always open, man. You know that."

The last client of the day, a musician pleased with the sleeve of skulls and snakes and roses Rachel had designed, rolled off Rachel's tattoo couch. She chatted to him as she cleaned him up, then dealt with the payment, trying not to notice the time ticking by.

In half an hour it would be seven, and she was due at Levi's.

"So, going to Gino's?" Xavier asked from his own station after the musician had gone out the door and Rachel had begun the process of cleaning up and sterilizing her gear.

"No, not tonight." She didn't look at Xavier, not wanting to get into more tedious explanations about moving in with Levi. Having to tell Zoe about it had been bad enough. "I'm kind of tired."

"Uh huh." Xavier sounded unconvinced in the extreme. "All that moving must be tiring."

Oh, fuck.

Rachel shot him a glance. He was leaning against his tattoo chair, one eyebrow raised in wordless question.

"Don't you have a client soon?" she asked.

"In a couple of minutes, yeah. But don't change the subject."

"Who told you I was moving out?"

Xavier lifted a shoulder. "Hey, it's a small neighborhood."

"Jesus." She turned around, busying herself with putting away the rest of her gear, mainly so she didn't have to look at him. "Okay, so I'm moving in with Levi. It's no big deal."

"Sure it's not." The edge of sarcasm in his voice would have done her proud. "And you're completely acting like a woman in love. Walking on air, can't stop smiling, mooning around, all that shit."

"So, I'm not demonstrative. I'm doing all that on the in-side."

Xavier laughed. "Bullshit, girl. What's going on?"

"Nothing." She shot him another glance. "Maybe I'm sleeping with him to see if I can get him to sign this building over to us."

Xavier stilled, his eyes widening. "Seriously?"

She hadn't meant it seriously. But now that she'd said it . . .

Weren't you going to treat the arrangement with Levi like a transaction? He's getting something from it, so why can't you?

Ever since Levi had gotten back here she'd felt as if she was at his mercy, that she couldn't argue with him, couldn't protest. The way she had all those years ago when her gran's heart problems had gotten worse and she'd needed more medication. It had been expensive, and Rachel had no job, no way of getting any money.

She'd only seen one way out of her situation at the time, and she'd done what she'd had to do so her gran could get her medicine.

Maybe the time had come to do what she had to again. And this time she'd do it for herself. She'd worked so hard for this studio, for her art gallery plans. She wasn't just going to let those plans go because Levi was being a demanding asshole.

Hell, he was getting a lot out of this deal. Why shouldn't she?

"Well, sure," she said, giving Xavier a grin, the decision crys-tallizing inside her. Finally she had a bit of direction. "Why not? We can't have him keeping this place, right?"

Xavier gave her an assessing look. "Just make sure you know what you're doing, okay? He doesn't strike me as a man you can screw around with. In all senses of the word."

He wasn't. But she had to remember that she did have one thing on her side—Levi wanted her. Which meant she could use that. At least, she had to try.

While Xavier greeted another client, Rachel, full of new purpose, went over to the rack of clothing and began leafing through what was there.

Levi had told her not to bother with dressing for the occasion, and she hadn't, settling for jeans and a T-shirt. But suddenly that didn't feel right. If she was going to get what she wanted out of this, making an effort seemed like a good idea.

Dressing like a hooker now?

Shoving that snide little thought aside, Rachel concentrated instead on what she was looking for.

There was a dress on the rack in the store that she'd had her eye on for a while now, a simple, formfitting dark-red mini that left one shoulder bare. Excellent for showing off her ink, since the fabric was almost the exact same color as the roses on her arm and across her chest. Plus it would show off her curves to perfection.

Pulling the dress off the rack, then making a note by the register to pay the designer for the dress later, she took it into the studio's tiny bathroom, undressed, then wiggled into it.

Smoothing down the fabric, she glanced at herself in the cracked mirror.

The color was perfect, highlighting the deep red in her sleeve and in the rose petals that drifted across her chest before disappearing beneath the material. It also gave color to her pale cheeks and made the rest of her skin glow.

The dress did a good job of following the shape of her figure too, ending at mid-thigh. Not too short to be classy, yet short enough to be sexy. Perfect.

Rachel pulled out the tie of her ponytail, shaking her hair out so it tumbled down over her shoulders and back, then she leaned forward and applied the finishing touch: deep red lipstick.

Now her outfit was perfect.

She gave Xavier a wave as she left the studio, but he was too busy chatting with his client to respond, which was probably just as well. She certainly didn't want any last minute wishes of good luck or knowing looks. This made her feel weird enough as it was.

It's not weird. It's just a transaction, remember?

Yeah. She was going to give Levi what he wanted—her in his apartment, in his bed—in return for signing ownership of her building over to her.

A thrill went through her, alien and unfamiliar. Reminding her of all the things she didn't want to think about. The sexual things. His hands. Her desire. Her hunger . . .

No. Think of the beach and the sand. Pretend.

The door to Levi's building opened as soon as she approached, and, as she walked in, she caught the red blinking light of a security camera that hadn't been there a couple of days before. Clearly Levi had been making some improvements.

Stepping into the cage elevator, she pressed the button and waited as old machinery clanked into life, laboriously hauling her up to the top floor.

She had to stop outside Levi's door to take a breath, to calm her racing heartbeat and get herself under control. Because she didn't want to go in there shaking. Didn't want to face him already vulnerable. Not when he knew how to take her apart so completely.

When she'd made sure her metaphorical armor was firmly in place, that there were no chinks to speak of, Rachel raised her hand to knock.

But the door swung open before her knuckles made contact with the wood. And Levi was there, standing in the doorway.

And her throat closed as the sheer physical impact of him hit her.

It had only been two days, and yet the sight of him brought everything she'd been so carefully not thinking about rushing back.

The strength of his hands as he'd shoved her hard against the wall. The heat of his body when he'd pinned her there. The feel of his cock pushing into her. The terrible aching pleasure of each thrust, the stretch and burn, his breath harsh in her ear.

Levi. Her friend. The first guy who'd made her laugh and think that the world might not be such a bad place after all.

The friend she'd destroyed.

Tears rushed into her eyes, and she had to blink hard to get rid of them. So much for her goddamned armor.

"Hey," she forced out, her voice husky. "Here I am."

He didn't say anything, propping one forearm against the doorframe and leaning against it, his uneven gaze scanning her from head to toe. And she caught it, the flare of heat in his eyes as he looked at her.

Good. The dress was obviously a success then.

"You dressed up," he said, the rough velvet of his voice rolling over her.

"I thought I would. It's an occasion, right?"

Again, he was silent, his gaze continuing to roam, and she had to fight to keep the shivers that chased over her skin locked down. Not letting him get to her was going to be a problem, especially when he looked so damn hot himself.

He wore a dark blue button-down shirt, the sleeves rolled up to reveal the black bands tattooed around his arms, the cotton pulling tight across the impressive width of his chest. The waistband of his worn jeans sat low on his lean hips, and there was a rip in one knee. He definitely hadn't dressed up, but then, he didn't really need to, not when he looked so . . . fucking good. When the easy, relaxed way he was standing with his arm on the doorframe, a confident, dominant posture, made something inside her want to roll over and beg.

He *wanted to make you beg too.*

She swallowed, ignoring the thought, the silence deepening, becoming tense and loaded with undercurrents, both emotional and physical.

She didn't want to be the one to break the silence, but right before she opened her mouth to say something, anything, he abruptly dropped his arm and stood to the side, indicating she should come in with a wordless gesture.

Without hesitation, she stepped through the doorway and into the apartment, catching his scent as she went past him, woodsmoke and spice, like a forest fire. It made some part of her want to stop and turn to him, bury her face in his neck, have him put his arm around her and hold her like he'd used to.

But those were dangerous thoughts. He wasn't her friend anymore, and she wasn't going to think of him like that. So she didn't stop, continuing on down the short hallway until she'd come out into the living area.

It wasn't as empty as it had been a couple of days earlier.

There were a low, black leather sectional sofa and a coffee table that looked carved out of a single, thick piece of battered wood arranged in the middle of the room. An empty shelving unit stood against one wall, and against another was a long console table with a massive, flat-screen TV on it.

But that wasn't all.

There was an armchair standing near the window. It was old, the red velvet covering it worn and stained, parts of the fabric coming away from the base. It should have looked out of place with all the new furniture around it, with the new white walls and the freshly varnished floor. But for some reason it didn't look out of place at all. It looked . . . right.

Her gran's chair.

Rachel's throat closed up, and for a second it was difficult to swallow. Because it wasn't only the armchair that was here. On the coffee table were two of her favorite knickknacks: a small antique vase her gran had given her, made out of pink glass with gold patterns on it, and a little china statue of a black cat curled up and fast asleep, the closest she'd ever gotten to a pet.

And on the wall, near the armchair, was a framed picture, one she recognized. She'd drawn it in her last year of high school, a self-portrait for an assignment. Her own face looked back at her, overlain with the sugar-skull imagery she'd first started using around that time, roses for her eyes and birds around her head. It was very similar to the mural she'd drawn on Sugar Ink's wall.

God, where had he gotten that? She thought she'd chucked it, along with a whole lot of other drawings she'd done back when she'd thought she'd go to art school and maybe one day be a famous artist.

The sound of Levi's footstep came from behind her, but she didn't turn, still staring at the picture on the wall.

"Why?" The question sounded far too blunt in the silence of the room, but she didn't make any effort to soften it. Or explain.

"I told you this was our apartment," he replied. "So your stuff is here too. Most of it is in storage in an empty room downstairs, but I pulled out some of your favorite things to have up here now. You can go down tomorrow and bring up anything else you might want."

A few of your favorite things . . .

He'd remembered. Even after all this time he remembered which things she'd treasured most.

"That picture isn't my favorite," she said.

"No. It's mine."

She turned, finding him standing close behind her, watching her. "I don't understand. What's all this for? I thought you wanted to punish me."

The expression on his face was unreadable. "There are lots of ways to punish someone, Rachel. And this could have been us eight years ago."

"No, it couldn't. We didn't have the money. We didn't—"

"Not for this apartment, no. But this could have been us somewhere else."

Oh, *now* she understood. He was rubbing her face in it. Making her think about all those lost years. Years she'd deprived them of. And yes, it was a punishment all right.

Her heart felt like it was drying up in her chest, becoming brittle and cracked like fall leaves.

You're not supposed to let him get to you.

She wasn't, but somehow he'd found a gap in her armor and had launched a sneak attack, hurting her deep inside. How was she supposed to protect herself against that?

Use the same dirty tactics as he does?

That was one answer. But it would probably only make things even worse. No, the quickest way to end this was to take the hits and hope that once he'd gotten the measure of hurt he wanted, he'd leave her alone.

Anyway, she could bear it. She was strong.

Levi lifted his hand and cupped her jaw, the heat of his palm feeling like a beam of sunlight against her skin. She wanted to tell him to fuck off and not to touch her, but her throat had seized up.

"Yeah, I think you understand now, don't you?" he murmured, running his thumb across her cheekbone, his gaze dropping to her mouth.

"Yes," she said, her voice thickening. "I understand."

His thumb swept back and forth along her cheekbone in a slow, steady caress, and the scent of him wound around her, pulling tight.

The ache inside her deepened, her heartbeat beginning to race. She didn't want to feel this, but she was feeling it all the same, a rising, helpless need.

For years she'd kept sexual desire out of her life, yet now it was as if she were drowning in it.

"Good." Keeping his hand where it was on her jaw, Levi reached for her purse with the other, sliding it off her shoulder and discarding it onto the floor. "Are you ready for the rest?"

Think of the beach. . . .

She resisted the urge to turn her cheek into his warm palm, to look up into that dark, disturbing gaze and try to find the Levi she remembered there. The Levi who smiled at her, whose blue eyes were always full of warmth, who always had a hug for her no matter what.

She closed her eyes, fighting the pain of that loss. "Yes," she lied. "I'm ready."

Levi's hand fell away unexpectedly, and she opened her eyes again. The last rays of the sun came through the windows, highlighting the perfect, vivid lines of his face. Straight brows of dark, tawny gold, the silver ring gleaming. The shadows in his one dark eye were deep, the silver blue of the other blazing with something that looked very close to satisfaction.

Of course he'd be pleased with himself. She was here, at his mercy, ready to take whatever it was he was going to give her. Relishing her pain.

Anger stirred, an ember of it catching alight inside her. Okay, so maybe she was here to take his damn payback, but he didn't have to look so fucking smug about it.

"So are we going to get to it then?" she asked, an edge in her tone. "Come on, Levi; don't leave me hanging. What do you want me to do this time? Ditch the dress? Get down on my knees and suck your cock? What?"

One corner of his beautiful mouth curved in a tiger's smile. "Actually, what we're going to do is have dinner."

Chapter 9

Rachel's eyes went wide. She hadn't been expecting that. Good. He wanted her off balance. Wanted her guessing about what was going to happen and what he was going to do.

Tonight he'd remember both his control and his patience.

Tonight this was his goddamn show.

The warmth of her cheek lingered against his fingertips, tempting him to rush straight to the part where he had her naked. But he'd planned this evening meticulously, and this time he'd remain firmly in charge.

First they were going to have a dinner he'd ordered in specially, since prison hadn't exactly improved his cooking skills. A fancy dinner on white china plates and with candles. A real fucking date. A date he'd never gotten the chance to ask her on.

They were going to talk, and she was going to tell him exactly how she'd spent the last few years, find out what Gideon had meant when he'd told Levi that she'd had some "shit" go down. Maybe they'd compare war stories; he'd tell her how Mace, one of the gang leaders in prison, had nearly killed him. And how, months later, after he'd recovered, Levi had decided that his former self was a pussy who needed to be put down. So he'd paid one of the older inmates—one no one ever fucked with—to teach him how to fight. Then he'd gotten Mace alone in the same prison library where he'd been beaten, and had taught that motherfucker a lesson.

Yeah, maybe she'd like that story.

Is that what you're doing now? Teaching her the same lesson?

Levi ignored that thought, just like he ignored the uncomfortable feeling behind his breastbone. The one that had started up as she'd looked around at her things he'd put in the apartment, and then told her he'd essentially put them there just to hurt her.

No, that painful feeling needed to get the fuck out of there. All he had room in his heart for was anger and lust. He didn't need anything else. Regret and friendship, love . . . All that shit only took up space, weakened you.

Only anger made you strong—as long as you controlled it. It was the perfect fuel to get you what you wanted.

"Dinner?" Rachel sounded disbelieving.

"Yeah, dinner." He had to resist the urge to curl his fingers around the warmth left by her skin on his palm.

"But I thought—"

"I imagine you thought a lot of things. But you're not the one who's calling the shots tonight, Rachel. I am. So dinner it is."

Her mouth flattened, but she said nothing, and when he gestured through the doorway that led from the lounge area into the dining room and kitchen area, she turned and walked obediently through it.

He followed, watching the sway of her hips in the sexy red dress she wore. Stupid, but he liked that she'd dressed up, that she'd made an effort even though he hadn't asked her to.

She looked good. Fucking hot. The fabric of the dress clung to the rounded shape of her ass, while leaving bare a good quantity of skin. Her shapely legs for a start and one graceful shoulder. The color brought out the red ink of her tattoos too, made her pale skin glow.

Christ, black hair and red lips, his Snow White. A tattooed and tough Snow White.

His dick hardened right on cue, obviously liking that idea very much. Too bad it was going to have to wait.

Tonight he'd have what he wanted. Her begging for him. And not because he'd told her to or because he'd kick her business out, but because she couldn't help herself. Because she wouldn't be able to think of anyone—*anything*—else but him. But the orgasm he'd give her.

Rachel stopped short just through the doorway, looking at the table he'd laid out especially.

He'd bought it from the same place he'd gotten the bed and the coffee table, a store in Midtown that sold furniture made out of wood and other materials from some of Detroit's abandoned factories. The pieces were all one of a kind, heavy and industrial, which he personally liked, but he'd thought Rachel might appreciate them too, especially where they'd come from. She was an artist and into recycling shit.

Since when does it matter whether she would like them or not?

It didn't matter of course. But it was all part of the building-the-perfect-apartment plan. To show her what they could have had.

"Like it?" he asked, coming up beside her.

She glanced at him, her black brows drawn down. "What the hell is this, Levi?"

"I told you. Dinner."

"Why?"

"So we can catch up." He put a hand in the small of her back, just letting it rest there, enjoying the warmth of her, feeling her muscles tense in response. "We're living together now, and that means we're going to eat together too." He brushed his thumb over her in a caressing movement. "Can't be all about sex all the time, Sunny."

She tensed even more. "Don't call me that."

"Why not? That's what you were to me."

"But I'm not now."

"No, you're not. Which is why I'm using it."

Her dark eyes blazed with sudden anger. "Another reminder of what happens when people fuck with you?"

"You could call it that."

"Well, thanks for that, but I'm aware of what happens when people fuck with you, Levi. They get hurt. So you don't need to use that name. You don't need to . . . taint it like that."

A hot feeling curled through him, an emotion he hadn't felt for a long, long time. Shame.

Too far, man. Too far.

Sunny . . . because she'd been like sunshine to him with her smart, snarky wit and those warm smiles, the ones she saved for him only. And suddenly behind that hot, ashamed feeling was something else, an ache. A yearning for what he'd lost. He wanted those smiles again. He missed them.

You miss her.

Shit, he couldn't give in to that feeling. He couldn't; not again. It only led to pain, to anguish.

To a man dead on the pavement. A man you killed.

Guilt coiled inside him like a massive snake, along with shock and confusion and a thousand other emotions he'd cut from his life while he'd been inside. They tightened around him, squeezing him.

But he crushed them, along with the yearning and the ache, giving her only a feral smile and increasing the pressure on the small of her back, urging her toward one of the chairs around the dining table.

She clearly didn't want to go, but went with him anyway, waiting while he pulled the chair out for her.

"So is this like a prison thing?" she murmured with a ghost of her usual sarcasm as she sat down. "Candlelight dinners and pulling out chairs?"

The comment stirred something like amusement in him. He'd always liked her sharpness, even when she turned it on him.

"How did you guess?" He pushed her chair in. "And we all went dancing in the exercise yard afterward."

She snorted. "I'm not dancing with you afterward."

"Don't worry. It's not dancing we'll be doing afterward."

Stepping away from her chair, he moved over to the counter that separated the dining area from the kitchen, skirting around it to get to the oven where the food was being kept hot.

Italian meatballs and spaghetti, another of her favorites.

He dished it out, carrying the plates over to the table, then going back for some crusty garlic bread and the wine he'd bought and opened half an hour earlier.

She watched him, the look on her face guarded. "Very domestic," she said as he poured her a glass of red and pushed it over the table to her. "You'll make someone a lovely wife. Is this going to be what happens every night?"

He sat down, pouring some wine for himself. Only one glass, since that was all he ever allowed himself in the way of alcohol. Becoming a drunk like his old man did not feature highly in his plans.

"Sure," he said easily. "Except you can cook next time."

"No thanks. I hate cooking." Rachel picked up her glass and took a sip of wine.

"You didn't used to. You used to cook for me a lot."

Her expression tightened. "So is that what you want to talk about? Old news?"

Levi leaned back in his chair. "Gideon mentioned some shit went down not long after I left."

She lifted a shoulder, putting her wineglass back down on the table. "You know Royal. There's always shit going down."

He almost smiled. It was the truth. "Gideon mentioned you specifically."

She picked up her fork and started eating, her attention on her food. "Did he? Well, it wasn't anything I couldn't handle."

Typical Rachel. Wouldn't admit to anything. She was protecting herself, as usual. "What happened?"

"Gran died. And I had difficulty paying for her funeral."

The blunt, flat way she said it made something catch in his throat. He had to force out the question. "You didn't go to Gideon?"

Rachel turned her fork in her spaghetti, slowly winding the pasta around the tines. "He was a little short on cash." Her gaze remained on her plate. "Mainly because he'd spent a fortune on lawyers."

The catch in his throat got worse, accompanied by a yawning feeling in his gut. A feeling a lot like guilt.

He'd known Gideon had spent money on his legal fees. Too much money. Which was why as soon as Levi had managed to get some returns on his investments, he'd paid his friend back, every last red cent of it.

But naturally that hadn't been till at least three years later.

"What happened?" he asked, shifting slightly in his chair.

Rachel lifted the fork and ate the spaghetti, chewing slowly, clearly in no hurry to answer him. "What do you think?" she said at last when she'd finished. "I used my savings."

Her savings? Jesus. Rachel had some money that her mother had left her when she'd died, and he'd made her put it into a savings account that wasn't easy to access so she could keep it, use it to pay for art school once she was ready.

It was supposed to be for her, not to pay for her grandmother's funeral.

Christ, so that's why she was stuck in Royal in a tattoo studio. She hadn't aimed higher because she hadn't been able to afford to.

It made him angry. "You used your fucking savings? That was supposed to be for art school."

"Gran deserved a decent funeral, okay? And that was more important than going to college." A spark of temper glowed in her dark eyes. "Besides, I didn't have any other option."

He didn't know why the thought of her using that money angered him so much. It was just that her dreams had always been important to him too, and the thought that she hadn't been able to do what she'd always wanted to, what she had the talent for, was wrong.

Shouldn't you be glad? There's some punishment for her right there.

Yeah, maybe he should have been glad. But he wasn't. Some part of him had always believed that the reason she didn't visit him was because she'd gone to art school and was too busy achieving her dreams the way they'd talked about.

Obviously that hadn't happened. She'd been trapped in Royal just as surely as he'd been trapped in that jail cell.

"So what happened? You used it all on a funeral?" It came out as a demand, but he didn't soften the hard edge to the words.

Rachel put down her fork and reached for her wine again, taking another long sip. "Not all of it."

"Not enough left for college?"

"No, not enough left for college." She put her elbows on the table, swirling her wine in her glass, the candlelight flickering over the ink on the bare skin of her shoulder. "I used the rest and some other money Gran left me, after she died, plus a bit from Gideon for Sugar Ink."

Levi shifted in his seat again, again irritated for reasons he couldn't figure out. She'd worked hard and created a job for herself doing something she loved, which was success however you measured it. Except . . . it wasn't what she'd told him she wanted to do all those years ago. She could do better. She *should* do better.

"Why didn't you use all that money for college then?" he demanded, unable to keep the sharpness out of his voice. "I mean, that's what you were always telling me you wanted to do."

She stared at him, her wineglass held between her fingers, the spark of anger glowing hotter. "Because earning money was kind of a priority for me. Anyway, why the hell should you care?"

He didn't care. Of course he didn't. So why he was angry with her about it, he had no idea.

"So you've spent all this time getting your business up and running," he said after a moment. "What else?"

"Nothing else." She took another sip of wine, long dark lashes veiling her gaze. "Sugar Ink's been my main focus. Anyway, if you wanted to compare histories, shouldn't you be telling me your story?"

"My story? Sure." Leaning forward, he picked up his fork and attacked his food. Jesus Christ, it was good. After years of prison food, the meatballs were fucking ambrosia. "What part do you want to know about? My getting kicked in the head? Or where I took my revenge on the prick and broke his arm? Maybe you might want to know about when my dad died and I wasn't allowed to go to the funeral. I could tell you about that if you like."

Her mouth tightened.

You could stop rubbing her nose in it, you fucker.

But why should he? Shouldn't she know everything that happened to him? It was her handiwork, after all.

"Your tattoos," she said quietly after a moment. "Tell me about those."

He put his fork down and leaned back in his chair again, allowing himself another sip of his wine. "Like I told your asshole colleague, I paid a guy to do them for me. He stole some ink and used staples."

"Staples?" An expression of distaste crossed her features. "God . . ."

"You use what you can inside."

"I guess so. Do they mean anything?"

He held her gaze, made sure she could see everything in his. "I got one every week for the first year. One for every week that went by where I heard nothing from you." She paled, but he didn't stop. "I was going to get more but after that first year of nothing, I realized you weren't going to contact me and that I didn't have enough room on my arms for eight years' worth of silence."

Her gaze flickered to his arms, then back to his face again. Then she lifted her glass and drained it. "Okay, so I think we're caught up now." She thumped the glass down on the table. "You want to fuck me or what?"

She didn't want to hear any more. Didn't want to sit here pretending they were two old friends reconnecting after years apart, or two people on their first date. All this fine white china and candles and food she liked, conversations about what they'd been doing after so long . . . It was a lie.

Levi hated her. They were enemies.

Which made what she'd come here for that much easier. He wanted to fuck her? Well, then, he could fuck her. She didn't give a shit.

He looked at her from across the table, the light flickering over his beautiful face, drawing golden reflections from that dilated black pupil and gilding the silver blue of his other eye. Softening the cynical twist to his perfectly shaped mouth.

And in spite of herself, her heart clenched painfully. This was going to be the real punishment. To live with him, be with him in a terrible parody of their old relationship. Knowing he was never going to let her forget or forgive what she'd done.

"In a hurry, Rachel?" His voice was low and deep, the roughness in it making her shiver deep inside.

"Not particularly. Just this 'catching up' business is bull-shit." She wanted some more wine, anything to dull the ache in her chest, but when she reached for the bottle, he nudged it away, shaking his head minutely.

Her anger coiled, twisting in on itself in frustration. "Ass-hole," she said bitterly.

He remained silent, watching her.

God, she hated how he did that. As if he were waiting for her to say something or do something, watching her with that unnerving gaze.

She pushed away her bowl of food, suddenly not even the slightest bit hungry. "Why did you come back here? Why didn't you go somewhere else? If you hate me that much, you should have."

Levi shifted in his chair, the sound of his big body moving making her even more physically aware of him. "I told you. I came back because I had fucking dreams. And you were part of them."

"So you have me and this dream apartment of yours. What else were you planning on doing?"

The light in his eyes glittered strangely, his mouth curving in a smile that was the very definition of enigmatic. "You'll see."

"Wonderful. So in the meantime I get to be your emotional punching bag?"

"You don't have to be here, Rachel. And you can leave when-ever you want."

"But if I do, you'll kick me out of your building."

He tilted his head, the ring in his eyebrow catching the light, the lines of his face hardening. "Yes."

Okay, so that was clear. This *really* was nothing more than a transaction. And if he wanted to play hardball, so could she.

"In that case, I want something out of this," she said, flat and hard. "I want something for me."

Levi didn't move, and yet a distinct air of menace gathered in the air around him. Suddenly he looked every inch the big, rough, dangerous ex-con. "Something for you?" he echoed. "Were you the one in jail? I don't fucking think so."

"Yeah, yeah. I think I got by now where you've been." Her voice was sharp, but she didn't care. What was the point in being careful with him if he wasn't going to be careful with her? "You're blaming me for everything that happened to you, and yet you're not even taking responsibility for that guy you punched in the face. The guy who died."

Still, Levi didn't move, the menacing atmosphere between them getting denser, the tension pulling tighter.

But she was done with being afraid of him. She knew her truth. Maybe it was time he faced up to his. "Yeah, Levi. He died. And sure, some of that's on me, but it's on you too."

His hands were on the arms of his chair, his knuckles beneath the layer of ink gone bone white.

Maybe this is a mistake?

Maybe it was. Too fucking bad.

"You want your pound of flesh?" she went on recklessly. "Fine, you can have it. But I want mine too. I want Sugar Ink's building. I want you to sign ownership of it over to me."

He stared at her, the expression on his face utterly unreadable. But the taut stillness in the air around him wasn't. He was royally pissed, and like a lion he was poised to attack.

With a certain amount of deliberation, he pushed back his chair and rose to his feet. "And why the fuck would I want to do that?"

"Because I asked." Then, hating the way he loomed over her, she stood up too, holding his gaze, daring him to do his worst.

For one impossible, stretched-out minute, a silence filled the room. The kind of silence that happened before a storm broke or the instant before an earthquake.

Then Levi was moving, kicking aside the chair with one booted foot so it skittered across the floor and hit the wall. He skirted around the side of the table in a slow, intent stalk that had her heart racing.

Dimly, a small, primitive part of her brain screamed a warning, but she ignored it. She wasn't going to run, not from Levi. Not this time.

He came closer and closer, the expression on his face intent, and her heart battered itself against her ribs. She had no idea why the fear inside her felt like excitement, because none of this should be exciting. All she should be feeling was rage.

Yet when his hand came up and slid around her throat, his palm lying heavy and hot on the pulse at the base of her neck, it wasn't only rage she felt, but something else. A thrill that shot straight down between her legs.

Jesus Christ. He had his hand on her throat, and yet all she felt was . . . turned on? What the hell was wrong with her?

She inhaled sharply, but his grip was firm and it didn't hurt, didn't choke. She could breathe.

"And why the *fuck*," Levi said quietly, his tone rough with menace, "would I give you anything you asked for?"

The thrill inside her deepened. Her throat had closed up, and it wasn't to do with his grip. It was the heat of his hand, the aching awareness of his fingers on her skin, and the dominant way he was holding her. She didn't want to be aware of any of that, but she was. She couldn't seem to help it.

With gentle, inexorable strength, Levi walked her backwards until she hit the wall behind her, then, still holding her throat, he leaned in close, his body almost covering hers, his mouth near her ear. "This isn't about what you want, Rachel. Remember?"

His hand was a hot, iron collar around her throat, his body a wall of heated muscle at her front, the smell of his aftershave like a drug. She wanted to shove him away just so she could breathe, but she was afraid to touch him. Not because of what he might do, but because she wasn't sure of her own reaction. "Kick out Sugar Ink if you have to," she forced out, her voice croaky. "I don't care. But if you want me, you'll give me that damn building."

There was a moment's taut silence, and then Levi pulled back, staring at her.

Shadows moved in the depths of his eyes, currents of heat and darkness. Desire and fury. The lines of his perfect features hardening.

She'd pushed him, maybe too far. But it was too late now. She needed something from this. She *had* to have it. She wasn't going to put herself through this and walk away with nothing.

Sure, he could refuse, and then she'd have to figure out where to go from there, but until then, it was worth the gamble.

It all depended on how badly he wanted her.

Levi's hand dropped from her throat, and he stepped back, the sudden loss of his touch a shock. "Take off your dress," he ordered flatly.

It took a moment for it to sink in. He wasn't refusing.

She straightened against the wall, staring at him. "Does that mean—"

"Take off your fucking dress. I'm not going to ask again."

No, he was going to say it. She would make him. "The words, Levi. Give me the goddamn words. Or else this dress is staying on."

That menace, that danger, was back. It glittered in his eyes, thickened the atmosphere in the room. And it made that trembling, excited part of her lie down and roll over in surrender.

"Fine," he said coldly at last. "You can have the fucking building."

She didn't smile; that would have been pushing things too

far. But she allowed herself a tiny sliver of satisfaction all the same. Then she stepped away from the wall and reached behind her for the zipper of the dress, pulling it down, then shrugging out of the fabric, letting it slide down her hips and thighs until it pooled at her feet. Kicking it to one side.

She hadn't worn a bra—not when the dress left one shoulder bare—so all she wore was the black lace thong she'd put on earlier and her black platform Mary Janes.

Then she got rid of the thong too.

It wasn't cold, but his gaze roaming over her made her shiver and her nipples harden.

She looked away, down at the floor, imagining the sun on her skin and the sand under her feet, distancing herself both from him and from all the sensations she didn't want to feel.

There was a long silence.

"You don't want to look at me?" Levi murmured. "Fine. You don't have to."

His footsteps retreated, and, when she glanced up, she saw him going over to the kitchen area and pulling open a drawer. He took something out, something white, and then returned to where she stood.

"Turn around," he instructed, his voice hard.

She turned without hesitation, already pulling away from the situation, not letting it touch her.

And then something white and soft was laid over her eyes.

She tensed in shock, her hands going to the piece of material that Levi had put over her face. "What the hell?"

The material tightened as he knotted it behind her head. "I'm blindfolding you."

"Why?"

"Because I want to." His hands settled on her hips, pulling her hard against the heat of his body, the buttons of his jeans digging into the small of her back. "Because I know what you're trying to do."

Her heart lurched, a sinking sensation in her gut.

"That's right," he murmured in her ear. "You're trying to keep me at a distance, turn this into some kind of transaction, right? Well, I'm not going to let you. This is not a fucking transaction, and there will be no goddamn distance. I'm going to make you feel, *Sunny*. I'm going to make you beg. I'm going to make you fucking scream."

Chapter 10

She had no time to protest the use of that name, no time to protest the blindfold. No time to figure out how he knew what she'd been thinking or even hold out against that fiercely stated intention.

One minute he had his hands on her hips; the next, her world was tipping sideways as he swept her up into his arms, gathering her close to his chest. Then he was walking, and she thought he was carrying her back through into the living area, though she wasn't quite sure until he bent and she was deposited onto something cool. Leather, which meant the couch in the living room.

Her heartbeat was a loud drum in her head, her whole body starting to shake.

She didn't want to feel. That had been the point of the last eight years. That was the reason she'd made herself into who she was now. So she didn't have to feel the hurt or the guilt or the grief. Or the shame and humiliation.

So she could be hard. Cold. Sharp.

Like the roses etched into her skin, she'd been forged in

pain. And, like them, nothing would erase her; nothing would wash her away. Fragile-seeming blossoms that were nevertheless permanent.

Nothing could crush her. Nothing could tear her apart.

Except Levi. He can do both.

No. She couldn't let him. She just wouldn't.

His hands were hot on her shoulders, pushing her back onto the couch so she was lying stretched out on it. And then the cushions dipped as he put one hand near her head, rough denim rubbing against her skin as one powerful thigh eased between hers. Then he eased his other knee there too, so her legs were forced apart, held spread open on either side of his.

"Hands above your head."

She was breathing fast, trying to visualize the waves of her beach and not feel the desperate vulnerability opening up inside her, the ache of a desire that was getting too big to ignore.

Clearly she hadn't moved fast enough because suddenly his big, warm hands were taking her wrists and lifting them, putting her arms up and back on the soft, cool leather of the couch. "Keep them there." Another flat, hard order.

Rachel took a deep, silent breath. She could do this. Sure, last time, up against the wall, she'd lost her head, but she wouldn't now.

Levi trailed his hand down the length of her body, from her throat down between her breasts, over the trembling plane of her stomach, and farther still, through the curls at the apex of her thighs and down to cup her sex. The wake of fire that followed the touch of his fingers made her skin tighten and the breath catch in her throat.

"You're going to have to beg for your orgasm, Sunny," he said softly, using that name again, the one that hurt so much. "You're going to have to want it. And not because I told you to, but because you'll die if you don't come. Understand?"

That name might have hurt, but his hand didn't as it moved from her sex, trailing back up to her throat, then down again in a long, easy stroke. "I want you to say my name." His fingers were unexpectedly gentle, warm as they brushed her skin, stroking her like a cat, awakening every single nerve ending she had. "I want to hear it all desperate and sobbing."

The heel of his hand pressed down slightly on her clit, an electric shock of sensation, making her breath catch. Then he shifted it in a gentle grinding motion, increasing the intensity of the sensation.

She tried to swallow, but there was no moisture left in her mouth. The movement of his hand was light, but insistent, making the deep, dragging ache between her thighs get fiercer.

It was such an exposed position to be in, with her arms over her head and her legs spread around his. He must be able to see everything. It made her want to turn her head away, run and hide.

You're lying on the sand. The sun is on your face, and you feel like going for a swim because you're hot.

Yes, she was. So goddamn hot. Because the pressure on her clit kept changing, his hand moving in small, hard circles, making her hips shift restlessly, trying to relieve it.

"This feels good, doesn't it?" There was a soft, dark note in his voice, one she'd never heard before. Full of sensual heat and smoky desire. "I can tell. You're moving around, wanting to rub against me, aren't you?"

She stared into the blackness behind her blindfold, trying to see the waves and the sand. Trying to be there, not here, but the terrible, insistent pressure between her thighs kept growing, kept pulling her out of her fantasy.

"Y-yes," she stuttered, because that was clearly the answer he wanted, and, if she gave that to him faster, then this would be over faster.

But then he shifted, the pressure of his hand easing. And yet that didn't make the ache any less intense. If anything, it only made it worse.

His hands were on the insides of her thighs, pushing them farther apart, increasing her sense of exposure. She tensed in instinctive resistance, but he ignored her, pushing her thighs even wider.

Stop. You're letting this get to you.

Oh God, she was. And she really needed to keep thinking of that fucking beach, but it wasn't working. Why the hell wasn't it working?

Her breathing was coming faster now, his palms burning against the inside of her thighs, holding them apart. "You keep running away from me, Sunny. I can feel it. But that ends tonight, understand? I don't want you running from me anymore." One of his hands moved, and then his fingers were sliding through the folds of her sex like they had that night in Gideon's office, a slow, leisurely caress.

And yet there was nothing slow about the pleasure that exploded in the darkness behind her blindfold, a cascade of violent sparks that seared her already sensitive nerve endings, and she had to bite her lower lip hard to prevent the ragged gasp from escaping. But somehow the sound got trapped in her throat, releasing in a low groan.

The cushions beside her head dipped again, and she felt Levi move, the heat of his body along hers as he leaned over her, his breath against her throat. "Christ, I've wanted to touch you for so long," he whispered. "Wanted to stroke that pretty little pussy of yours, feel your cunt all hot and tight around my fingers." His hand shifted, one finger slowly, gently, circling the entrance to her body, around and around. "Tell me you want that too, Sunny. Say it."

Her head was shaking in denial almost before he'd finished

speaking. Because she didn't want that. She really didn't. Pleasure threatened everything; it cracked the armor and made all those other feelings she hated slide in through the fissures. The painful feelings that tainted everything, that made her feel worthless.

Well, isn't that what you are? Worthless?

His finger was relentless, circling and circling, making her back arch and her hips lift toward the touch, as if he was right, as if she craved more.

No, she damn well wasn't worthless. That was fucking pathetic. She was strong, and she was stronger than this.

The teasing finger stopped. She felt his breath against her throat and then his mouth. Then his teeth as he bit her, a gentle pressure, not hard enough to hurt, but enough to send a jolt arcing through her. And this time the sound escaped her before she could stop it, a shuddering gasp of shock that ended on a harsh cry as he followed up the bite with two fingers thrusting deep into her pussy.

She shuddered, the scalpel-sharp edge of pleasure beginning to peel her open, cutting through her ridiculous beach fantasy as if it were made of tissue.

He licked her, then bit her again, his thumb finding her clit, his fingers pushing deeper. She gave a sob, her hips lifting into his hands, her body wanting more even if she didn't.

"Come on, sweetheart," Levi murmured, husky and hot in her ear. "Don't hold out on me. Give me the words." He drew his hand back, his fingers withdrawing before pushing in deep again, driving that sharp, piercing edge of pleasure against her skin.

His thumb stroked over her clit, and another sob collected in her throat, because it felt so good.

His mouth was trailing down her throat, his tongue on her skin, licking her. "You want it. I can feel it." His breath was hot against her breast now. "God, I love how you're all hot and so fucking wet." He thrust again with his hand as if to illustrate the point, his fingers slow and slick inside her. "But you're holding back, and I'm not going to let you." His thumb circled, everything inside her drawing into a tight, aching knot. "I had eight years of being alone. All those nights I thought about you. All that time I missed you. It was too long, Sunshine. Far too long. And now I want it. I want you. Let me in, sweetheart."

She was shaking, trying to resist the thread of emotion in his dark voice. An emotion that wasn't cold or distant this time, but hot, ragged, pulling at her. Yet something in her wouldn't let her surrender. And she didn't know why, only that to give in would be to destroy herself.

Hot, wet heat around her nipple. The pressure of suction drawing hard on her, adding a layer to the almost unbearable pleasure. His fingers slowing, the circular movement of his thumb on her clit matching the tempo.

"You promised me," he whispered against her breast. "You promised me you'd give me this."

She had promised. In return for her building she would give him this.

A simple transaction. Just like the one she'd had with Evan.

But this isn't Evan.

Her throat tightened, her eyes prickling as realization knifed through her. She'd been lying to herself. Of course this could *never* be a simple transaction to her. Of course it couldn't. Because it *wasn't* Evan. It was Levi, and that made everything different.

Levi, who hated her. Levi, her enemy.

Who'd missed her.

And now his thumb was on her and his fingers inside her, pleasure undermining her resistance, desire making her desperate. And it was wrong to feel this way, so goddamn wrong, but she couldn't stop it. Couldn't hold it back any longer.

Sensation was swamping her, drowning her, overwhelming all the barriers she'd erected, closing the distance.

The pad of his thumb did another slow, aching circle, and this time she couldn't stop the words coming out of her. "Oh God . . . please . . . Levi . . ." His name sounded as if it had a hundred cracks running through it, the truth pouring out of each and every one.

"Yes. Tell me, Rachel." The dark satisfaction in his tone made her forget everything she'd told herself. Shattered the fantasy of her stupid beach as if it had never been. All that she was aware of was the touch of his hand, his heat, and the rough sound of his voice in the flaming blackness behind her blindfold.

"I want you." It spilled out of her, just like it had before when he'd had her up against the wall and she'd pleaded.

"What do you want me to do?" His fingers spread apart inside her, stretching her, making her arch her back in ecstasy.

"I want your hands on me," she gasped, trembling, hardly even aware of what she was saying. "I want your mouth. I w-want you to make me come."

Everything went quiet except for the sound of her panting breaths, so loud in the silence.

Then she felt him shift, the hands on her body falling away, the feel of his breath moving away from her breast. But he didn't get off the couch; the rough denim of his jeans stayed against her thighs.

"Don't stop," she whispered, caught in the grip of a hunger so intense she could hardly breathe. "Please don't—"

"I won't. Just tell me who you want."

"Y-you."

His hands were on her thighs, gripping her. "My name. I want to hear it." There was a ragged edge to his voice now, an edge of desperation.

"I want you, Levi." It came out hoarsely, but she didn't care. Not now.

"Yes. *Fuck* yes." He was pushing her legs apart even wider, his fingers trailing through her slick folds. "And this, all of this is mine, isn't it? *You're* mine."

She shuddered at the touch, every nerve ending sensitized. "Yes." Because it was. *She* was. Somewhere deep inside, she'd always wanted to be.

"Yeah, that's right. You are." His hands slipped beneath her thighs, lifting them, and then there was warm cotton and shifting, powerful muscle along the backs of her legs, hot breath feathering against her exquisitely sensitive skin.

Oh God . . .

"Where do you want my tongue?" Hot palms sliding up to cup her butt in blatant possession, making her shift in his hold and arch her back again. "Tell me what to do, sweetheart. Tell me where you want it."

Her fear had dropped away now, her body relaxing into his touch.

She swallowed and stuttered shakily. "I w-want it . . . on me."

"Where?" His thumbs slid up her sex, gently spreading her soft flesh like the petals of a rose. "Exactly. Tell me exactly."

Evan never did this. He never touched you like this. Never spoke to you like this.

The thought was brilliant and clear in her head. No, he hadn't because their arrangement had been for his pleasure, not hers.

But this was for her.

Unless Levi was planning to use that pleasure to hurt her again.

She began to tremble, Levi's breath against her making it worse. Because she didn't think she could bear it if he did. "Don't . . . leave me l-like . . . you did before. At Gideon's." There was a husky note of desperation in her voice, and she couldn't seem to make it sound any less stark. "Don't . . . use this as a punishment. Please."

God, she was pathetic.

He was silent, and, with the blindfold on, she had no idea what that meant, though she thought she heard him curse. Then he said softly, "No. I won't. I promise."

His promise. Another relic of a past that was dead and gone. Yet just like that, what was left of her fear, what was left of her resistance, all melted away, as if he were still the one person she trusted most in the world.

"This is for me," he went on. "Not going to lie. But it's also for you." His mouth brushed her inner thigh, his voice deepening, becoming even rougher. "Now . . . you haven't told me where you want my tongue."

"I want it in . . . my pussy." This time she didn't care how husky she sounded. "I want you to lick me, make me come. Please, Levi. Please . . ."

"Good girl." There was rough heat in the words and something else. Approval. He'd said that to her before, too, up against that wall. "Such a good girl." She shivered, feeling the roughness of stubble along her inner thighs as he rubbed his jaw against her tender skin. "You need me, don't you?"

Something empty yawned wide inside her, an emptiness she'd been trying desperately to pretend wasn't there. "I do." A cracked sound. "I do need you."

He kept pushing. "You missed me, too." The rough feel of his jaw was replaced by the softness of his mouth, kisses up her inner thigh. "You missed me a lot." The thread of hot emotion wound through his voice again, edged with a desperation that sounded an awful lot like her own. Almost as if he wasn't telling her what she felt, but asking her if she did . . . *You missed me? You missed me a lot?*

The material of her blindfold felt wet. God, was she crying? "Every day."

"You don't need to anymore." That soft, dark note in his

voice was full of intent, full of certainty. "I'm here now, Sunny. I'm here."

Then there was no more talking, his wicked tongue gliding straight up the center of her pussy in a long, leisurely lick, tearing a hoarse scream from her, the pleasure wild and electric as a lightning storm.

His fingers dug into the tender flesh of her buttocks, his grip hard, and he pushed his tongue deep inside her, making her pant and cry out his name as pleasure arced and crackled over the entire length of her body.

She couldn't keep her hands where they were any longer, reaching down and finding the thick silk of his hair, pushing her fingers into it and holding on for dear life.

"Fuck, you taste good," he whispered huskily. "Hot and sweet." He gave her another lick, his tongue circling her clit, drawing a sob from her. "I used to imagine what your pussy would taste like and what you'd do when I finally got my tongue on you. How you'd sound." His fingers squeezed her buttocks, making her back arch even more. "I wanted to make you scream my name. I wanted to make you cry. And you're going to do both, aren't you?"

But she couldn't form words anymore, and, when his tongue pushed back into her sex, she could barely even think. He fucked her with his tongue, slow and deep, taking his time. And then he used his fingers, adding pressure to her clit until she was shaking so badly she couldn't stop, his name a sob in her throat.

He didn't need to tell her to beg, the words came out of her all on their own, hoarse and desperate, her fingers curled tight in his hair, the warmth and solidity of him holding her up, grounding her as the pleasure expanded inside her, getting hotter, more intense.

She was a firework, and all she needed was a lighted match to go up. She'd fly all the way to the fucking moon.

And then that terrible, wicked tongue of his provided the spark, the pressure of his thumb the flame. And she ignited.

Not falling, but shooting up into the wide-open freedom of the sky as the orgasm broke over her, a streaking, brilliant comet, a roman candle in the night. Flaming in ecstasy, only to drift back slowly to earth.

It took her a long time to come back to herself, to remember where she was, hearing the echo of her own scream in the silence of the room.

At another time that would have embarrassed her, but there was no time for that. No time to even try to get herself together, because she could feel Levi moving. There came the rustle of fabric and the sound of a zipper being undone. And then bright light stabbed her eyes as he leaned forward and ripped off her blindfold.

She turned her head instinctively, flinging an arm over her face, but he pulled it away. She didn't resist, blinking hard, trying to get her breath back. Trying to get her whole goddamned mind back. Because she was pretty sure he'd just made her lose it.

Then, as her vision cleared, he made her lose it all over again.

He was kneeling between her spread thighs, naked. And he was just so fucking beautiful she couldn't look away.

Smooth, dark golden skin. Each muscle perfectly outlined and exquisitely carved. Wide shoulders, broad chest, his stomach ridged and hard. Narrow hips and crisp, dark blond hair leading down to his cock, hard and ready for her.

Jesus, he was perfect. Utterly perfect.

She was shaking from the intensity of the orgasm, and she could feel wetness on her cheeks, and there was a small, frightened, lost part of her that wanted to run away and hide, protect herself. Because surely this kind of beauty wasn't for her, could never be for her.

He was always too good for you.

But she didn't want that voice in her head, not now. Because he was here, looking at her, his face taut and intense and hungry. The dark and light of his eyes glittering. And she found herself reaching out to him, desperate to touch, and yet half-afraid that, if she did, he might vanish or pull away.

Perhaps he sensed her uncertainty because he took her wrist and guided her hand to his chest, her breath catching at the feel of warm skin like oiled silk beneath her fingertips. She could feel the flex and release of all that hard, delicious muscle too, as she trailed her fingers over his chest, then down further over the dips and hollows of his abs.

He made a sound, harsh and guttural, as she reached further down, his grip on her wrist tightening. "No," he said. "Jesus, not now."

She looked up at him, suddenly feeling desperate and not too proud to beg. Hell, she'd been doing so ever since he'd laid her down on the damn couch. "Please. I want to touch you."

"I said no."

His gaze was fierce on hers, and she could hardly meet it.

"I thought you weren't going to punish me?" she asked, unable to help herself.

"It's not that. I just can't have you touching me right now." He looked away, down at something he held in his hand. A condom. With a series of short, sharp movements, he ripped open the packet, then rolled the condom on. Then he raised his gaze to hers again. "I've been celibate for eight years, and, you touch my dick now, I'm going to explode."

Oh. Right.

He leaned over her, one hand gripping the arm of the couch near her head, and she shivered uncontrollably, because he was so close. That hard, hot wall of muscle over her, the musk of sex and the spice of his aftershave heady in the air around them. His gaze, so intense, staring into hers.

Keeping his hand by her head, he reached down with the

other and slid it beneath her thigh, raising her leg up high and around his waist. The head of his cock pushed against the entrance of her body, making the breath catch in her throat. All it would take would be a shift of her hips, just a little . . .

"Sneaky girl," he murmured. "Not yet. When I say."

She quivered, the pressure of him right there maddening. "Levi . . ."

"You want me to fuck you, Sunshine?"

She looked up at him, into his eyes. Shadows and light, because that was Levi. The light of her long-gone friend, the shadow of the man he was now. And for a moment she didn't know which one she wanted more. "Yes," she said thickly. "I want you to fuck me. Right now. Please, Levi. God, please."

He shifted his hips, teasing her, pressing his cock against her clit, gliding it, sending jolts of pleasure through her. "Maybe I should make you wait. Keep you here all night without any satisfaction." He flexed his hips again, and she gasped, another white-hot spear of pleasure piercing her. "I could do that. I could play with that little pussy until you're desperate. Until you can't think of anything else but my cock inside you."

She panted, trembling. Wanting to move and yet holding herself still because he'd told her not to move. "You p-promised me you wouldn't."

But then he lowered his head, his mouth so close to hers, his eyes inches away. Watching her. "Yeah, I did." Then he shifted a third time, pushing inside her slow and deep, drawing a ragged gasp from her as her whole body arched upward, pleasure rising like a sweet, dark fire. "And I keep my promises."

"Levi." Her voice was shaking, a hoarse whisper. "Oh my God, Levi."

But that was all she managed to say because he covered her mouth with his, the kiss as deep and as wet and as carnal as the feel of his cock inside her.

He moved, slowly at first, a rhythm that had her curling her leg tighter around him, tilting her hips so he could go deeper. Then he moved faster, harder, his kiss hungry, demanding.

She lifted her hands to his shoulders and ran them down his spine, feeling the massive muscles of his back shift beneath her touch, pressing her body hard against the incredible heat of his.

He lifted his mouth from hers, came up on his hands, bracing himself above her, thrusting harder, driving into her, shoving her against the arm of the couch with each thrust.

The burn of pleasure was so fierce she couldn't move, could barely breathe, could only lie there and take it, staring up into his eyes. There was fury there and hunger and desperation, and something else she didn't recognize. Something intense.

Then he changed the angle of his thrust, hitting her clit with each stroke, making her sob, making her scream, the dark intensity in his eyes growing darker, deeper. A fire of need, flames leaping high. Engulfing both of them.

She screamed again when the climax hit, when she felt herself shatter into pieces. And the only thing that kept her together was his arms.

Chapter 11

Levi woke up hard and ready—pretty much like every other morning. But this morning was different. There was a woman in his arms, soft and warm, her scent musky-sweet and totally delicious.

Rachel.

Her back was against his front, and he had his arms wound around her waist, holding her close. The curve of her butt fit nicely against his groin, pressing along the length of his dick, which only added to his satisfaction with the entire situation.

In fact, he couldn't think of a morning when he'd woken up feeling better than he did right now. Made a nice change from waking to the sounds of his cellmate jerking himself off in the bunk above.

Levi turned his face into the wealth of silky black hair that flowed down her back, inhaling the delicious, sensual scent of her.

Last night had been incredible. There was no other word for it. The feel of her. The taste of her. The shock of pleasure when she'd touched him, when she'd come around him . . . Christ.

Every single goddamn thing had been just as he'd dreamed. No, God, she'd been *better* than any of his dreams.

After she'd given up everything to him on the couch, he'd picked her up, carried her into the bedroom, dumped her on the new bed, and they had then proceeded to christen it pretty thoroughly. Half the night even.

Which should have meant he'd be pretty sated now, and yet he wasn't. He was just as hungry for her now as he had been the night before.

Well, he had a lot of time to make up for, not to mention years of fantasies to live out.

He ran a hand down her side, her skin smooth and silken beneath his palm, and she made a sleepy sound, rolling onto her back, turning her face toward him.

Her eyes were closed, long, thick lashes lying still on her cheeks. And he couldn't stop looking at the soft pout of her mouth, all red from last night's kisses. There were faint marks on the pale skin of her throat and, further down, on her breasts.

He liked having his marks on her body, especially where people could see them. It made her his. And if that made him some kind of primitive Neanderthal, then shit, he was a primitive Neanderthal.

Bending his head, he nuzzled her throat gently, then moved further down to the rose petals inked across her chest, falling from the drooping rose that covered her shoulder. They were pretty, and yet there was something sad about them too. A rose dying and dropping its petals . . . She hadn't had those tattoos when he'd left.

He traced one with his finger. What the hell did they mean?

She'd laid a lot of stuff on him last night, first all that crap about wanting the building, then accusing him of not taking any responsibility for what he'd done to that fucking dealer. Which was bullshit.

But was it, really?

He shoved that thought away, far, far away, concentrating instead on her tattoo, tracing it over and over.

She'd also been trying to distance him, which he didn't like, not one bit. Her being all guarded and protecting herself wasn't what he'd envisaged.

Are you surprised, given the way you've been acting toward her?

The thought made his gut feel unsettled and his chest tight. Yeah, he'd been a prick to her; he knew that. But he'd had good reason. She was why he'd done time. And then to add insult to injury, she'd ignored him for so goddamn long. Years and fucking years.

He slid his finger to the next petal, stroking.

She'd made him promise not to punish her again the way he had at Gideon's, and there had been a note in her voice, a raw plea that had cut through him like the edge of a razor. That vulnerability had made him confess stuff too, stuff he hadn't meant to say, "*You missed me.*" And then she'd said, "*Every day.*"

His finger stopped, resting on her skin, the tightness in his chest suddenly enough to make him almost stop breathing.

How could she have missed him? When she hadn't even cared enough to visit? That made fuck-all sense.

At that moment Rachel made another sound, her back arching as if she were seeking more of his touch.

He forced the tight feeling away, concentrating on the satisfaction instead. Yeah, this was more like it. She couldn't hold out on him now, and she wasn't going to ever again, not if he could help it. Not with this chemistry between them. He'd always known it would be incendiary when they finally got together, and he hadn't been wrong.

Glancing down into her sleeping face, he let his finger trail down over the curve of her breast, circling one hardening nipple. She sighed, her lashes fluttering. She was close to waking now.

He circled her nipple again, watching the color rise under

her skin and her mouth open, pleasure flickering across her lovely face. She wasn't fighting it like she'd fought it the night before, holding out on him right to the last minute. At the time he'd been so hungry for her surrender, he hadn't thought to ask why that was.

Maybe you should?

Yeah, maybe he should. Because whatever the reason was, he needed it dealt with. Rachel warm, willing, and wet, and in his bed was absolutely nonnegotiable, and anything that interfered with that had to be gotten rid of.

He bent his head, kissed one of the petals on her chest, felt her shift restlessly beneath his mouth.

"Levi?"

Thank Christ. She'd finally woken up.

"Good morning." He kissed the next petal, lazily circling her nipple with his finger at the same time. "Was wondering when you were going to wake up."

"Hmmm. What time is it?"

Did it matter? He didn't have anything on his agenda for the day. He'd planned to meet with Ryan so the guy could get a look at the neighborhood and Levi could talk through his ideas, but that wasn't until next week.

Not that he was going to tell Rachel about those plans quite yet. He wanted to get everything signed off on first. And besides, if he told her about his ideas for development, she might say something to Gideon, and Levi *definitely* didn't want Gideon involved. At least not until Levi had gotten the investment dollars confirmed at the very least.

Levi rolled over to glance at the clock on the heavy wooden nightstand beside the bed.

Eight o'clock. Thank fuck for that. Plenty of time to deal with the morning hard-on that was becoming quite insistent.

"It's eight," he said, turning back to her. "No need to get up yet."

She gave him a brief glance, then passed a hand over her face. "Yeah, I have to."

"Why?" He slid an arm around her waist again, drawing her up against him the way she'd been before, so his aching dick was pressed against the delicious curve of her butt. "I haven't finished yet."

There was a certain stiffness in her muscles, as if she was trying to stop herself from pulling away from him. Which was annoying, especially when he thought they'd dealt with that particular issue the night before.

Sweeping aside her hair, he brushed his mouth over the sensitive skin at the nape of her neck.

"Levi . . ." She gave a shiver.

"What? Don't tell me that studio of yours needs to be open. No one wants to get a goddamn tattoo at eight in the morning."

"No, I just . . ." She stopped.

He pulled at her shoulder, easing her onto her back so he could see her face. "You just what?"

Her dark eyes were guarded, her expression unreadable. And all the satisfaction he'd been feeling earlier abruptly drained away, that tight feeling back again. Because he didn't want to see that wary, shuttered look. He wanted what he'd had last night, when she'd been panting and desperate and sobbing in his arms. Telling him she wanted him. Telling him she had missed him.

She was keeping a part of herself locked away, and he wanted it.

But maybe she saw the intention in his gaze, because she moved, twisting out of his arms and sliding out of the bed.

"Hey." He made a grab for her and missed. "Where the hell are you going?"

"Bathroom," she said over her shoulder, heading for the adjoining bathroom.

He lay there for a moment as she disappeared through the door, debating whether or not to follow her and force the issue, use pleasure to make her tell him what the problem was even. But for some reason, he didn't like that idea.

You want her to tell you not because you made her, but because she wants to.

He frowned, uncomfortable with that thought. Uncomfortable with the memories it bought back, of when she used to come to him and talk to him about anything.

There was no hope of her doing that now.

He glanced toward the bathroom again, the unsettled feeling back with a vengeance.

This wasn't part of your dream, was it?

No, it fucking well wasn't. He'd wanted Rachel the way it had been before, when she'd shared everything with him, with the added bonus of lots of sex. He didn't want her guarded and wary, protecting herself the way she was doing now.

Levi let out a breath. Maybe he could give her the Sugar Ink building, the way she'd demanded last night. He'd given in because he'd wanted that dress off her, but he hadn't promised her. It was supposed to be the centerpiece of his plans for the area, and changing those plans wasn't going to happen. But maybe he could work some deal with her, grant her a permanent lease for her studio or something.

Or you could just get her to trust you again. Rebuild that old friendship.

The unsettled feeling slowly began to creep back inside him, tightening his chest and making him ache. Yeah, well, that wasn't going to happen anytime soon, was it? Whatever trust there had been between them was gone, shattered years ago and probably beyond repair. Certainly he had no hope of fixing it. Which meant if he was going to get what he wanted, he'd have to use either blackmail or business.

Blackmail had only gotten him so far, which left business.

Luckily along with the MBA he'd gotten inside, he'd also gotten a very good understanding of the business world.

You want her trust. You know you do.

Levi shoved the thought away. Trust had never been part of this particular deal, and he didn't want it anyway, not when it would mean opening himself up to her in return. Because the last time he had, she'd left him in a police station with a manslaughter charge on his rap sheet.

Not again. *Never* again.

He got up, pulled on some clothes, and went into the kitchen to make some breakfast. Cooking wasn't his strong point, but he could do a mean bacon and eggs and coffee.

By the time she got out of the shower, he had breakfast on the table all ready for her, and his satisfaction was starting to return when she came out of the bedroom, pausing in the doorway and staring at the food on the table with obvious surprise.

In black skinny jeans and a tight, black T-shirt that had the mural painted on the wall of her studio printed on it, she looked hot. Her hair had been pulled back, the marks on her neck covered imperfectly with makeup.

It irritated him that she wanted them hidden, but he let it go. Give him another week, and she'd be showing them off to anyone who wanted to see them.

"What's this?" she asked.

"What does it look like? Breakfast."

"I guess you didn't order this in."

"No. This is all me." He put the coffeepot down onto the table. "Come on, eat. You're going to need to get your strength back today."

She glanced down the hallway as if she were checking to make sure the front door was still there, reluctance clear on her face.

The irritation gathered tighter in his gut.

What? Did you think you were going to sit here with her and have a nice, friendly breakfast?

Yeah, actually he kind of had.

Doesn't work that way, asshole, and you know it.

His mood darkened. Of course it didn't work that way, and he was a fucking idiot to expect that it did.

"Don't worry," he said, a rough edge creeping into his voice. "I'm not staying. Going out for a run."

"Oh."

He didn't miss the flicker of relief that crossed her face, and it only made him angrier. Yeah, it was better to get out of here, leave her to enjoy the food he'd cooked for her alone. And maybe in the process he could figure out just what the fuck his problem was.

Digging into his pocket, he pulled out his keys and worked one off the ring, putting it down onto the table. "Apartment key. I'll text you the code for the front door too." He stuffed the keys back into his pocket. "Enjoy breakfast."

And he didn't look at her as he brushed past, heading into the hallway.

As he strode down to the front door, a small, traitorous part of him waited to hear her call him back.

But she didn't.

The following week Levi pushed open the cracked glass door of Gino's, Royal Road's original bar, and stepped into its familiar dark interior, the memories of too many rowdy nights spent in its alcohol-soaked atmosphere assaulting him.

They were good memories for the most part. Nights with Gideon and Zee, watching them downing boilermakers, racing each other to see who could drink the most and still speak at the end of the night. Nights with Rachel, sneaking her in while she was still under twenty-one and buying her illicit beer when she'd had a tough day with her gran. Nights with the whole crowd once Zoe turned twenty-one, no less rowdy or wild. Laughing as Zoe got drunk for the first time and had a stand-up, screaming fight with Gideon about something that Levi couldn't even remember now.

Nights spent dragging his father's drunken ass home after another vodka-fueled binge.

Levi stopped in the entrance, looking around. Same grimy, slightly sticky carpet. Same stained walls. Same cracked vinyl booths and wobbly barstools. Same musty scent of spilled alcohol and stale cigarettes.

Shit, some things never changed.

The place was virtually empty apart from the usual drunks—not unusual at lunchtime—and a couple of men leaning on the bar. Men who stood out from the rest, purely because they were wearing suits and had expensive haircuts.

Ryan and some other guy. Who the fuck was that?

Ryan looked sharp in his dark suit, but the other man's was custom-made, Levi would have bet anything on it. He was older too, late sixties maybe, with a fine head of silver hair and the well-preserved look that only the very wealthy or the very important had. Levi had seen enough men like him before he'd gone inside, when he'd used to hang around downtown, watching the suits go to work. They'd given him hope back then. Hope that since they were men like him, he could do what they were doing. Going to work in a big city building every day, earning big city dollars to take back to their lovely wives in their equally lovely apartments. No drunken dad to keep out of trouble. No drug dealers threatening you and the people you cared about with knives.

Yeah, he'd looked up to those men. He'd wanted to be one of them.

And now you are.

Levi smiled. Yeah, he fucking was. Tattoos and criminal record and all.

Ryan turned as the door opened and raised a hand in greeting. He didn't actually smile—he didn't smile much, anyway—

but then maybe the suit at his shoulder was the problem. That guy didn't smile either, only stared at Levi with disturbingly direct dark eyes. He seemed familiar somehow, though Levi couldn't place him.

"Rush," Ryan said as Levi approached them. "Nice place you got here."

Levi ignored that, shifting his attention to the older man standing behind Ryan. "Didn't know we were going to have another guest."

Ryan shifted. "Yeah, about that—"

"It's all right, Jason," the man said, his voice deep and cultured. "I can introduce myself." And this time he did smile, perfectly friendly, even charming, as he held out his hand. "My name is Oliver Novak, and I'm very pleased to meet you, Mr. Rush."

Novak. Okay, now it made sense.

While he'd been inside and studying, Levi had made it his mission to read the business pages of the local and national newspapers every day, and Novak's name came up quite frequently. He was old Michigan money and head of Novak Incorporated, a national company that had fingers in all sorts of different pies, from real estate to manufacturing to investment. An important man, very important. Even more so since, the last Levi had heard, the guy was gearing up for a political career, a senator's position in his sights.

So what the fuck was he doing in Royal?

"Likewise," Levi said, taking the man's extended hand and shaking it.

"I hope you don't mind my crashing your party. But Jason came to me a couple of days ago raving about the plans you have for this area, and I have to say, I was intrigued."

Levi flicked a glance at Ryan. It was difficult to imagine him "raving" about anything—the guy had a total poker face when it came to business—and it was even more difficult to imagine Novak's being intrigued with Levi's plans.

It wasn't that Levi didn't think they were good—he knew they were—but they were centered totally on a small Detroit neighborhood. So what would this guy find so intriguing about those plans?

"Raving, huh?" Levi raised a brow at Ryan.

The other man shrugged. "I might have mentioned your ideas a couple of times."

"A good thing he did," Novak said. "I'm always looking for new investment opportunities, and this seemed . . . very attractive indeed."

Levi leaned his hip against the bar. "I hope you don't mind my saying, but I'm finding it difficult to believe a guy like you would be interested in an area like this. Or in development plans from an ex-con."

Amusement glittered in Novak's eyes. "I'm not interested in your record, Mr. Rush. I'm interested in your ideas. And an area like this is just what I'm looking for." He nodded around the grimy bar. "Somewhere with the potential to be something greater, bigger. And Royal Road has that potential, I think."

"Why?" Levi asked bluntly. "I mean, what's your interest in developing someplace like Royal?"

Novak's mouth curved in a slight smile. "Good. You ask questions. I like that in a man, Mr. Rush. It speaks of intelligence. What's my interest? I believe Detroit's due for a renaissance. And I'd like to be the one to put that in motion."

Of course he would. With buildings cheap enough to offset the cost of construction and lots of people looking for alternatives to the rapidly rising rents of downtown, now was a great time to be investing in gentrification. There was money to be made, and Levi was betting Novak had his eye on making more.

But money alone didn't explain his interest in Royal. There had to be other reasons, and Levi bet he knew what they were.

He gave the older man an assessing look. "Nothing to do with your senatorial campaign, I guess?"

Ryan had gone still, beer lifted to his lips. A warning flashed in his blue eyes.

Levi ignored him. "I mean, it's going to look good for you, isn't it? Investing in a rundown part of the city. Kicking out the dealers and whores, and giving the old buildings a new lease on life. Stuff like that."

It was a gamble, being so confrontational. But Levi had no time for bullshit. Plus he'd developed a healthy distrust of rich men in positions of power. He liked to know where people were coming from so there were no surprises. Especially not when such surprises could potentially affect the success or failure of his plans.

Far from being offended, Novak only laughed. "You're very blunt, Mr. Rush."

"Sorry, but when money's involved, my bullshit threshold tends to be low."

"As it should be. As it should be, indeed." Novak reached for his beer bottle sitting on the bar and took a sip. "Another point in your favor. And since you've mentioned it, yes, providing the money behind such a positive revitalization project wouldn't hurt my campaign." He smiled. "In fact, I'd like Royal Road to be the centerpiece of that project. An example of how great we can make this city with a little hard work and an injection of cash. You see, I want to make Detroit big again, Mr. Rush. I want to make this city proud of itself the way it used to be. The way it should be. Wouldn't you like to be part of that?"

Stupid question. And yet there was something about the way the guy said it that deepened the distrust inside Levi a little more. Which was crazy when an opportunity like this was just what he was looking for. His plans needed investment dollars and lots of them, and Novak here was just the man to provide them.

"Sure, I would," Levi said slowly, keeping his expression guarded, not letting any of his distrust show. "What sort of things are you thinking about for this project then?"

Novak smiled, a distinguished and important businessman who nevertheless had the common touch. "You're the ideas man, Mr. Rush. I'm just the money. You tell me."

It couldn't hurt. Levi wouldn't lose anything by doing it, though there might be issues if Novak decided to cut him out of the deal and handle it all himself. Then again, considering Levi now owned the more important buildings in Royal, Novak might have a few difficulties with that.

"Sure you need me?" Levi asked, testing the waters. "You don't want to go it alone?"

Novak stared at him a moment. "You're right to be careful. But I'm a busy man, and I haven't got the time to plan something like this myself. All I want to do is find a project already up and running that I can put some money behind. You're the brains behind this, and I'd like it to stay that way."

Well, okay then. This was getting better and better.

"Mr. Novak also agreed to allow a formal presentation of the project to some of Detroit's other major players," Ryan put in. "In fact, he's offered to host it himself."

Now *that* was a big deal. Ryan had a certain reach, but Novak was a much bigger draw. He had the reputation and the contacts, and moved in circles that Ryan didn't have access to. Novak could potentially pull in a whole lot of people. Valuable people. People with money.

"You have?" Levi met Novak's gaze. "That's a pretty major vote of confidence."

"Like I told you," Novak said levelly, "I'm intrigued and ex- cited by the vision you have. And I think there are many people out there who'd want a piece of it too." He smiled again. "So why not?"

Yeah, why the fuck not?

Well, that sense of distrust for one. Then again, Levi didn't trust anyone. And this was an opportunity he'd be stupid to turn down.

"Okay," he said. "I guess I'm good with that."

"Excellent." Novak put his beer down on the bar with a click. "In that case, Mr. Rush, would you care to show us around the neighborhood?"

Chapter 12

"You want a phoenix?" Rachel asked dubiously.

"Yeah," Tamara said. "One like Zee's, only little and on my shoulder."

Rachel glanced at Zoe, who only rolled her eyes.

Tamara had decided she wanted a tattoo as a surprise for Zee and had sworn both women to secrecy about it. Rachel had even closed Sugar Ink for the night so Tamara could get it done in privacy. It wasn't something Rachel would do for just anyone, but she'd decided she liked Tamara, and, since that made the other woman nearly family, concessions could be made.

Especially when Tamara had turned up with a jug of ready-made margaritas.

Since Rachel was the one doing the tattooing, she'd made do with one drink, but Tamara and Zoe clearly had no such qualms, both of them already starting on their third.

Now they were all sitting on the couch, Tamara in the middle looking through the book of tattoo designs, while Zoe peered over her shoulder and Rachel tried not to wince when

Tamara pointed out something hideous. Which was quite frequently.

It seemed like alcohol wasn't Tamara's friend when it came to choosing a tat.

"I'm thinking maybe something like this." Tamara reached out and pointed to a brightly colored design. "That looks cool."

"Sure," Rachel said patiently. "If you want your entire upper back covered."

Tamara pulled a face and reached for her glass, taking a healthy swig. "Uh, no, that's what I do not want." She leafed through more pages, then stabbed a finger down on another design. "What about that one?"

"That's a sleeve."

"Oh."

"Could look cool," Zoe offered, squinting over Tamara's shoulder. "If you don't mind the baby deer."

"Baby deer?" Rachel frowned at the picture. What the hell was Zoe talking about? Rachel didn't include baby anythings in her designs.

"Oh, no," Zoe muttered. "They're not deer."

They weren't. They were supposed to be flames.

"Jesus, Zoe." Rachel stared across at the younger woman. "Are you drunk?"

Zoe blinked, her eyes even more owlish than normal behind her glasses. "No. Just shortsighted."

"Like hell."

"Like hell that I'm shortsighted or like hell I'm not drunk?"

"You're drunk," Tamara confirmed, patting Zoe on the shoulder. "But don't worry, you can get a tattoo too."

Zoe frowned. "I don't want a tattoo."

Meaning, Gideon wouldn't let her have one.

"Hey, you're twenty-five," Rachel said. "What does it matter what Gideon thinks?"

Zoe's frown deepened. "It's got nothing to do with Gideon."

"Sure it doesn't," Rachel muttered.

"I heard that." Zoe leaned forward and grabbed her glass from the table in front of her. "And I don't give a shit what he thinks."

Rachel shot Zoe a glance, picking up on the undercurrents that Tamara, still happily leafing through the designs, wouldn't.

Was something going on with Gideon and Zoe? It wasn't a big secret that Zoe had a major crush on the guy, though Gideon had never given any sign that he felt the same way about her. He wouldn't though. Gideon would probably rather chew his own leg off than think of Zoe as a woman.

Zoe was sipping moodily on her margarita, her basketball-booted feet crossed at the ankle and up on the table. She wasn't a person who hid what she felt; it was all right there to read on her face. And right now her face was saying "I'm fucking pissed."

"Something up, Zoe?" Rachel asked.

Zoe shrugged. "Gideon was in a bad mood this afternoon." She took another long sip. "He yelled at me."

Actually, that was kind of shocking. Gideon was almost never in a bad mood, and still less frequently shouted at people. Especially Zoe.

"Oh," Rachel said. "Why?"

Zoe scowled. "I didn't do anything."

"Hey, I never said you did—"

"It was just that he was being a tool about seeing Levi walking around Royal with some guys in suits today. So I told him to stop giving Levi such a hard time."

"Actually," Tamara murmured, "you told him he was being a dick. I know; I heard you."

Zoe scowled even harder. She drained her glass and put it back on the table with slightly more force than necessary. "I think I might go home," she announced. "Have a nice tattoo party." Then she got up and headed for the front door.

Rachel stared at her in shock. Zoe in such an obvious temper wasn't something you saw every day. If at all.

"Zoe, wait." She half got to her feet only for Tamara to grab her arm.

"Leave her," the other woman muttered. "I think she needs some space."

"What?" Rachel only half heard her, her attention on Zoe's retreating back.

"Gideon also told her that if she didn't like it, she should stop following him around twenty-four seven."

Oh, hell. That would hurt. That would really hurt.

The door of the studio slammed.

Slowly, Rachel sat down and glanced at Tamara. "What happened? You heard it?"

"Zee was doing something on his Trans Am at Gideon's, and I was waiting for him. I heard Gideon and Zoe arguing upstairs." Tamara pulled a face. "Like Zoe said, Gideon saw Levi showing some guys around Royal, and Gideon wasn't happy about it. God knows why."

"Some guys? What guys?"

Tamara shrugged. "I don't know; I didn't see them. Not locals from the sounds of it though."

Rachel frowned, trying to make sense of it.

The past week or so of living in Levi's apartment hadn't been as bad as she'd first expected.

Waking up in his arms that initial morning had been the worst moment, when her stupid, sleep-deprived brain had thought it meant something more than it had. That his arms around her and his mouth on her skin had been a sign of some tenderness, when all it had been was the usual male response to a naked woman first thing in the morning.

She'd felt suffocated. Not by him, but by the feeling unraveling in her chest. The need, the sheer, painful yearning for that long-gone friend. And the ache of knowing that nothing was going to bring him back.

She'd been glad when he'd gone out for a run, while eating the breakfast he'd cooked for her alone in the dining room, trying to ignore the stupid fucking feeling of hurt.

They'd spent the day apart, but that night she'd come back to his apartment—after checking herself when she had automatically headed toward her old place—and there hadn't been any candlelit dinners or talks of dates.

There hadn't been any talking at all.

Only Levi, hard and hot and demanding, pushing her up against a wall and taking her so fast she'd barely gotten a breath.

Which was kind of what they'd spent the last week doing, in between cursory attempts at stilted conversation. Her attempts, at least. He didn't attempt to talk about anything. The past two nights he'd sat on the couch with his laptop, fiercely concentrating on whatever it was he was doing.

It was a weird sight, the massive tattooed guy with the ring in his eyebrow, tapping away on a sleek piece of silver technology. She'd asked him once what he was doing, but he'd only said, "Business."

She hadn't wanted to watch him after that. Looking at him only made her aware of the distance between them, of everything she'd lost.

Maybe whatever he'd been working on had something to do with these guys in suits. But then, what about them would piss Gideon off? It had to be something major to put a dent in Gideon's normally chilled-out personality.

Curiosity gathered inside her. She wanted to ask Tamara more about it, but since the other woman had only overheard the details from someone else, questioning her wasn't going to get Rachel any more information.

Clearly Rachel was going to have to ask Levi himself. And

maybe at the same time she could push him more about her building. She'd tried bringing it up with him a number of times, but he'd told her she was going to have to wait. That he was still sorting some things out. It was blatant bullshit, but she hadn't pushed.

Perhaps it was time to push again.

Tamara was eyeing her. "You don't know what's going on?"

"No. Levi hasn't mentioned anything to me about it." He hadn't said anything to her about anything, period.

"Zee thought it was weird. Especially Gideon's getting mad."

"Yeah, that *is* weird. Gideon doesn't let anything much bother him." She paused. "Unless it's something threatening his hood."

Tamara's pale brows arrowed down; she was obviously remembering what had happened with Zee and his father a couple of months or so earlier, when Joshua Chase had threatened Zoe. Gideon had been pissed then, though pissed was kind of an understatement.

"What could be threatening about guys in suits?" Tamara said. "No, scratch that. Plenty of guys in suits are threatening."

"This is true. I'd better ask Levi what's going on. No one wants Gideon in a mood, that's for sure. He's a fucking pain in the butt when he is."

Tamara nodded, glancing back down at the book of designs. Her eyes widened. "Oh, what about that one?"

Rachel sighed. "That's not a phoenix. It's an eagle, and it's supposed to go over your chest. You really want an eagle head on your left boob?"

Tamara's look of distaste said it all. "Not so much. What I want is something pretty, but not too over the top. Small, but not so small it looks stupid. Maybe with some color, but not too much. You know what I mean?"

Yeah, Rachel did. It was the same thing she heard from every client ever. And there was only one answer. "Why don't I design you something? It means you won't get it now unfortunately, but if you're happy to wait, I could draw you something really cool that I think Zee would find really sexy."

Tamara's eyes widened. "Oh, would you? I'd love that!"

Rachel grinned at the other woman. "Sure. Just give me a couple of days. I'll draw a few things so you can choose." She liked doing custom design and didn't get to do enough of it since most of her clients were either conservative in their tattoo choices or balked at the cost.

The door to the studio banged opened.

Rachel lifted her head, ready to tell whomever it was that the studio was closed for the evening, but the words died in her mouth when she saw whom it was coming toward them.

Levi.

But it wasn't the Levi she was familiar with, the guy in battered jeans and a T-shirt. This Levi was different. Because he was wearing a suit. It was an elegant dark-charcoal color that perfectly set off the width of his shoulders and his chest, the blue of his business shirt making the silver blue of his eyes more intense. She could even see the fine rim of color around his one dilated pupil.

He wasn't wearing a tie, the collar of his shirt undone, and she couldn't believe the sexiness of the exposed skin of his throat. It was difficult to drag her eyes away.

"Whoa," Tamara breathed. "Maybe I should get Zee a suit."

Rachel rose to her feet, her heartbeat accelerating all of a sudden. Which was ridiculous given the amount of sex she and Levi had had over the last couple of days. She should have been inured to him by now, but clearly she was not.

"What are you doing here?" The question sounded almost accusatory, but she didn't take it back. He hadn't come by the studio since she'd moved in with him, not once, and she hadn't been expecting him, still less dressed like that.

"What do you think?" He stared at her. "I want a tattoo."

"Um, you know what? I think I have . . . a thing . . ." Tamara slid off the couch. "Let me know about the design, Rach. Oh, and mind if I leave the margarita stuff here?"

Rachel barely heard her, all her attention focused on Levi. A tattoo? He wanted a fucking tattoo?

He didn't say anything, standing not far from her, his hands in his pockets, staying utterly still as the door of the studio closed behind Tamara.

A taut silence fell.

"What do you mean you want a tattoo?" she asked inanely.

"I mean, ink me up. That's what you usually do in here isn't it?"

"Why?"

"Because I want one; that's why."

"Levi . . ." She didn't know why she was protesting, because seriously, what did it matter why he wanted it? And why she didn't want to do it was anyone's guess. Clearly she was insane.

"What? Last time I checked this was a tattoo studio."

Yeah, so what's the big deal?

Getting a grip on herself, she shrugged. "Fair enough. What's with the suit?"

"I had a business meeting." His gaze dropped to the margarita glasses on the table. "Did I interrupt something?"

"Oh, Tamara's thinking about getting a tat. We were just discussing designs. But don't tell Zee, okay? It's supposed to be a surprise."

"Sure." His intense, uneven stare returned to her again. "Do I get a kiss?"

A delicious tension had crept into the space between them, tugging at her, a pull she felt all the way down between her thighs. He'd been demanding the night before, keeping her up till way past midnight, and yet it felt like years since he'd touched her.

Dealing with the desire she felt every time he came near was difficult, mostly because it wasn't purely sexual. She didn't like it. Didn't want to feel it. But it was there all the same, just like it was there now, making her want things from him that it was clear she was never going to get.

She let out a silent breath and skirted around the table, walking slowly over to him. A kiss was nothing—hell, they'd kissed so many times before. So why she should feel reluctant now she had no idea. Maybe it was because he was here, in her space, instead of the other way around.

Stopping in front of him, she looked up into his face. She should have gotten used to the intensity of his focus by now, but she hadn't. Every time she met his gaze it felt like being plugged directly into an electrical socket.

"You look like you're afraid I'm going to kill you, not kiss you." The deep rumble of his voice was unexpected.

Dammit. Did he really have to pick up on her every emotion? She was usually way better at hiding things than this.

"I'm not afraid you'll kill me, Levi."

She placed her hands on his chest and rose up on her toes, pressing her mouth to his. His lips were warm, and she wanted to open them with her tongue, taste him. But she restrained the urge, keeping the kiss to a mere brush of her lips before stepping back.

He made no attempt to prolong the contact, continuing to stand there with his hands in his pockets, staring at her. "And that's not a kiss."

Her mouth tingled, the deeply physical pull she felt toward him tugging harder. But she ignored it. "I thought you wanted a tattoo."

"I do. But I'd like a proper kiss more."

"I'm at work. If you want a proper kiss, you'll have to wait till we get home." She was *not* going to be doing this now, not in her studio. "Where do you want this thing then?"

He didn't say anything for a second, his gaze narrowing, and she had the impression he was weighing up something. Then he abruptly shrugged out of his jacket, throwing it carelessly on the couch where she'd been sitting, and undid a few more buttons on his shirt.

She couldn't stop looking. At the slow movement of his fingers as he undid the buttons. At the tanned skin revealed under the cotton of his shirt. It was dumb; she'd seen him naked so many times by now it shouldn't have had any impact on her whatsoever. Yet like the force of his gaze, the sight of his body caused a fierce, electrical thrill to go through her.

Levi opened his shirt all the way down and pulled aside the fabric to reveal his bare chest, then put a palm over his heart. "That's where I want it. Here."

"Okay." She stared at his big, long-fingered hand. At the letters tattooed on the back, the first four letters of the word *patience*. She'd seen those letters a lot on various places on her body in the past week. He hadn't explained why he had that word on his hand, but he hadn't needed to. She knew. Seemed as if everywhere she looked there were reminders of what she'd done.

She turned away from him, moving over to the table where Tamara had left the book of tattoo designs. "I have a book of designs you can—"

"I already know what I want."

Of course he did. He was that kind of guy.

She stopped and turned back. "What?"

"A sun."

He saw the flare of shock in her eyes. Which wasn't totally unexpected. After all, he hadn't given her any reason to think he'd want something like that over his heart unless it was yet more punishment. But he'd decided that actually, he'd lost his taste for punishment. He had something better in mind.

He'd been thinking it over for the past few days. Specifically about how he was going to broach the topic of giving her Sugar Ink's building in return for the trust she was so obviously withholding.

But he'd put the issue on the back burner for the past few days, irritated by the wall she seemed to put between them every time he tried to initiate any kind of conversation.

Every night it was the same: another awkward conversation in which he'd try to get something out of her and she would withdraw. He kept hoping she'd eventually open up without his having to ask her or force her, but that had clearly been a stupid fucking hope.

Nothing had changed.

Even though he wasn't entirely surprised by this, he did find the disappointment of it unexpectedly sharp. Which was stupid, given that he hadn't exactly opened himself up to her either.

But he felt disappointed anyway.

He'd thought that maybe with enough sex, he wouldn't care. Yet he found he did. Which meant if he wanted it to change, he'd have to be the one to make the first move.

The meeting with Novak and Ryan had gone on much longer than Levi had expected, finishing back up at Gino's where he'd bought a couple of rounds, oiling the wheels of commerce a little more. Not that he needed to, when Novak was so obviously enthusiastic about Levi's plans and Royal in general.

Levi had felt good after Novak had departed, sliding into the evening traffic in a black chauffeur-driven town car. And positive too. More positive than he'd felt in months, as if everything was finally coming together.

Which was why Levi was here now, making that first move.

He was done with waiting.

Naturally, as a businessman, he'd use whatever leverage he

could find to convince Rachel to open up. And if that meant going into her territory and getting her to give him a tattoo, then that's what he'd do. Especially a tattoo that would be meaningful for both of them.

Rachel stared at him. She was looking especially hot today, in a tiny blue denim miniskirt and a tight white T-shirt with a sugar skull printed on the front of it. Her legs were bare, pale and elegant and strokable, her feet in black platform sandals with lots of buckles and straps.

He wanted to run his hands up those pretty legs and under her miniskirt. See what color panties she was wearing today. Then rip them off.

"Why a sun?"

He met her gaze. "Why not?"

"Because that's not what we are to each other any longer," she said without hesitation. "Because that's not what I am to *you*."

"You got one on your back." He'd run his fingers over it the night before, while she lay asleep on her stomach, tracing it as if he couldn't help himself.

She flushed. "That's different."

"Why? If I want a sun, I'll get a sun." He didn't know why he was arguing with her when he quite easily could have gotten something else. Problem was, he didn't want anything else. He wanted a goddamn sun.

Her mouth flattened into a line. "So that's it? You're coming in here just to get a tattoo of a sun?"

"No. Actually I thought we could talk while you're doing it."

She'd turned toward the row of tattoo chairs. "I don't talk while I work."

"Bullshit you don't."

Moving over to the long counter where all the tattoo gear was stored, she began pulling out various items. "Sit down," she said shortly.

He walked over to the chair she'd indicated, but didn't sit, not quite yet. "I want to talk about this building."

Rachel stilled, then flicked him a surprised glance. "What about it?"

"You wanted it."

"Yeah, and you told me you'd give it to me, then I got nothing but silence."

"I'm considering doing it."

She stopped what she was doing, staring at him. "What?"

He didn't answer immediately, sitting down in the chair as she'd asked him to, stretching out, and crossing his ankles. "I think you heard."

Rachel stared at him a moment longer, then she reached for the rolling chair at her station and sat down at the long counter than ran the length of the room. She'd gotten out a piece of paper while he was sitting down, and now she pulled a pen from the cup at the edge of the counter. She looked down at her paper for a second.

Then she began to draw. "You've been considering all week. Has something changed?"

He watched her as she drew, her hand strong and sure and without hesitation as it moved over the paper. A sense of familiarity reached into him and held on tight.

He remembered this, sitting and watching her draw. She was never without a pen in her hand or a ratty old notebook, and some nights, when her gran had finally been put to bed and Rachel had needed company, he would come to her apartment and sit with her, and they'd talk. Or after one of his father's binges, Levi cleaning up while she cooked him dinner, then he'd sit and eat while she'd drew.

He was always amazed at the pictures that took form beneath her hand, at the sheer creative talent that poured out of her. He'd found it humbling that someone so gifted could be his friend, could create such beautiful pictures in a place where there was no beauty at all.

Those moments had been precious, and he'd used to day-dream about the time when they would be together in their own place, and he could watch her in her very own studio, creating magnificent pieces of art.

Like now?

No, not like now. Because even though this was her studio and she was creating art, it wasn't the kind of art he'd ever imagined for her. He'd envisaged her in New York, showing paintings to the artistic elite, or even in Paris, studying the works of the great artists.

Certainly not in a tattoo studio in shitty Royal, in abandoned Detroit.

Something had happened to make her settle for this, and he was going to find out what it was.

"I want to know why didn't you go to art school like you planned."

She didn't look up from her drawing. "I told you; I had to use the money for Gran's funeral."

The way she said it didn't sit well with him, though he couldn't quite pinpoint why. A funeral was expensive, so it made sense. Maybe it was how she said it, as if it were no big deal. As if spending the money she'd been saving to achieve her dreams hadn't been important to her. And that was weird, because they'd had conversations about her going to art school. Her eyes would light up whenever they discussed it, all her barriers and walls dropping, revealing the passionate, excited girl behind the sarcasm and the barbs.

But now . . . it was like that didn't mean anything at all.

"I thought you had your heart set on it."

"People change. And so do circumstances." She leaned over the picture she was drawing, making some tiny, precise movements. He couldn't see what it looked like yet, as her hand was in the way. As she shifted over the paper, a lock of glossy black hair drifted over her shoulder, and he wanted to touch it. Then he found himself getting distracted by the pull of her T-shirt across her breasts, by the lace of her bra clearly visible beneath it.

Goddamn. Sex, for once, wasn't what he was after here.

"Tell me why," he said, shifting his attention back to her face, drawn in tight lines of concentration. "The real reason, not that funeral bullshit."

"There is no other reason."

He ignored that. "I'm considering giving you a permanent lease for Sugar Ink. I know it's not the entire building, but it means you won't be able to be kicked out."

Her hand slowed, then came to a stop. She turned, flicking him a glance, the look in her eyes unreadable. "Why would you do that?"

"I'd do it if you told me what you're hiding from me."

"I'm not hiding anything from you."

"Give me that shit again, and the offer's off the table."

Her expression tightened. She looked away, back down at her drawing, studying it a moment before making a few last adjustments. Then she put down her pen, picked up the paper, and got to her feet, moving down the counter a little way to where a small machine sat. She pulled out another piece of paper and began messing around with the machine, looking as if she were preparing to send a fax. One push of a button later and she was coming back to her station with a perfect copy of her drawing on a piece of carbon paper. She put down the drawing, then began to pull out various different things—a pair of disposable gloves, a razor, and some wipes.

He watched, fascinated as she put the gloves on with a series of short, sharp movements, then got a disinfectant wipe and stepped over to his chair. She said nothing as she leaned over him, pushing aside the fabric of his business shirt and studying the area above his heart.

"So you've got nothing to say?" he asked.

Rachel bent and gave his skin a couple of passes with the wipe, leaving behind it a cool feeling. "I'm not quite sure what you want me to say."

"I thought you wanted your ownership of this place to be secure."

"I wanted the entire building." She got rid of the wipe and picked up the razor, bending lower over him, her breath warm on the area she'd cleaned.

He almost shivered at the feel of it, her scent mixing with the astringent smell of the disinfectant. Fuck, this was different from those times with the guy who'd inked him in prison. He preferred Rachel. Much.

"Why the entire building?" he asked, trying to concentrate on their discussion and not on the soft press of her breasts as she leaned over him. "What's so important about it?"

She was silent a moment, moving the razor across his skin. "I wanted to turn it into an art gallery. Like, have the studio along with a café and maybe a hair salon or something on the ground floor. Then the other floors could be artists' studios and galleries for exhibitions. I thought I could even run art classes from here as well. Work with the outreach center to get some kids along too." She paused. "I always wished there had been something like that when I was younger, but there wasn't."

He stared at her dark head bent over his chest, at the way the light glossed her hair. At the fierce look of concentration on her face.

A fucking art gallery. And art classes. Studios and hair salons. Hardly aiming for the moon and hardly anything that was going to make a difference to the neighborhood, surely?

"Why art?"

"Because there are a lot of artists here. Because art kind of saved me, and I think it could save a lot of other people too. Because people need beauty, especially when there isn't any." She looked up, her dark eyes meeting his. "It gives people hope, Levi. Makes them see there's more to life than mere survival."

"So you're doing this for other people?"

Her gaze flicked away. "Someone gave me hope for a better future once, showed me that I had talent and made me believe it. Why can't I do the same for others?" She straightened, turning back to the counter where the drawing was.

Someone . . .

Was she talking about him?

You know she is.

"Rachel—" he began, starting to say God knows what.

But she interrupted. "What about you?" She'd picked up the piece of carbon paper she'd gotten from the machine, a copy of her drawing on it, and moved back to the chair with it. There was something fierce in her eyes. "What do you want the building for? Something to do with your little business meeting maybe?"

He hadn't wanted to tell her yet, not when he hadn't quite got things in place. Then again, she'd find out soon enough, so there wasn't any point being cagey about it.

"I want to develop it. So, yeah, it had something to do with my 'little business meeting.' I'm trying to get some investors to turn this place into apartments. I also own another building down the street I'm thinking would be great for some big-box stores to move into."

Her shock was obvious. "Apartments? Big-box stores?"

"It's been great for plenty of other neighborhoods, so why not Royal? And this is the perfect time, while real estate is cheap and construction costs are low." He watched her face, conscious that a part of him was looking for something in her expression and not seeing it. Excitement or enthusiasm or agreement at the very least.

Christ, you want her approval.

Levi shifted in the chair, uncomfortable with the thought. No, fuck, why would he need anyone's approval, least of all hers? He didn't. He could do whatever the fuck he wanted, and he didn't give a shit.

So why are you still looking for it?

Rachel frowned, and there was no approval and definitely no agreement there. "You're talking about gentrification." She said the word with a certain amount of distaste.

"Yeah, so?" He couldn't keep the belligerence from this tone.

"So you want Royal to be like all those other neighborhoods? With fancy apartments and pricey stores?"

He scowled, irritated. "I'm talking about encouraging more money to come into a neighborhood that could fucking use it."

"No," Rachel snapped. "What you're talking about is pricing locals out of the market and forcing them to move into even shittier neighborhoods than the one they're in already."

"That's not what I'm saying."

"Bullshit it isn't." She leaned over him again, making a couple of passes over his skin with a stick of deodorant, then dumping it back on the counter before pressing the piece of carbon paper onto his skin, right above his heart. "Why, Levi? Is it the money?"

Her fingers were on his skin, and the way she was leaning over him made him so aware of the heat of her body and the delicious vanilla scent of her. She was looking up at him as she held the stencil to his chest, temper sparking in her dark eyes.

Yeah, she definitely didn't like his plans, not one bit.

"No," he said roughly. "It's got nothing to do with money. It's about making Royal a place where people want to live. A safe place for people to bring their kids up in. It's about making it the kind of neighborhood we dreamed about, Sunny. Don't you remember? A place where there aren't fucking drug dealers on the corners and whores near the school and trash in the streets. So you didn't fear for your life every time you opened the damn door."

"We can have that without building fancy apartments and expensive stores. Without making it worse for the people living here already. I mean, that's what my art gallery idea is all about. I want to involve the locals, not alienate them. Get them excited about their own neighborhood and give them hope."

His irritation grew. Okay, so he hadn't thought she'd be as excited as he was about his plans, but he'd expected that she'd be a little more enthusiastic about them.

You more than expected it—you wanted it.

That fierce spark glowed in her eyes, the one he usually associated with her when she talked about her dreams of being a famous artist. Except the spark wasn't about those dreams now; it was for all this neighborhood art gallery bullshit.

"You've given up," he said abruptly. "All those dreams you had, the ones of going to New York or Paris and studying art, of having a career as an artist, you've given them up." And he didn't make it a question because it was obvious that's exactly what she'd done.

She looked away from him, back down at the stencil on his chest. "I haven't given them up."

"Sure you have. That's why you're settling for this local art gallery crap."

"It's not crap, asshole." Another sharp, dark look. "It's important."

"It's not what you wanted, Rachel."

"Yeah, well, I've changed." She lifted the paper from his chest, not even looking at the design she'd drawn, her gaze burning into his. "I've decided there are other things more important than stupid dreams."

His hand flashed out as she began to turn away, gripping her wrist, holding her tight. "Stupid dreams? Is that what you really thought they were?" Because he remembered her excitement and her passion for art. Remembered the hours he'd spent with her discussing plans for how she could turn those dreams into reality—how they both could. They hadn't been stupid dreams then.

Rachel froze, half turned away from him. "Let me go, Levi."

"No." He tightened his grip. "Something happened. Something killed those dreams for you. Tell me what it was."

"Why?" She turned her head, glancing at him, her tone bitter. "So you can rub my nose in them again?"

"No. So I can help you reach for them." And he meant it; in that moment, he meant every word. "Why the hell do you think I came back?"

She didn't look away, a ripple of what looked like pain moving in those dark chocolate eyes. "Wasn't it to pay me back for every mistake I ever made?"

His heart lurched, missing beats like an old engine trying to start and failing.

Something in the way she said it, something in her voice made him suspect she wasn't talking about that night in the alley behind Gino's, the night they'd both made the biggest mistakes of their lives.

She was talking about something else. Something she was never going to tell him.

Not the man you are now. But she would have told Levi, her friend.

The realization made that tight, uncomfortable feeling in his chest shift. How the hell could he be that friend anymore? He'd forgotten how.

If you want this, you'll have to try.

Fuck.

Levi adjusted his grip, gently tugging her back against the chair as he did so. "Tell me, Sunny," he said softly. "Tell me what's wrong."

Chapter 13

He wasn't holding her so tightly anymore, but his fingers around her wrist felt like an iron manacle all the same. But that wasn't even the worst part of it. The worst part was the look in his eyes, the look that reminded her of the old Levi, whenever he'd been trying to get her to tell him something. Direct, level, understanding. And yet somehow uncompromising too, as if he wasn't going to leave without an explanation.

She hadn't wanted to tell him then. She desperately didn't want to tell him now.

In fact, she'd been going along quite happily not thinking about it at all for eight whole years until he'd shown up and started making her feel things she didn't want to feel.

She should have said something to him all those years ago, when he'd still been her friend and not the terrible, intense stranger he was now. But she'd been so ashamed of herself, so afraid of disappointing him that she'd kept quiet and pushed it to the back of her mind.

Maybe it's easier now. Because now you don't care what he thinks of you.

That was a fucking good point. And maybe that was the way to see him. As a stranger she didn't care about, his opinions of her utterly irrelevant. In fact, what was the point of worrying about the friend who was dead and gone? There was only the stranger, and he didn't matter.

Except . . . he wasn't looking at her as if he were a stranger anymore, and, if she didn't notice the ring in his eyebrow, his tats, or the fact that one of his eyes had gone dark, he might have been the Levi she had known and loved once.

It hurt.

"Why should I?" she asked, unable to keep the sharpness out of her voice. "When you'll probably use it against me at some point."

His jaw hardened, and the darkness of that one pupil seemed to swallow the light from the other. But the gentleness of his hold didn't change. "I won't. That's over and done with now, I promise."

"Sorry, but I'm not sure I believe your promises anymore, Levi."

Anger leapt briefly in his eyes, but then, weirdly, it vanished, leaving nothing but that direct, level look. The one she knew so well. "You can believe this one."

Her heart wanted to so badly. But if she got it wrong now, if she trusted him and he used that trust to hurt her like he had been doing with everything else, she didn't know if she'd ever recover. "So, that's it? You've got your pound of flesh now? Sure you don't need any more?"

"Something's wrong," he said quietly, ignoring her sarcastic questions. "Remember, Sunny, I know you. I know you like no one else does, and I can tell when you're feeding me bullshit."

He did know her. At least, he used to.

She didn't want to look at him, meet that understanding, knowing gaze. Her friend was dead and gone—that's what she'd told herself; that's how she'd gotten through this. Yet now, he was looking at her like that. . . . She didn't know what to do.

"Okay," she said, her throat feeling dry. "But if I tell you, I want my goddamn building. And I want you to promise in writing that you'll give it to me." At least if she kept some part of this as a transaction, she'd have something left at the end. Right?

He gave her a long, intense look, and she thought he was going to protest or object. But all he said was, "Give me a piece of paper and a pen."

She didn't hesitate, turning to grab both from her station and handing them over. He released her wrist and took them, scribbling something quickly down on the paper before signing and then handing the paper and pen back to her.

What he had written was terse and to the point. Reading it made her feel cheap and mean all of a sudden, that she was willing to trade her most personal secret in return for a piece of real estate, rather than just trusting him and telling him.

But that was the way the world worked, wasn't it?

Nothing came for free.

Forcing the emotion away, Rachel folded up the paper and stuck it in the back pocket of her miniskirt. "You have a deal then."

Levi stared at her, his gaze completely uncompromising. He was sitting back in the chair, his shirt spread open, the little stylized sun—a black center with curling black rays projecting out—dark against the golden skin of his chest. And the sight of him made her breath catch and that pulse of desire between her thighs grow stronger, more demanding.

God, she hated it. Hated wanting him so badly.

He lifted a hand. "Come closer."

Time's up. You have to tell him now.

Fuck.

She moved nearer, everything in her rebelling at the thought of sharing her secret. Of meeting his unnerving stare and having to give him the darkest part of herself.

He's going to be so angry with you.

His gaze narrowed all of a sudden. "You're scared."

She felt as if he'd peeled her open. "No, of course I'm not—"

But before she could finish, he leaned forward all of a sudden and grabbed her by the hips, lifting her and dragging her sideways into his lap. There was no time to struggle. One minute she was looking down at him; the next the hard length of his body was beneath her, and she was being held against the muscular heat of his bare chest, one arm tight around her waist, holding her there.

She struggled, even though she knew there wasn't any point, trying to push him away, to at least get some space. But he only tightened his grip.

"Don't be scared." His voice was soft and rough in her ear. "Please don't."

It was the *please* that did it, that and the soft note in the words. The one she sometimes heard at night, in his arms, when he gave her all that pleasure.

The pleasure you don't deserve.

She shivered, trying to hold herself away from him. "I can't tell you like this."

"Yes, you can." He settled himself in the chair, urging her back with him, and it felt almost tender, like he was cradling her.

Her heart was tight with that dull, yearning ache, the one she didn't think was ever going to go away, and she wanted nothing more than to put her head on his shoulder and rest against him, let him make it all better.

But she couldn't. She was all out of trust.

"You know what I told you about the ring in my eyebrow?" he said after a moment's long silence.

She blinked. Because that was *not* what she'd expected him

to say. "It was a reminder, wasn't it? Of what happens when people fuck with you?"

There was another silence.

"Sounded good, didn't it? It's really a reminder of how sticking a smuggled needle through your eyebrow in an attempt to look more badass can hurt like a motherfucker."

Rachel blinked again. Because, yeah, this was *so* not what she'd been expecting. Why the hell had he told her that? Wasn't he supposed to be pressuring her to tell him all her secrets?

"Now you're supposed to tell me what a dumb shit I am," he prompted.

"You're a dumb shit," she said inanely.

"Yeah, I know." His palm was on her hip, his fingers spread, and he began to move his thumb over her in an absent, stroking movement. "And I'm still a dumb shit."

She looked down at her hands clenched tightly in her lap, tried not to feel the heat of his body all around her or smell that familiar, sexy, dark, earthy scent. She had no idea where he was going with this, but as long as she didn't have to talk, she was okay with it.

"I'm still trying to stick that fucking needle through my eyebrow to prove what a badass I am," he went on. "Because it's fucking hard to act like a normal person after eight years inside."

She tensed, unable to help herself, preparing for some kind of barb about all those years again. That was the only reason he'd bring it up, right?

"I can't remember." His voice had gotten quieter and a little rougher. "I've forgotten how. So I need you. I need you to help me remember what it's like to be a friend."

Her aching heart had gone quite still, and all her muscles tensed up even further in shock. "I didn't think you wanted to be anyone's friend," she said hoarsely.

"I didn't think I did either. But . . . you need one, Sunny. And so do I."

Sunny. As if she was still that to him. As if she was all bright and warm, making people happy. She had no idea why he called her that when she was the opposite.

"You know how I told you that my mom left me some money?" As soon as the words came out of her mouth, she wished she hadn't spoken. But it was too late.

"Yeah. You were going to use that for art school."

Her jaw felt tight, her throat aching. "My mom didn't leave me any money, Levi. I got it from someone else."

"Where did you get it then?" His tone was utterly neutral.

She kept her gaze on her hands, on her white knuckles. "Do you remember Evan Saunders? He used to be the building superintendent."

"I remember. He was a prick." Levi's thumb kept stroking along her hip, back and forth. "What about him?"

She gripped her hands together tighter, her heartbeat getting faster. This was ridiculous. She just needed to throw it out there, stop making this into more of an issue than it was. Christ, it had been over years ago after all. "I got the money from him."

Levi's big body tensed beneath her. "What do you mean you got it from him?"

"I mean, he gave me the money."

"Why?"

She looked up then, into Levi's strong, handsome face. Because she was being a fucking coward staring at her hands. "I slept with him, and he paid me."

Shock rippled over Levi's features. "You fucking *what?*"

"He wanted me, and at first I said no. But then he offered me money and . . . I couldn't refuse. I needed it. If I wanted those dreams we talked about to be a reality, I had to get the money from somewhere."

Levi had gone rigid, every muscle beneath her gone rock hard, the arm around her waist like an iron band. The look on his face was frightening, and he wasn't stroking her anymore.

You shouldn't have told him.

No, but she couldn't take it back now.

Rage glittered in his eyes, and this time both had gone dark, the silver blue of his iris completely swallowed by black. "So, are you telling me you were fucking this guy?"

Pain caught at her. "I wasn't *fucking* him, Levi. I needed money, and he was offering it. How the hell else was I supposed to fund art school? There was no way I could get a job that would pay enough, not when I had to look after Gran and pay for her medications as well."

He stared at her as if she were a complete stranger. "So you decided that earning money on your back was a good idea?" His arm around her had tightened, squeezing her, making her feel as if something fragile inside her was imploding. "What the *fuck* were you thinking?"

His face, set in tight lines of fury, began to blur, stupid tears threatening. This was worse that she'd imagined, so much worse. She knew this had been a bad idea. "I wanted to go to art school. You kept telling me over and over how we had to fight for our dreams, how we had to work for it. How it wasn't going to be easy and we'd have to make hard choices, but we'd do it if we only tried!"

There was a hidden well of anger inside her, one she'd never guessed was there, and now it was rising up, erupting in a thick, hot wave. Anger at him and his optimism, at his insistence on the importance of dreams, of the future they'd talked of together. Anger that he'd made her want those things and want them enough to make the stupidest decision of her life.

She'd told herself she couldn't regret it, that if she did, it would have made what she'd done mean nothing. And she couldn't have it mean nothing.

All that shame you felt. All that humiliation would have been in vain.

His expression was molten with rage. "I didn't mean that you should start whoring yourself out!"

"How else was I supposed to do it?" she shouted, suddenly shaking with the force of all those suppressed emotions. "How else was I supposed to get the fucking money for those stupid goddamn dreams? Evan offered me more money than I'd ever seen in my life, so I took it. Every opportunity, right, Levi?"

He went very, very still, fury stamped all over his features. Then abruptly he shoved her hard off his lap, getting out of the chair and walking without a word to the couch where he'd left his jacket.

It was a rejection, pure and simple, and after that quiet moment of being held in his arms, it felt as if he'd stabbed a knife right through the center of her chest and left the blade in.

She turned sharply away, unable to watch him leave, covering her face with her hands. Wanting blackness, wanting silence. Wanting her armor back any way she could get it.

And yet there was no sound of the door slamming. No hard footsteps retreating.

"Why didn't you tell me?" His voice, full of hot rage. "Why the hell didn't you say anything?"

She dropped her hands, keeping her back to him. "Why do you think? I felt cheap and disgusting every time I did it, every time he left, and I couldn't bear for you to know. I couldn't bear for you to be disappointed in me, to find me cheap and disgusting too."

There was a silence behind her.

"You should have come to me, Rachel." All the anger had bled out of his voice. "I could have done something. I could have helped—"

"How? You had no money either. And you had your plate

full with looking after your dad. I didn't want to make any more demands on you."

Another deafening silence.

"And that night with the drug dealer? Is that what you were doing with him too?"

"No," she said hoarsely. "I'd ended things with Evan. But Gran's medication bills were mounting up, and I didn't want to start using my savings. So I thought I'd run a couple of packets of coke. Just a couple. But the dealer had heard about me and Evan, and he wanted to . . ." She stopped, remembering the feeling of cold that had seeped through her. All the despair and anguish. And then Levi, rescuing her. Saving her. Ending up killing someone because of her.

As if she'd ever been worth that kind of sacrifice.

"You want to know the real reason I didn't come and see you in prison, Levi?" She might as well say it, might as well admit the whole sorry state of her life. "It was because I was ashamed. Because you're right, all of this *is* my fault. If I'd never slept with Evan, that dealer wouldn't have touched me, and then you wouldn't have gone to jail. And I couldn't bear to see you, couldn't bear to tell you about all my stupid fucking mistakes." Her throat was sore, but she forced the rest of the words out. "And I was angry with you too. Angry with you for making me want what was always out of my reach. And for making me believe I could have it."

There was only more silence behind her.

"I've told you everything," she said thickly. "Now, if you want to be a real friend, you should leave me the fuck alone."

She looked so small, standing near her workstation, her shoulders hunched, her head bent. Small and fragile.

He wanted to go to her and wrap her up in his arms, hold her the way he knew he should, the way he'd done in the chair, but he couldn't. Not while he was *so* fucking angry. At himself.

He'd fed her all that stuff about dreams. He'd told her she could do whatever she wanted if she wanted it badly enough.

And clearly she'd wanted it badly.

Christ, whoring herself out to the building superintendent, who'd no doubt pressured her into it, because he'd been a creepy prick and someone Levi would have quite happily punched in the face.

Maybe, knowing Rachel, she'd told herself it was no big deal. That it was what she'd have to do to get what she wanted.

I couldn't bear for you to be disappointed in me, find me cheap and disgusting too. . . .

He felt like someone had taken his heart in a giant fist and was slowly crushing it. How the hell could she have thought that? How the hell could she have thought he would even consider something like that?

She'd been his sunshine, and nothing could have changed that. Sure, he'd probably have come close to killing Evan if he'd found out, but then he'd also have tried to help her. He certainly would *never* have judged her.

But she'd kept it a secret. She hadn't let him in because she hadn't wanted to make any demands on him.

And now she was doing the same thing, standing there with her back to him. Protecting herself from him. Because of course she felt she had to protect herself. He'd come to hurt her. Made her live with him, sleep with him, give him everything, while she got nothing in return.

You're as bad as Evan.

Oh Christ.

Self-loathing curled inside him, thick and bitter and hot. No wonder she was holding him at bay. All those times she'd had sex with him . . . Her body had been ready, wet, and open for him, but her mind had closed around itself.

Fuck, he couldn't bear the thought. He literally couldn't stand it.

Rachel's head bowed, and he saw it then, the slight shake of her shoulders, and he was moving before he was even conscious of doing so, no thought in his head but the need to show her that he was here, give her comfort the way he used to. Crossing the space between them and putting his hands on her shoulders, turning her around.

She tried to fight him, tried to knock his hands away, but he simply ignored her, one arm going around her waist to bring her close, the other rising to grip the back of her head, turning her face into his shoulder.

She went stiff, but he kept his hold on her, and gradually all the tension bled out of her muscles. She made a soft, hiccupping sound, then another. And then the soft sounds became sobs, her face pressed hard to his chest, her hands coming up to grip the edges of his shirt as she cried.

He'd seen her unsure and afraid. He'd seen her worried. He'd seen her sad. But he'd never seen her cry, not once. She'd always kept that part of herself hidden, staying strong and keeping herself protected. Yet she wasn't now. Now she was a woman in pain, and the only thing he could do was hold her, bend himself around her as if he could put himself between her and the thing that was hurting her.

That's all he'd ever wanted to do. Keep her safe. Keep her from harm.

"I don't think you're cheap. I don't think you're disgusting," he murmured in her ear as he held her. "You're my sunny girl, and I would never, ever, not in a million years think that about you. And you shouldn't be ashamed either. You were taken advantage of by that fucking asshole, and if he were here now I'd kill him."

"But it was my decision," she muttered thickly against Levi's chest. "I didn't have to do it. I could have told him no. I just thought it was nothing. That I'd be able to handle it because it was just sex. And I wanted the money."

His arms tightened, fury burning inside him. For her and the decision she'd made. A decision she shouldn't ever have been faced with. "And what would he have done if you'd said no? He would have taken it anyway."

She gave another sob. "I thought I was taking control of my life. I thought I was being strong. But afterward . . . every time . . . I felt so . . . dirty. Disgusting." She took a heaving breath. "I used to go away in my head. I used to imagine myself on a beach. But sometimes . . . it didn't work."

Ah, Christ, was that why she'd always held herself back when he'd touched her? Because she didn't want to feel anything?

The thought made him want to smash something, take apart the bastard who'd done this to her like he'd taken apart that dealer with his hands all over her. Levi had lost it then too, punching the guy so hard he'd fallen and hit his head on the curb. A fatal injury.

Levi regretted so much about that night. That he hadn't controlled his temper. That a man had died. But he'd never regretted saving her.

"That wasn't you," he said fiercely. "He never touched you. Not the real you."

She shivered against him. "I only wanted the money. But I couldn't even bring myself to use it. After what happened with you . . . it felt wrong to go to school, and that money was already tainted. So I used it for Gran's funeral instead."

Something inside him ached. She'd slept with that fucker for a chance at her dreams, and in the end it had all been for nothing.

He tightened his fist in her hair, the silky strands sliding over his fingers, easing her head back so he could look down into her face.

Her cheeks were wet with tears, her dark eyes fathomless and black. There was no guardedness there anymore, no walls.

"You're going to art school," he said. "I'll get you there."

"No. I can't."

"Why not? You think you don't deserve it?"

Her long, thick lashes descended, the light sparkling off the tears caught there. Hiding herself.

"Look at me."

She began to shake her head. "I can't . . ."

"I'm not asking."

Slowly, her dark eyes came back to his. Fear lurked in them, and grief, and he wanted to take both those things away, make sure she never felt them again.

"You deserve it, Sunny," he said softly. "You deserve everything."

"How? I made so many mistakes, Levi." The words were blunt and raw. "My whole fucking life has just been one mistake after another. And what happened with you . . ."

He put his hand against her throat, feeling the beat of her pulse beneath his thumb and the warmth of her body against him. Knowing the words he had to say, the words he'd been trying to avoid ever since he'd gotten out of jail, full of righteous rage and bitterness. To acknowledge what she'd flung at him the night she'd demanded her building from him.

"You're blaming me for everything that happened to you, and yet you're not even taking responsibility for that guy you punched in the face. The guy who died."

Ah, Christ, he couldn't avoid them any longer. Couldn't avoid the truth. That he'd been a coward too. That he'd forced her to shoulder the responsibility for his actions, because he couldn't handle the fact that he'd killed a man.

He'd been the one who'd landed the first punch. Sure, it had been in her defense, but that didn't make it better. That didn't make it right.

"What happened with me was not your fault." His voice had gone hoarse. "And I was wrong to blame you." He let his thumb stroke the soft skin of her throat, looking into her eyes.

"So stop punishing yourself." He paused a moment. "Or if it's punishment you want, then maybe you should be punishing me."

A tear slid down one cheek, her dark gaze searching his face. "I had a crush on you once—did you know that? Way back when."

The hand around his heart squeezed so tight he could barely breathe. She'd wanted him once. All this time and she'd wanted him. Somewhere deep inside, a part of him howled at the unfairness of what they could have had together if only they'd talked to each other, been a bit more honest, a bit older. But they hadn't. And now they were here with so many broken bridges between them, they probably would never be able to find their way back to each other.

He almost couldn't speak. "You never said."

"No. You never looked at me like that, so I didn't want to tell you. And after Evan . . ." She stopped.

He didn't want to ask, but he made himself all the same. "Do I make you feel those things? Do I make you feel dirty and cheap and disgusting?"

Another tear slid down her cheek. "No." The word was very, very faint. "I thought I would feel that afterward, but . . . I haven't. I keep waiting for it, Levi."

Maybe he should have felt relieved, but he didn't. He just felt angry on her behalf. Because she was still waiting to feel all those things, and those memories were still in her head. They needed to be gone.

He had to do something; he had to fix it. But he didn't know how.

Life had taken a lot from her, and it felt just plain wrong not to help her. He couldn't change the past, couldn't change the decision she'd made all those years ago, when she'd been so young, inspired by the dreams he'd told her were within reach. But he could give her back some of the things she'd lost. He could make her feel good, give her pleasure, give her some good memories instead of the bad.

Very deliberately, he stroked her throat again, looking into her eyes. Then he slid his hand up her neck, around and behind to her nape, pushing his fingers up into all that glossy, black hair, urging her head back gently.

She didn't resist, staring up at him, as if she had no fight left and was waiting for the next blow to fall.

Yeah, he was going to build all those bridges again. Every fucking one.

"I want to give you something," he said in a low, fierce voice. "I want to give you what we should have had together. What we missed out on. I want to make it like he never touched you, like he was never even there. Only me, Sunny. Only, ever me." He paused, scanning her face. "Will you let me?"

Before, he would have just taken what he wanted. But not now. Now, he wanted her to choose.

Her eyes were so dark, like bitter espresso, and there were so many emotions in them that he couldn't decipher them all. But all she said was, "Yes."

Which was all he needed.

So he bent over her, covering her mouth with his.

It wasn't like those raw, demanding kisses he gave her every night, the ones where he took everything and gave nothing back.

He didn't do gentle, didn't do soft, but he tried, running his tongue along the seam of her lips, coaxing her to open. Tasting her slowly at first and maybe even delicately, exploring her mouth as she let him in. Like a first kiss. Like it should have been between them.

She tasted all salty from her tears and yet with a lick of sweetness that had him wanting more, because it always did. Testing his patience and the grip he had on his control. No one tasted like she did. No one.

He eased her head back further, sliding his tongue along hers, still gentle, savoring the heat of her and that sweet, honey flavor. She shivered, responding to him, beginning to explore him, her mouth hot and wet, beginning to demand.

So sweet. And not enough.

He lifted his head, his fingers wound into her hair to keep her there. Her eyes were very, very dark, her mouth swollen from the kiss, her breathing fast and uneven.

Desire built inside him, a hunger for her that some part of him knew would be never ending. He would always want her, no matter how many years passed, no matter how many times they hurt each other. Other women had never done it for him the way she did. None of them had ever been right.

It would always be Rachel. Always.

"I want to know what you imagined when you thought of me," he said roughly. "I want you to show me." He released her and stepped back, moving over to the tattoo chair. "But I'm not going to force you if you don't want to do it. It'll be your choice." He glanced at the chair a moment, then he got into it and sat back. "And if you don't want to, I'll settle for that tattoo you promised."

Chapter 14

Rachel stared as Levi linked his hands behind his head, stretching out on the chair as if he were preparing for an afternoon nap. Except there was nothing sleepy about the look in his eyes or the aura of tension around him.

But it wasn't anger this time. It looked almost like . . . vulnerability.

Well, she knew how he felt because she was feeling like that now. Shaky, naked, and vulnerable. Every single protection stripped away. It was scary as hell.

She'd thought he'd gone, that he'd left her alone, and the tears had come whether she'd wanted them to or not. Tears she'd held back for a long time. Telling him everything had been the hardest thing she'd ever had to do and him leaving . . . Well, it was what she'd deserved, wasn't it?

Except, he hadn't left. His arms had come around her, turning her, and, before she knew what was happening, she was pressing her face against the hot skin of his bare chest, weeping as though her heart would break. And he'd held her the way he'd held her in bed, keeping her together, or else she would have fallen apart.

And now he was sitting there looking at her with that searing look in his eyes, as if he wanted her, even knowing all about Evan and what she'd done. As if she hadn't been tainted by that stupid, naïve decision she'd made back when she was so young.

Her mouth burned from the kiss, from the gentleness in it, desire gathering into a small, hard knot between her thighs. Desire she'd never wanted because it always reminded her of the bad things. Of the shameful things.

Of her little bedroom with its single bed and Evan on top of her. Of desperately hoping her gran wouldn't hear him moaning. Of thinking it would help if she shut her eyes and pretended she wasn't there.

"Why?" Her voice sounded all thick from crying. "Why do you want that? Why do you even want me?"

His focus never wavered from her. "Because I've always wanted you, and nothing will ever change that. Because I don't want you to have those memories. I want you to have something better. Because everyone's taken things from you, including me. And now I want to give you something back."

She swallowed, wanting, aching, and yet still afraid. "Every single choice I've made has ended up with my regretting it, Levi. What's to say this one will be any different?"

He stared at her for a long moment, and then his mouth curved slightly, an almost smile that did strange things to her heartbeat. A smile she recognized from years ago. "I'll make sure you don't regret it, Sunny. I promise."

I promise.

She shouldn't trust those promises, but her body was moving before her mind had a chance to catch up, going over to the chair, her heart thumping, her breathing getting short and fast and hard.

He reached out and pulled her into his lap like he had done before, only this time, he made her face him, straddling him. As her legs spread on either side of his hips, her miniskirt rode up to the tops of her thighs, no doubt giving him a prime view of her dark purple lace panties.

She shivered, the denim of his jeans rough against her bared skin, the heat of him like a furnace. She really should be used to him by now. But she wasn't. She was fully clothed, and yet she felt utterly naked.

Levi let her go, leaning back in the chair again with his hands behind his head. "So, you wanted me. Tell me what your hottest fantasy was."

She could feel heat rising in her cheeks, God, heat rising everywhere. "It . . . it wasn't very dirty."

"Yet you're blushing."

"It's embarrassing."

"No, it's not. It's fucking hot." His gaze traveled down her body, before settling between her thighs. "Tell me."

She took a shaky breath. "I used to imagine you touching me."

"Where?"

"Between my legs."

"Show me how."

Once she'd pushed those thoughts out of her head so hard, she'd almost forgotten they were there, not wanting them to be tainted by what had happened with Evan. Now it was impossible to think of anything else.

She stared at him. His eyes glittered, the flame of desire burning strong, his focus concentrated fiercely on her.

He knew what she'd done. He knew her darkest secrets. And yet he was still looking at her as if she were the only thing worth looking at in the entire universe. As if she were special.

As if she still mattered.

Something inside her relaxed all of a sudden, something that had been fighting a long time.

She could have this moment for herself. She was allowed. And if it all went to shit in the end, well, it would have been worth it just for this alone.

Rachel moved her hand down, her fingers sliding over the damp lace of her panties, watching his gaze move down along with them. "Like this."

"That's good, sweetheart. Show me more."

Her mouth had gone dry, her breathing getting faster. The pulse of desire had gotten stronger, but this time, as she watched that same desire reflected in his eyes, she welcomed it.

She moved her hand again, pressing down with her index finger, feeling the heat and softness of her own flesh. "Here," she whispered. "I imagined you touching me here."

His attention was riveted to where her hand was, color staining his high cheekbones, his rapidly hardening cock pressing against her butt. And she felt a certain kind of power flow through her all of a sudden.

Perhaps it was something she'd always known, that she could affect him as strongly as he affected her, yet she'd never fully grasped it until now.

It only added to the desire, building it higher.

He shifted restlessly beneath her. "I need to see you."

"Say please." She didn't know where she'd gotten the confidence, but it shot through her blood like adrenaline.

He blinked, his gaze flicking up to meet hers in surprise, and she smiled, unexpectedly enjoying having the balance of power tip her way for a moment.

The look in his eyes flared, hunger burning there, and his mouth curved as if he was enjoying the change, too. "Please." The word was rough and raw and sounded like a demand, but hell, he'd said it.

She eased her miniskirt farther up her thighs. "Better?"

"Oh yeah," he murmured, his attention flicking down again. "Much."

And, Jesus, but that made her feel good. The desire on his handsome face, the evidence of how much what she was doing affected him.

She'd never known there was power in this, had been too afraid to even try to understand it. But somehow, now she wasn't. Somehow he'd taken her fear away.

It made her want to explore this newfound power further.

Easing her thighs apart to give him a better view, she moved her finger, sliding it up the center of her pussy, then back down again, shivering as the sparks of pleasure became tiny flames.

"Fuck," he said roughly, his voice low and guttural. "Is this what you wanted me to do to you?"

"Yes." Her own voice was unsteady as she looked into the dark shadow and silver blue of his uneven gaze. "I wanted you to stroke me. Your fingers on my pussy just like . . . this."

"Where? I want to see it."

"Here." She pressed her finger down on her clit and circled around it, those tiny flames of pleasure licking higher.

He shifted restlessly beneath her, and she could feel him, long and hard and thick. "And how did I make you feel?"

She slid her finger back and forth, the material of her panties getting damper, getting wet. "So good, Levi. God, you made me feel so good."

It was impossible to look away from him.

He wasn't leaning back now, but forward, his gaze pinned to the movement of her hand, his face drawn in lines of fierce hunger. And she couldn't stop staring at the way the light hit the perfectly carved angles of his face, creating shadows that hid his eyes and made his cheekbones stand out. It caught the gilt in his dark blond hair too and the stubble along his jaw.

He was so beautiful. She wanted him so much; she always had.

"Keep going," he said hoarsely, and reached forward to tug aside the crotch of her panties. "Please, Sunny."

Ah, that *please*. It undid her. Like the look on his face undid her. It made her want to give him whatever he wanted.

So she slid her fingers over her own slick folds, stroking over and over, the pleasure winding tighter and tighter.

"More." His voice was a dark whisper. "Show me more."

She slid one finger deep inside her sex, feeling her muscles grip on tightly, gasping at the sensation. She shut her eyes, hardly even aware of doing so, remembering being in her bed before it had all happened with Evan, thinking about Levi. Touching herself, tentatively at first, then harder, faster. Imagining his hand instead of her own, his mouth on hers, the feeling indescribable.

"How does it feel?" he murmured.

"Incredible." She eased another finger inside herself, sliding them out, then back in again. "Your fingers inside me made me feel . . . so fucking good."

"Yeah, I know." His hands were on her knees, pushing them even wider, and he made a soft growling sound of approval. "You're so wet you're glistening. And I can smell you, too. Christ, it's delicious."

She'd begun to shake, the movement of her hand and the tight grip of her sex around her fingers increasing the pressure inside her, building it higher and higher.

"Did you imagine my cock inside you?" Levi's voice wound around her, rough and heated. "Did you imagine what it would feel like to have me fuck you?"

"Yes, God, yes . . ." Her thighs were trembling, her muscles tightening. "I wanted it. I dreamed about it."

"And did you make yourself come, Sunny? Did you imagine my doing that too you?"

"Yes . . ." Her voice had gotten so thick. "Every time."

"Good. Because I'm going to do it now too." And then his fingers were wrapping around her wrist, pulling her hand away, and it was his fingers on her wet, swollen flesh now. His hand.

She gasped, her body arching helplessly, her thighs shaking even more.

"Open your eyes," he ordered. "Look down."

And she did, obeying him without thought, looking down between her spread legs, at the hand moving on her, the ink of his tattoo dark on his knuckles.

It was the most erotic sight she'd ever seen in her life.

Then his finger pushed in deep, tearing a groan from her throat, making her flex against his hand, shuddering with the indescribable pleasure of it. And he sat up, sliding the fingers of his other hand into her hair, drawing her head back so all she could do was look up into the shocking beauty of his face.

"Take it, sweetheart," he whispered. "Come for me."

He pressed his thumb down on her clit, making everything get so bright and so intense she couldn't even cry out. All she could do was shudder in his arms as the orgasm crashed over her and swept her away.

He covered her mouth, taking her cry of release, holding her as she trembled and shook against him. He was so hard it hurt, the clutch of her pussy around his fingers insanely erotic, and he wanted nothing so much as to lift her up and bury himself inside her.

But he didn't quite yet, waiting until her shudders had quieted and her soft cries died away. Then he lifted his mouth from hers, staring at her. Her lashes had come down, veiling her gaze; her cheeks were flushed. She leaned forward, pressing her forehead to his chest and he let her, gazing at the light glossing her hair.

Watching her touch herself while she'd told him what she'd

228 / Jackie Ashenden

imagined him doing to her had been so fucking hot. Watching her give in to her own desire, explore her feminine power, had been incredible.

He felt half desperate, and when he lifted his hand to stroke her hair, it was shaking. "Sunny . . ." The word was all ragged. "Sunny . . . Jesus Christ."

She'd imagined him doing all that to her. Imagined him as more than a friend even back then. All that time they'd both wasted . . .

What about your plans?

Ah, fuck, what did they matter? He had his dream right now, sitting on his lap, shaking from the effects of her orgasm. And not only that, she'd let him hold her as she'd wept, had leaned against him wanting support.

No more walls. No more barriers.

This was what he'd wanted. What he always had wanted.

She shifted in his lap, lifting her head to look up at him, her eyes so dark they were almost black.

"Tell me what you want." He could hardly speak. "I'll give it to you. Anything, it's yours."

She lifted a hand and touched his mouth. "You. I want you."

"Then fucking take me." He held her gaze, letting her see the intensity of his desire. "I need you."

For a long second she didn't move, staring at him. Then she let out a breath, her attention dropping down to his chest, and lifted her hands to touch him. Her fingers were cool, trailing over his pecs and down, brushing his nipples, causing him to inhale sharply as sensation flickered like electricity through him. She leaned forward and pressed her mouth to his throat, and he couldn't stop the shudder that shook him. God, the feel of it . . . so soft. So hot.

She began to kiss him, his neck, his collarbone, down further, her tongue on his skin, licking. Around his nipples and down, her hands sliding over his abs, her hips moving against his. Jesus Christ, she felt amazing.

"I always imagined what it would be like to touch you," she whispered against his skin. "How you'd feel. How you'd taste. Hot . . . hard . . ." She stroked his stomach over and over, lovingly following the lines of his abs as if he were a work of art, making his muscles tense in reaction. "You're better than I imagined, Levi. So much better."

Again he felt that strange tightness in his chest. The way she was touching him, her hands shaking. The way she was looking at him, as if she were so desperately hungry, as if she'd die if she didn't get a taste. . . .

Finally.

He couldn't speak as her hands trailed lower, to the button of his pants, then one hand tracing the length of his cock through the material while the other tugged down the zipper. Jesus, she was going to kill him.

She pushed open the fabric, her fingers sliding into his boxers, circling his cock, drawing him out.

Holy shit, he was so hard. He wasn't going to be able to hold on long.

Rachel shifted back, bending her head, her hair an inky spill over his chest and stomach. But he reached for it, twining his fingers in the silky mass of it and holding on. "Wait." His voice was so hoarse it didn't sound like his.

"What?" She looked up at him, her brows drawn together. "Do you not want—"

"No, fuck, I want this." She hadn't ever gone down on him, and he'd noticed she'd been actively avoiding it. He hadn't insisted, though, deciding to address it when they'd spent more time together. He thought he knew the reason now. "Did you do this for him? Is that why you didn't want to do it with me?"

Her dark eyes flickered. "Yes."

Levi twisted his fingers tighter in her hair. "I don't want this to be bad for you."

Something fierce entered her gaze. "It won't be. Because it's not him I'm thinking about."

He almost smiled, because this was the Rachel he remembered. Determined and passionate. A fighter. "You better not be," he said, answering her ferocity with his own. "Because there's only going to be one cock in your mouth, and that's mine. Understand?"

The look she gave him burned him all the way through, and then she was shifting back and bending her head again, an explosion of heat engulfing him as she wrapped her mouth around his dick, taking him in deep.

A groan escaped, helplessly drawn from him, the pleasure indescribable. He looked down, pushing her hair out of the way so he could see, the visual so fucking erotic he nearly came right there and then. Her lifting her mouth from him, gripping him in one hand so she could circle the head of his cock with her pink tongue. Then her full, red lips opening and taking him between them, swallowing him whole.

He growled, gathering her hair into one fist and winding it around his wrist, pulling on it. "Harder. Faster."

Her flushed cheeks hollowed as she obeyed him, increasing suction, her movements more rapid, her hand squeezing him tighter.

Jesus Christ, he was so close, already shaking like a teenage boy getting his first blow job. Pleasure coiled and twisted, an animal inside him demanding to be freed.

Rachel's free hand stroked him, over his stomach and up, trailing over his skin, leaving a forest fire blazing in its wake. While her mouth worked magic on his cock, the heat of it driving him insane.

Too much; it was too fucking much.

The orgasm exploded like a lightning bolt chasing the length of his spine, tearing a ragged groan from his throat, his hips pushing up into her mouth as he pulled hard on her hair. And for long minutes he couldn't speak, could hardly breathe through the intensity of the pleasure, closing his eyes and free-falling in the darkness.

Then he felt Rachel shift slightly, her mouth brushing over his stomach, her fingers tracing lazy circles on his skin. "You're amazing." Her voice was husky. "Everything about you."

When she said it like that, after giving him the best damn blow job he'd ever had, he felt amazing too.

Levi opened his eyes to find her curled in his lap, continuing to stroke his abdomen and chest as if she couldn't keep her hands off him. He was holding a fistful of her hair, and he didn't much feel like letting it go. Didn't feel like letting go of her, period.

"Was that okay?" There was a hint of uncertainty in her tone. "I mean, it's been a long time and—"

He tugged her head back before she could finish, leaning down to give her his answer in the form of a hard, deep kiss, tasting himself in her mouth, mixed with her own sweet flavor. "That was more than okay," he murmured against her lips. "That's the best fucking thing that's happened to me all day."

"You're easy to please."

"I'm a simple man." He pulled back, staring down into her dark eyes. "Two minutes, then I'm inside you."

A slow smile curved her mouth, rare and sweet, making that tight, impossible feeling in his chest intensify. Then her hand on his stomach moved lower, her fingers running down the length of his cock, sending electric jolts through him. "I don't think you'll need two minutes."

No, he damn well wouldn't. Not with her touching him like that.

He reached into his back pocket, taking out his wallet and extracting the condom he kept in it. Then, discarding the wallet, he held tight to the condom packet as Rachel circled her fingers around his dick, stroking him, squeezing him, leaning forward to trail kisses all over his chest.

The carbon paper outline of the sun was long gone from his skin, rubbed away first by her tears and then her mouth, but he didn't care. There would be plenty of time for that later. First pleasure, then the pain.

She straddled him, tugged aside her panties, rubbing her sweet little pussy all over his cock, her eyes glazed, her cheeks flushed as she touched him. She looked almost drunk on him, on the pleasure that was being generated between them.

His breathing was getting ragged as her hips flexed and she ground herself against his rapidly hardening dick, her fingernails scratching lightly at his chest. And he liked that, oh yeah, he liked that a lot. Her hunger, her need.

"You want me, Sunshine?" He stared into her eyes. "You want me inside you?"

She shivered. "God, yes." Her voice was husky. "Now, Levi."

Yeah, fuck, he couldn't wait.

He ripped open the condom packet and took it out, sheathing himself. Then he reached for her, gripping her hips and lifting her up, settling her back down onto him, both of them gasping as the slick heat of her pussy closed around him.

For a second they both were still, staring at each other, the connection between them alive and electric with pleasure and something else, something deeper.

Because in this moment nothing mattered. Not their past and all the mistakes they'd made. Not all the anger and the pain. Not even all the missed opportunities and wasted time.

All that mattered was that right now, they were both here.

They were together. They were one. The way it always should have been.

Levi slid his arms around her, gathering her close, cradling her. Then he began to move, deep and slow, and she was all tight flesh and molten heat and soft, panting breaths. Her eyes were wide and black as the night outside.

He let himself fall into them and lost himself.

Chapter 15

Zee leaned against the body of the Firebird and folded his arms, watching silently as Levi finished fiddling with the car's engine.

Goddammit. Clearly his friend had something he wanted to talk about. And no prizes for guessing what that was.

Levi straightened, slamming down the hood of the car. "What?"

They were in the garage, Zee having finished up some work he was doing on his Trans Am. Gideon wasn't there, which was probably a blessing. Levi wasn't looking forward to having to broach the topic of his investment project with Gideon. And Levi was going to have to do that at some point—at least before construction started.

You'll have to do it sooner than that. If you don't, Gideon'll be even more pissed because you didn't tell him earlier.

Yeah, Gideon would be. Not that he wouldn't be pissed about the whole situation anyway. He was notoriously protective of Royal, and Levi suspected Gideon would have the same attitude toward Levi's plans that Rachel did. And speaking of, that was another issue Levi was going to have to work out.

Since the night in her tattoo studio a couple of days ago, things had been so much better between them. The tension had eased, and, though they hadn't talked again of anything major—certainly not his plans for Royal—they'd gotten back a little of their old relationship. And whenever there was any awkwardness, there was always sex. That, at least, they didn't have any problems with.

Zee's expression was neutral. "What's up with you and Rach?"

"You know what's up with me and Rach."

"She was afraid of you. At least it looked that way to me."

Yes, and now Levi knew why. It wasn't for the reasons that Zee thought either. "We've sorted that out. Not that it's any of your fucking business."

Zee only shrugged. "Just looking out for her, man."

"Yeah, okay. But I'm back, and I'm looking out for her now."

"Okay, sure." The narrow expression on his face didn't change.

Fucking wonderful. "What?"

"You've got something else going on, haven't you?"

"What makes you say that?"

"You, walking around Royal a few days ago with a couple of suits."

"That's none of your fucking business either."

Zee shifted against the car, his gray eyes piercing. "Since when did you become such as asshole? The Levi I knew wasn't this much of a prick."

An uncomfortable feeling turned over in Levi's gut. He scowled, biting down on the instinctive angry comeback. Rachel had been helping him relearn a few things, such as not treating all direct opposition as an attack, but overcoming the habit of eight years was difficult.

"Yeah, well . . . I'm sorry." The words came out stilted. "I picked up some bad habits inside, okay?"

Zee's expression relaxed. "I get that. But we're your friends, okay? You've known us a long time. You don't need to treat us like strangers and ones you don't particularly like."

Levi turned his gaze to the paintwork of the Firebird, examining it. "You've all had years together that I didn't have, Zee. So my long time isn't quite as long as yours." Levi hadn't realized until that moment how much he'd resented that too. That his friends had shared experiences together, ones that he'd missed out on.

Jesus, he'd missed out on so much. Sometimes he just couldn't think about it, otherwise it made him want to smash something.

That's not Rachel's fault, is it?

No, of course it wasn't. He'd already told her that, right?

Zee let out a breath. "Sure. That's hard, man. But there's always gonna be stuff you missed out on. You can't keep holding that against us. Or against Rachel."

Intellectually that made perfect sense, but something inside Levi didn't like it. That something wanted to keep hold of his anger at the unjustness of the whole thing.

Because then you won't actually have to feel your own responsibility.

Bullshit. He'd admitted it. He knew what he'd done.

"I'm not," he said, rubbing at a spot of rough paint. "Rachel and I are fine."

Behind him the door to the garage slammed.

Zee turned his head. "Hey, Gideon."

Levi cursed silently. He hadn't been actively avoiding Gideon; he just hadn't been actively trying to find him either. Levi only needed a few more days, until after the function Novak had organized for the following week. When there were a few more investors on board, so Levi would know definitively it was all going to happen and he could convince Gideon. Because no matter what Levi told himself, he wanted the other man on his side.

"Can you give us a moment, Zee?" Gideon's deep voice came from behind him.

Zee glanced at Levi, then back to Gideon. "Uh, sure." He eased away from the Trans Am, flashing Levi another look. "Remember, man. Doesn't matter how long you've been away. You're still a Royal, okay?"

Levi stared at him, slightly taken aback by his friend's vehemence. Seemed as if Levi wasn't the only one who'd changed in the last decade. Zee had too. He'd always been reserved, quiet, and intense, yet there was an ease about him now. Though perhaps that wasn't the years. Perhaps that was Tamara.

Zee headed toward the door, pausing to say something to Gideon that Levi didn't catch before continuing on and out of the garage.

As the door clanged shut behind Zee, Gideon stared at Levi for a second. Then he came over to where Levi stood beside the Firebird.

The expression on the older man's face was impossible to read. But there was something in Gideon's eyes that Levi didn't like one bit. He thought it was maybe anger, though Gideon never let slip anything he didn't absolutely want anyone to know about.

Christ, had he heard about Levi's plans? If so, how the hell had that happened? Levi had told no one.

Levi straightened. "You after an interrogation too?"

Gideon said nothing for a moment, his gaze impenetrable. Then he said, "Saw you a few days ago, walking around Royal with a couple of suits."

"Yeah, so?"

"What's that all about?"

There was no reason to feel defensive. No reason at all. No reason Levi shouldn't tell Gideon what was happening either. Gideon wasn't Levi's father. Levi didn't need his approval.

Jesus, you sound like a child.

Irritated with himself, Levi leaned back against the body of the Firebird, pushing his hands into his pockets. "I bought a couple of buildings here while I was inside. Investment purposes and possible development. I have a guy who's going to be getting some financing for me, and I was showing him around, along with another guy who's interested in providing the finance."

Gideon's expression didn't change. "Who?" The question was almost barked out, a harsh sound.

"Jason Ryan from Ryan Investments. And—"

"Oliver Novak," Gideon finished for him, his voice hard.

Levi frowned. "Yeah, that's right. How do you know?

"I asked around."

"You know Novak?"

"I know of him. He's an asshole."

"Of course he's an asshole. Those guys always are."

But there was something sharp in Gideon's tar-black eyes. A glimpse of a man you wouldn't want to cross. "I don't like the word 'development,' Levi. I don't like it at all. Especially in connection with Oliver Novak."

In spite of himself, in spite of everything he had told himself he didn't give a shit about, in spite of everything he'd been trying to learn, Levi felt defensive anger twist in his gut. "Why? What the fuck is your problem with it?"

"Do I really need to tell you?"

"Yeah, actually, you really do."

Gideon remained absolutely still, his gaze like a laser. But instead of explaining, he asked, "What are you planning?"

Levi had nothing to hide. Nothing to be ashamed of. What he was planning was for Royal's benefit, to make it a better place. "I want to get some decent apartments happening. Nice enough to attract people away from downtown, bring some more money here. Maybe some more cafés, some bars. A big-box store or two. Nothing major." It didn't escape his notice that as he spoke, Gideon's expression changed. Becoming harder, more set. Colder.

Levi met his gaze head on. "You got a problem with my wanting to make this neighborhood a better place?" Might as well come right out and say it.

"Money doesn't automatically make this neighborhood a better place. Especially when you're using Oliver Novak to do it."

Levi's anger twisted tighter. "Why? What's the issue with Novak?"

"He's just a rich prick with lots of money who doesn't give a shit about this neighborhood or anyone else."

"And how would you know?"

Gideon's expression looked as if it had been carved from stone. "I just do."

Great. Well, if Gideon was going to be a cagey bastard, that was too bad. "Okay, that's fine for you. But as far as I'm concerned, Novak's ready to put his money where his mouth is, and that's all that matters to me."

The hard glitter in Gideon's eyes was a warning. "Don't do this, Levi. Developing apartments for other rich pricks isn't the way to make Royal a better place. Talk to Rachel, she's got some great ideas that—"

"I know what Rachel wants," he interrupted, angry and unable to fully fathom why. "And maybe I'll incorporate something like that. But at the moment, developing those buildings, creating places people want to live in, with a safe environment for their kids, is more important than a fucking art gallery."

Gideon's gaze narrowed. "Why? How do you know what's important to the people here?'

Levi found his hands had bunched into fists in the pockets of his jeans. What kind of dumb fucking question was that? "You remember who you're talking to, right? I'm from here, Gideon. I know what's important because—"

"You haven't been here for eight years, Levi." It was Gideon's turn to interrupt, and he did so quietly and utterly without mercy. "What the hell would you know about Royal now?"

It felt like the other man had whipped out a knife and slid it between Levi's ribs. Levi took a couple of steps toward him, unable to help himself. "What the fuck do you mean by that? It wasn't like I had any fucking choice about it!"

Gideon just stared at him, unmoved. "No, I know you didn't. But whether you did or not, fact is, you've been away a long time. And you can't just come in here, telling everyone what's good for them without asking them yourself."

The knife in Levi's gut twisted. He hadn't had much of a family life, not with his mother dying when he'd been a small kid and his father being drunk most of the time while he was growing up. But he'd never felt like he didn't belong, never felt like he was alone, not when he had Gideon and the others. Like his friendship with Rachel, it had been something he'd never questioned.

Until now.

Levi stared at the other man who'd always been like a big brother to him, the uncomfortable tightness in his chest becoming a painful ache. "So what are you saying? That I'm not part of Royal now? I'm not one of you?"

The look on Gideon's face was stony. "I can't make you part of Royal or otherwise. That's a choice you make yourself. And all I'm saying is that you coming here, acting as if you've got something to prove, isn't going to earn you any friends."

"I'm not—"

"Drop it, Levi. That's my advice to you. Think about doing something else with those buildings. Something that doesn't involve Novak or any of those other downtown fucks. We don't need them, and we don't want them. This is our neighborhood, and that's how it's going to stay."

Levi's gut tightened, but he buried the strange hurt beneath a wave of righteous anger. "Really? Who died and made you mayor all of a sudden? Have you actually asked people in Royal what they want?" He took another step toward the other man. "Have you asked any of the store owners whether they'd like a cut of some of the money those rich dicks spend? Whether they'd like more people spending in their stores? Whether they'd like to be able to walk around at night, knowing some asshole isn't going to hold them at gunpoint and take their wallets?"

He didn't know what he was trying to do, maybe make Gideon angry, get some kind of reaction from the other man, but Gideon only stared back, the hard glitter in his eyes unchanging.

"Perhaps the real question is, why is this so important to you, Levi?" Gideon's voice was level, betraying no hint of rage or other emotion. "Why is doing this so important that you'd piss off the people who care about you the most?" Gideon paused, his eyes narrowing. "It's like you broke something and now you're determined to fix it."

There was a tangle of emotions all caught up inside of Levi, knotted together so tightly that it was impossible to untangle and figure them all out. It was easier to focus on the one that was familiar to him, the one he knew best of all. Anger. "I didn't break anything," he said harshly. "And as for what I'm trying to fix, just this entire shitty neighborhood. I've been working toward that for fucking years, and I'm not going to stop now, so whatever it is you think of my plans, I don't care. They're happening, whether you like it or not."

Gideon said nothing for a long, uncomfortable moment, his gaze impenetrable. "Don't kid yourself into thinking this is about Royal," he said. "This is about you."

There was no answer to that, because Gideon was right. It *was* about Levi. About the dreams he'd had. The dreams he'd had to put on hold while he'd looked after his fucking drunk of a father.

Another person who'd never showed his face while Levi had been in jail. It was as if Levi had been forgotten by the world, dropped down a hole and off the face of the earth, no one giving a shit.

You know that's not true. This is about that life you took. And the life you fucked up yourself.

But he was too angry to consider that now. Too angry to consider anything. The only thing that made sense was the plan he had in his head. The plan that had kept him going all these years.

"Yeah," he said harshly, meeting Gideon's gaze without even a flicker. "Yeah, maybe it is about me. And it's about fucking time."

Gideon opened his mouth to no doubt issue some other directive or homily in the way that Gideon did, but Levi was done listening to that bullshit. "No. I'm done."

"Levi . . ." Gideon began.

But Levi ignored him, stalking to the door of the garage and letting it slam shut behind him.

Rachel stood in the light-filled, expansive space just off the bedroom of Levi's apartment. He'd told her to decide what kind of furniture or equipment she'd need for it since he was going to take her out to get some supplies. Make it an actual art studio, the kind she'd always dreamed of for herself.

It should have made her deliriously happy, all things considered. And yet as she stood there, looking around, there was a part of her holding back even now. As if this was all too good to be true and she was waiting for the other shoe to drop.

It was stupid. She'd told Levi everything, and they each knew where the other stood. There were no secrets between them. And yet things weren't entirely comfortable between them either. He was trying, but he was still so angry. She could sense it, an animal prowling just beneath the surface of his skin. A great cat pacing before the bars of its cage and looking for a way out.

She'd thought after that night at Sugar Ink that maybe the

poison would have been drained from him the way it had been for her, but that didn't seem to be the case. She'd considered pushing him for more answers, yet broaching the topic of his anger with him felt like taking the first step into a minefield, and she wasn't ready to potentially misstep and lose a leg or an eye or anything else.

At least not while things between them were good.

She wandered over to the far end of the room, studying the way the light fell. She could set up an easel or something here. Or maybe get a giant canvas and lean it against the wall. Not that she was particularly set on painting. She could just as easily get a drafting table and draw here.

She pulled a face. It was all very well, Levi's magnanimously granting her space for a studio and telling her she could outfit it, but he was still operating on the assumptions of eight years ago, when life had been different.

She had her own studio already; that was the problem. Her dreams had changed. He seemed to think they'd gotten narrow, that she should be aiming for more, that she should go to art school and New York and Paris, and all that shit.

As if what she wanted to do now wasn't good enough, as if she were settling.

But she wasn't settling. This *was* what she wanted to do. Because she wasn't the same woman she'd been all those years ago. She was different. Levi hadn't been there for her nor she for him, but Gideon and the others had. Royal had. And now she wanted to give back to it. And if that was all part of her guilt, then so be it. She was okay with that.

She let out a breath, staring around the white-painted space. Levi wouldn't be happy when she told him she didn't want this, but he was going to have to accept it. She wasn't the only one who needed to move on from the past.

The door slammed out in the hallway, and she heard the heavy tread of Levi's boots on the floorboards, coming closer.

She turned to the doorway, and, sure enough, a minute or so later, he appeared. It only took one glance at his face to know he was in a towering fury. The force of it hit her like a blast wave from a nuclear explosion, almost knocking her flat. The lines of his beautiful face were hard, fixed, and his one light eye was as dark as the other. He looked as if he wanted to level the entire city.

She took a couple of steps toward him, then stopped, held at bay by the fury radiating from him. "Hey, what's up?"

"Nothing," he said curtly. "Just a little disagreement with Gideon."

No, it had to be more than just a "little disagreement." Especially judging from the stiffness of his shoulders, the tension in his entire posture.

The old Rachel would have gone to him and demanded the truth, but things were still too new between them, too uncertain, and she didn't know quite what to do.

Of course you do. The new Rachel would demand the truth too.

Pulling her hands out of her pockets, she closed the distance between them, coming right up to him, lifting her palms to his chest and spreading her fingers out on the warm cotton of his T-shirt. Using the warmth of her touch to let him know everything was okay.

His gaze was fierce on hers, as if he were looking at her to take all his fury away, to help him.

She remembered years ago, when his endless patience with his father's binges ran short, as it did from time to time, she used to drag him out to the movies, where they could both sit in the dark and escape for a couple of hours. It was the cheapest way to forget about life for a while.

"Want to go catch a movie?" she asked now, rubbing her thumbs over the material stretched over his chest in a soothing caress. "You look like you could do with one."

Unexpectedly he reached up and covered her hand with his

as if he needed her touch, but the hard look on his face didn't ease. "A movie's not what I need right now."

Oh. No need to guess what he did need right now.

Her heartbeat accelerated, a familiar tight ache building inside her. Well, she had no problem with that. Beat the hell out of the movies, that was for sure, and it was a lot more effective than actually talking about whatever was bothering him.

"Uh huh." She let her free hand trail down over the hard, flat plane of his stomach. "I guess this disagreement with Gideon isn't quite so little, then?"

There was heat in his eyes, the anger there beginning to change into something far hungrier. He slid an arm around her, his palm curving over her butt, pulling her close, one powerful thigh pushing between hers, making her breath catch. "I don't really want to discuss Gideon right now."

"Yeah, I know you don't." She didn't really understand why she was continuing to talk when it would be so much easier to do what he obviously wanted them to do. But somehow she found herself saying, "Maybe it would help, though?"

A dark expression crossed his face. The hand on her butt pressed harder, forcing her more firmly against his thigh, the hard line of her zipper a subtle pressure against her clit, sending little sparks though her.

"No," he said, as if that were the last word on the subject. "It wouldn't."

Unable to help herself, she flexed her hips, rubbing herself against him, watching the embers of heat in his eyes catch fire. No doubt about it, she liked watching his reaction to her, liked watching all that anger change, be replaced by something else. Liked being the one who changed it. Who made it better for him.

She lifted her free hand, trailed her fingers along his jaw, stroking. "Come on. If you tell me, I'll give you a blow job." It was meant as a joke, and she had her reward in the faint easing of the hard line of his mouth.

"I might consider it if I didn't know how little it takes for you to get down on your knees and do that anyway."

Well, that was true. The last couple of days, she'd lost a lot of her inhibitions, creating new memories for herself. Memories of Levi instead of Evan. The taste and scent of Levi. The way he touched her, the way she touched him in turn. Reclaiming her body and her sexuality for herself.

It had been good, so good. And yeah, she did like a bit of cock worship, as long as the cock was Levi's.

She looked at him, considering. "In that case, maybe I won't. Maybe I have an urgent client instead."

His hand on her behind firmed, his thigh insistent. "No, you don't."

Damn him. If he kept doing that she'd forget what she was doing. "Oh, come on. Gideon's been a bear the past couple of days, so it's no wonder—" She stopped short as Levi suddenly let her go, putting her from him with gentle but firm pressure.

She blinked, staring at him in surprise, the rejection hurting, though she tried not to let it. "What?"

He turned away, brushing past her to pace over to the wall then back again, his movements sharp and restless as he ran a hand through his dark, tawny hair. Then, just as suddenly he stopped and faced her, his expression fierce. "I don't want to tell you because I don't want to have the same argument with you that I had with him."

"What argument?" And then she remembered what Zoe had said that night in the tattoo studio. That Gideon had been pissed about seeing Levi showing some guys around Royal. Levi's little "business meeting." "Oh," she said, as understanding began to dawn. "This is about those guys in suits, right?"

"Yes." The word held a note of challenge in it.

Development. That's what Levi had told her when he was in the tattoo chair. He wanted to develop Royal, attract a better class of people. Make it safe or some such crap. "You told him about your development plans?"

Levi's shoulders went back, his whole body straightening, becoming a huge, muscular wall of stony determination. He folded his arms. "Yeah, I told him. Actually, I'd prefer to have showed him my plans, but he preempted me because he saw me with Ryan and Novak."

Rachel frowned. "Who are they?"

"Ryan manages my investments, and Novak's going to be a backer. He's going to be hosting a function for more potential investors next week too." Levi's expression became even stonier. "For some reason fucking Gideon doesn't like him."

She had no idea why Gideon wouldn't like whoever this Novak guy was, but she knew for a fact that he had a healthy distrust of the wealthy and the powerful. And as for Levi's plans for Royal . . . Well, the fact that Gideon had argued with Levi about them came as no surprise. He felt as she did. That the kind of gentrification Levi was planning would only cause harm to the people already living here. The people who couldn't afford the fancy apartments he was planning, or the big-box stores that would move in. And who eventually wouldn't be able to afford the rents on their own apartments should the gentrification process ensure massive rent hikes the way it had in every other city in the world.

"I'm sure it wasn't only him Gideon didn't like," she said, trying to keep her voice neutral.

Levi's straight tawny brows drew down, the ring threaded through the left one glittering in the sunlight. "No," he said flatly. "Gideon didn't like my plans either."

"Can't think why," she muttered, unable to help herself.

Instantly Levi's expression became like granite. "Like I said, I'm not having this argument with you as well."

She didn't know what to say, because she didn't want to have that argument with him either, and the way he was standing, the look on his face—it was all very familiar to her. Uncomfortably so. He reminded her of herself when she felt threatened. Withdrawing behind her armor, the one with the spines that warned off all intruders.

Levi's armor didn't have spines. His was built to withstand all assaults, standing firm and cold and immovable. Resisting everything that was thrown against it. Unbreakable.

Why? Why did he find this threatening? What was so important about these plans of his? Yes, there was all that stuff about dreams and futures, but what was driving it?

"This is important to you, isn't it?" she asked carefully, because she had to do this right. Looked like she was entering the minefield whether she wanted to or not.

"Of course it's fucking important to me," he said roughly. "I've got money invested in this."

"It's not about the money though, is it?"

"You really have to ask me that? You know what this is about."

She studied him. "You mean the reason you told me or the reason you told yourself?"

He scowled, and, just like that, all that latent anger was back on the surface, prowling around and looking for a target, looking for prey. "I expect that kind of shit from Gideon, but not you, Sunny."

"Oh, what? You mean the truth?" What the hell, she might as well explode a few mines.

His arms dropped to his sides, fingers curling into fists, all aggression. "What the fuck is that supposed to mean?"

She didn't flinch. "Chill out. I'm not attacking you. I'm only pointing out that I'm not the only one who doesn't like to be confronted with stuff I don't want to think about."

"Stuff?" The question was almost barked out. "What stuff?"

"The investment and development plans you have." She

kept her gaze on him. "What's behind them? There's something there, Levi, something you don't want to talk about."

"Bullshit!" he spat. "I'm more than happy to talk about it. I'm doing it for my dad. For your gran. I'm doing it for this whole fucking neighborhood." The cotton of his T-shirt pulled tight as he heaved in a breath. "I'm doing it for you!"

Her heart gave a hard, thudding beat. Because there was something under the harsh words, a thin thread of what she thought was uncertainty or desperation. Something he was trying to hide, and yet it bled through all the same.

But she knew. She understood. He was afraid.

She went over to him and reached out, taking his white-knuckled fists in her hands, covering them gently with her fingers. "I know," she said. "I know."

"Don't fucking patronize me." His voice was harsh, his body vibrating with tension. But he didn't pull away.

She tightened her fingers around his. "I'm not. But this isn't just about me or your dad or Gran. This is about something else." She didn't take her gaze from his face, looking straight into his eyes. "What is it, Levi?"

Chapter 16

Her fingers around his were cool, but she was looking at him as if she saw something he couldn't. And he didn't know what that was.

Of course he was doing this for her. For them. For his father who'd lost everything when he'd been made redundant from his job. For her gran and her lack of decent medical care.

Levi was making things different. He was changing things. He was fixing the things that were broken to help the people he cared about. That was the start and end of it. There wasn't anything more than that.

Are you sure about that?

Fuck, yeah, he was sure. All this about him doing this for himself was bullshit. Gideon didn't know what the hell he was talking about, and Rachel . . .

Rachel does. Rachel knows.

Levi wanted to pull his hands away from her, from the cool touch of her skin that somehow eased the heat inside him at the same time as it incited a different kind of heat. He didn't know how the hell she managed to do that. She really was magic.

"No," he growled. "There's nothing else. Don't make this into something it isn't. I'm here to help people, Rachel. That's all I'm trying to do."

Christ, he sounded pathetic. Why the hell was he justifying himself to her like this?

You know why. Because she matters to you; she always has.

His throat was dry, and his chest ached, and he did *not* want to feel shit like this. But he couldn't deny the truth. She *did* matter. And though he could tell himself he didn't give a shit what Gideon thought of him, he couldn't do the same with Rachel. Not while she was standing there, holding his hands.

"I'm not trying to make this into anything." Her gaze saw so much, and he wanted to turn away. Do something else so she wasn't looking at him like that. "But this is about more than just helping me, and you know it." She paused, her hands tightening on his as if he were a live electrical wire and she was trying to ground the current. "I appreciate what you're doing; don't think I don't. But my life is how I want it. And your dad and Gran are gone. Things are different now."

Different. Yes, everything was different. Everyone had moved on.

Except you.

He opened his mouth to say that her life wasn't the way she wanted it, that she was kidding herself, but that wasn't what came out. Instead he said in a voice that didn't sound like his own, "I missed it. I missed everything. Dad. Your gran. You. I missed the whole fucking thing. Everything I wanted to do, everything I wanted to fix . . . It just went on without me like—" He stopped abruptly, clamping his mouth down on the words before they could escape. The words he didn't want to say to anyone because he hadn't fully understood them before.

Until now.

Until she stood in front of him with her hands covering his

and her dark eyes seeing right through him the way they always did. As if they had no secrets from each other anymore.

"Like what?" she asked softly. "Like you don't matter?"

How did she know? How did she manage to understand him better than he understood himself? But, God, how he hated the vulnerability implicit in her questions. Hated how it stripped him bare, left him exposed. He'd learned all about vulnerability in prison, how you couldn't ever show it, not if you wanted to survive. So keeping himself defended every moment of the goddamn day was just instinct.

Yet now she'd taken his defenses from him.

"Don't say that. Don't say—"

She lifted a hand, cupped his jaw, the heat of her touch taking away every single word in his head. Because there was gentleness in it, and a tenderness he'd forgotten was even possible.

As if you even deserve that from her, after how you've treated her. Blaming her for everything when you're the one who fucked up.

He didn't deserve it, and yet she didn't stop touching him, her fingers tracing his cheekbone and then up to his left eyebrow and the ring threaded through it. "It's okay," she said quietly. "It's only me, Levi. And you can talk to me, just like I talked to you. We're friends, remember?" Her eyes were the color of dark chocolate, and she smelled like something delicious to eat. And he didn't want to talk. He wanted to do other things instead. Yet there was a pressure in his chest. As if something were trying to push its way out, a yearning for more than a warm body against him. A need for something deeper.

"I have to fix things, Sunny." He stared into her eyes. "It's the only way it's going to get better."

"I know, but it's already better. Don't you see? The studio, my plans for the art gallery . . . Maybe it wasn't what I dreamed then, but it's what I want now. It makes me happy."

"You didn't need me at all, did you?" He couldn't stop the

question; it just spilled right out of him whether he wanted it to or not. "You didn't need me to help you. You didn't need me to be there for you. I might as well not have even fucking existed."

Her eyes widened in shock. "No, you know that's not true. Why would you think that?"

"Well, my old man didn't need me." More words spilled out, words he'd never intended to say to anyone. Words he hadn't even realized existed inside himself. "My old man just drank his fucking life away whether I was there or not. He didn't need me to clean up after him; he didn't need me to drag him home from Gino's. He didn't need me to do anything for him at all. He just sat there with his fucking bottle, and nothing I did made any kind of difference." Anger welled up inside him, a never-ending current of it as if from an underwater volcano. "I was trying to fix him. I was trying to make it better for him. But do you think he cared? No, he didn't give a shit. He just kept drinking. I might as well not even have existed for him either."

There was sympathy in Rachel's eyes, in the lines of her beautiful face. And understanding too, such a terrible understanding. One that cut him open and spread him out, all his insides on display. "I know," she said simply. "I didn't really exist for Gran either. She didn't know who I was, and at the end she was even scared of me every time I came to visit her in the hospital." Rachel's hands reached up and cupped his face. "But we did matter to them, Levi. You have to know that, deep down, we did. We helped them, we made their lives better, and I think we did believe that, because why else did we keep doing it? And in the end, we were doing it because we loved them. Isn't that what you used to tell me?"

Did he? Jesus, he couldn't even remember. He only knew that once he'd had hope; once he'd had optimism and belief that things were going to get better. That things would change.

That was before you killed someone.

Yeah, and now he was trying to fix that too.

"I don't know." His voice sounded like it had been scraped raw. "Did I?"

Something in her face softened. "Yes, you did. You said that was the bottom line. We weren't helping them for acknowledgment or reward or anything like that; we were helping them because we loved them. And that's all that mattered."

Maybe he had said that once. Sounded like something his younger, stupidly naïve self would have once believed. Problem was, he didn't believe that now. Just like all that other bullshit about love being its own reward.

"Yeah, well, it was a stupid thing to say." Even to himself the words sounded petulant.

Her mouth curved. "I don't think you believe that. I think you believe it's still true. Why else are you arguing with Gideon? Why else are you so insistent that this is about the neighborhood? About me?"

"I killed someone, Sunny." The admission was a harsh whisper of sound. "I can't ever change that. All I can do is try to fix it. I *have* to." What else was his life worth otherwise?

That lovely smile faded, and he felt the weight of the three lives he'd changed forever with one stupid punch. And it was crushing.

Then her fingers skimmed back down the side of his face and along his jaw, tracing his lower lip, making his skin feel all tight and sensitized. "You've paid for that, Levi. You've done your time. You don't have to do anything else. Just being here is enough."

Just being here is enough.

There was a deep ache inside his chest, getting deeper with each swipe of her fingers.

"It's not that simple," he said, because it couldn't be. "If all I had to do was be here, then Dad wouldn't have drunk himself to death."

The look in her eyes darkened. "You know I tried to—"

"Gideon tried to look out for him too." He cut her off, not wanting to go into it. "But it was too late. Nothing could stop it." Levi reached up, took hold of her hand, feeling the fine, fragile bones beneath her skin. "Nothing could fix it. And now . . . Now I can." He tightened his fingers a little, kept his gaze on hers. "And you have to let me, otherwise the last eight fucking years of my life might as well have been for nothing."

Her mouth softened, her gaze searching his. "I didn't know," she said quietly. "I didn't realize you saw it like that."

"Well, I do." He brought her hand down and turned it over, cupping the back of it in his palm. "Next week Novak is hosting a function for potential investors, and he's going to be presenting my plans for Royal's development. I want you to be there. I want you to see for yourself what I'm thinking of for Royal." He could see the doubt cross her face, her hesitation as loud as a shout. But he didn't look away. Because he hadn't realized how important it was to him that she be there until now.

She let out a breath. "Levi, I . . ."

He bent, pressing a kiss to the middle of her palm. "Please, Rachel." He'd never asked like that before, never wanted to reveal that kind of vulnerability. But he would for her.

Because she mattered.

Her gaze dropped to her palm, where he'd kissed her, and for a long moment she just stared at it as if he'd branded the center of it instead of merely kissing it.

Then she said, "Okay. I'll come."

"I like that one."

Rachel stared at herself in the full-length mirror that had appeared on the wall in the bedroom a couple of days ago. Levi was slowly but surely adding furniture to the apartment. Some things she appreciated, and some she didn't. The mirror—another one of his rough, recycled finds—was one she definitely appreciated, especially when all she'd had before had been the cruddy one in her gran's bathroom.

Behind her, Zoe sat on the bed, nibbling on a nail and offering advice on Rachel's wardrobe choices. Again, some of the advice was appreciated; some not so much.

"This? Really?" Rachel narrowed her gaze at the black leather miniskirt she was currently wearing, a favorite of hers. It was very short, very sexy, and sadly, she suspected, also very inappropriate for this function of Levi's. "I think it's probably a bit short."

Zoe wrinkled her nose. "Can a skirt ever be too short?"

"Says the woman who never wears skirts."

"Hey, you wanted some advice. I'm giving it to you." She sighed. "Though really, you need Tamara on this, not me."

This was probably true. Tamara's family was society all the way, and if anyone would know what was appropriate "function-wear" it would be her.

Of course, Rachel could rock a sexy miniskirt, or the dress that left her shoulder bare, not giving a shit whether she was appropriate or not. But the problem was she did give a shit.

Levi had asked her along to this thing, and she'd told him she'd go, mainly because refusing him hadn't been an option. Especially after what he'd told her the week before. This was important to him, which meant it was important to her—even if she didn't agree with it.

"I really do," she muttered, pulling a face at herself in the mirror. "Wanna text her for me?"

Half an hour later, Tamara arrived carrying a garment bag and looking very determined. Rachel eyed the bag suspiciously. "I'm guessing that's not margarita mix."

Tamara grinned, flinging the bag on the bed and unzipping it, revealing what looked like a cloud of floaty, gauzy silks in various different colors. "I don't know if these will fit you or not, but I thought it was worth a try." She took the items on hangers out of the bag, and the silks resolved themselves into gowns of vary-ing lengths and styles.

Rachel stared at them. They were beautiful, the kind of dresses she'd dreamed about as a little girl. The kind she'd never be able to afford now she was all grown up. "Tamara . . . I can't—"

"Yes, you damn well can." Tamara laid down a couple of the dresses, holding up a black silk number with what looked like an honest to God train. "They're just sitting in my closet doing nothing, and it's not as if I'm going to be wearing these any time soon." She thrust the black dress at Rachel. "Now go try this one on. And if it's no good, we can try the others."

Rachel took the dress and disappeared into the bathroom to try it on, though part of her felt weird about it, as though she were trying to be someone she wasn't. She'd always been very in-your-face with her clothing and her hair color, a loud shout to the rest of the world that she didn't care what they thought of her.

Yet this was different; this was definitely caring about what someone thought.

She pulled on the first dress, feeling uncertain. She tried the dresses on one by one, twisting and turning in front of the mir-ror in the bedroom, then standing still while Tamara stalked around her, pulling bits of fabric this way and that.

As nice as the black was, and the rest of them, it was always going to be the red dress that was the hit.

It was simple, elegant, the silk wrapping around Rachel's curves and snaking over one shoulder to fasten in a knot, the tail of it draping down her back in a fall of scarlet gauze. The cut of the gown didn't hide her tattoos, but the red fabric com-plemented the color of the roses and the pale tone of her skin.

Rachel stared at herself in the mirror as Tamara began mat-ter-of-factly pinning Rachel's hair up into a loose bun on top of her head, letting a few strands fall around her face. Rachel let the other woman do it, studying the stranger in the glass in front of her. It was weird seeing herself like this, all elegant and refined, her tattoos looking like the small, precise works of art they were. She was different, and she wasn't sure she liked it. Wasn't sure she *didn't* like it either.

"Wow," Zoe said from the bed, her eyes round behind her glasses. "You look amazing."

Tamara stepped back, examining her handiwork. "Yep," she said after a critical moment. "You really do."

Rachel met Tamara's gaze in the mirror, then Zoe's. "I feel weird."

Zoe slipped off the bed and came to stand next to her. "You shouldn't. Levi's going to freak. And I mean that in a good way."

Rachel hoped he would. She hoped he'd like it and wouldn't think she looked ridiculous. And that was strange too, wanting someone to like the way she looked, having it matter to her.

"What's all this for anyway?" Zoe asked. "I mean, this thing you're going to with Levi?"

Rachel turned, looking at her in surprise. "Gideon didn't tell you?"

Zoe's gaze fell to studiously examine the floor. "No. He wouldn't talk to me about it." There was a note of hurt in her voice.

What the hell was going on between Gideon and Zoe? It wasn't like them to fight, and it certainly wasn't like Gideon to hurt her. He was protective of all of them, but most especially of Zoe. What made matters worse was that Rachel had a horrible feeling it all had something to do with Levi's plans. Something to do with the investors he'd been showing around.

She should talk to Gideon about it, see what the problem was. In fact, she should have done it before now, but she'd been . . . busy. Busy as in spending the time she wasn't at Sugar Ink with Levi, at least what time he'd been able to spare.

Because he too had been busy, going out all suited-up for "meetings" that lasted all day. She didn't inquire too deeply about these meetings, knowing that they were all connected with his development plans. She'd find out soon enough anyway.

And when he wasn't going out for meetings, he was at Gideon's doing God knew what. It wasn't talking to Gideon, that was for sure, because Zoe had mentioned to her that Levi spent most of the time in garage and only when Gideon wasn't there.

She'd decided to let that lie for now. Things were going too well to upset the situation with pointless arguments. She and Levi weren't quite back to where they'd been before he'd gone to jail, but, give them another month or two, and maybe they would be.

However, she didn't like this new rift between Gideon and Zoe. It wasn't right, and it didn't make sense. And she hated to think that it was something to do with Levi.

Rachel gave Tamara a wordless, inquiring look, but the other woman only shrugged.

"Why not?" Rachel asked Zoe after a moment. "What's his problem?"

Zoe lifted a shoulder, her gaze staying on the floor. "God knows. But, hey, I don't give a shit. If he doesn't want to talk to me, that's cool."

But it wasn't cool; that much was obvious.

"You want me to talk to him?" Rachel offered, not liking the set expression on Zoe's face. "I don't mind."

"No." The word was unequivocal, and, when Zoe looked up, there was an unfamiliar, fierce look in her amber eyes. "I'll deal with it."

"Zoe—" Rachel began.

"It's okay, Rach," Zoe interrupted. "Really, it is. Now, what's this thing you're going to? You never said."

It seemed like Gideon wasn't the only person who didn't want to talk.

"It's some kind of thing to attract investors for some development plans of Levi's."

Zoe pulled a face. "Oh," she said, as if that explained everything. And knowing Gideon, it probably did.

"Yeah, I know," Rachel said, turning back to the mirror, giving herself another critical look. "I don't agree with it either. But I told him I'd go, and so I am."

In the mirror Tamara was looking at her. "Because it's important to him, right?" she murmured. There was understanding in the other woman's eyes, a knowing look.

Rachel's heart felt suddenly full and large in her chest. "Yes," she said quietly, because that was the reason. The only reason.

Zoe, clearly having seen the look they'd exchanged, snorted her disgust. "If you two are going to be mooning over guys, I'm leaving."

Rachel wanted to point out the irony of that particular statement given the mooning Zoe did over Gideon, but that wouldn't help matters. And she didn't want to make things worse for Zoe. Instead, she gave Zoe a brief hug. "Thanks for coming over."

Zoe grinned back, her face lighting up in the familiar Zoe way. "No problem. I want all the details when you get back, okay?"

A couple of minutes later the other two women had left, and Rachel was pacing around the room nervously, holding the little red satin purse Tamara had given her that was barely big enough to carry a lipstick let alone the silly little thing she'd bought to make Levi smile.

He'd told her he'd pick her up, which she'd thought was odd considering they lived together. But he hadn't been home when she'd gotten back from work, and then she'd gotten a text telling her he'd be coming for her at seven sharp.

She stopped in the middle of the room, feeling stupidly unsettled. It was ridiculous, considering it was only Levi, who knew her better than she knew herself. Who'd seen her naked and clothed and everything in between.

But no amount of telling herself this helped the feeling inside her, as if she had a thousand butterflies flying around in her stomach. A thousand that became a million when she heard the front door shut and the sound of Levi's familiar step.

She turned to the doorway, and her heart came to slamming halt against her breastbone.

Jesus Christ. He was wearing a tux.

And he looked . . . God, he looked incredible. The black jacket and white shirt accentuated his wide shoulders and broad chest. In fact, the tux should have had a civilizing effect on him, yet it only seemed to highlight the wild aspects of him. He'd made no effort to hide the signs of being the rough ex-con, the ring in his eyebrow glinting in the light, the black lines of his tattoos visible at the cuffs of his shirt, his uneven, disturbing gaze.

There was no apology to him, no hiding who he was and who he'd once been. It was all out there, as arrogant as the man himself.

He was magnificent. He made her heart go tight, made her mouth dry, made her want to run her hands all over him, touch him, kiss him, do anything and everything she wanted to him.

He didn't say anything for a long moment, the light and dark of his gaze sweeping over her, taking her in. Heat glowed there, a heat that warmed every part of her, that turned her nervousness into a satisfaction that went bone-deep.

She lifted her chin. "What do you think? Am I presentable?"

He smiled, and there was a hint of feral hunger in it that caused a shiver to chase over her skin. "Come here."

She obeyed, letting the silk of the dress sway enticingly as she walked, her own smile turning seductive.

As she came within reach, he lifted his hands to her hips, pulling her close. "Forget presentable," he murmured in her ear. "Try fuckable." And then he leaned in closer, pressing his mouth to the sensitive skin beneath her ear, trailing it down.

Rachel shuddered, relaxing against the heat of his body. "I'm not sure that's the look you want for this party of yours."

"I meant to say you look fuckable in an elegant way." He nipped the side of her neck, then released her. "Which is perfect."

She didn't want him to let her go. She wanted to stay here, strip him bare, then make love with him right here on the couch. Then afterward lie in his arms and talk like they used to.

Unfortunately she couldn't.

She stepped back, smiling up at him. "So what's with the whole picking me up thing?"

He took her hand, lacing his fingers through hers, the look on his face enigmatic. "Come on. I've got something to show you."

What he had to show her was parked at the curb right outside the apartment. A long, sleek, vintage Firebird, all glossy black paint and gleaming new chrome.

Years ago, she remembered him talking about his dream car. Now she was looking at it.

"Wow," she breathed, moving up to it and running her fingers down the side of it, careful of the paintwork. "This is beautiful." She turned to look at him where he stood beside her. "Where did you get it?"

Satisfaction gleamed in his eyes. "I've spent the last week restoring it."

The gorgeous, secretive bastard.

She touched a gleaming side mirror. "Ah. So that's where you've been all this time. At Gideon's. And here I was thinking you were actually doing some work."

"I've been doing that too. But mostly making sure this baby was ready for tonight."

She wanted to ask him how things were with Gideon, but

she didn't want to broach that topic just yet, not while he was looking so damn pleased with himself.

Instead, she said, "I've got a surprise for you too."

He lifted his pierced brow. "Oh?"

Flicking open her purse, she removed the packet she'd stuffed into it and held it out to him, watching his face.

It was a beautiful sight, the smile that dawned over his features as he saw what was in her hand. A smile of delighted surprise and then of deep amusement.

His gaze came to hers, and, just like that, the old Levi was back. "You're kidding, right?" There was laughter in his eyes, genuine, honest-to-God laughter. "Pixy Stix?"

She couldn't stop her own grin. "They're still your favorite, right?"

"Damn straight they are." He whipped the packet from her and stuffed it in his pocket. "And I'm going to eat them. Tonight." The laughter in his eyes became wicked. "Maybe off your skin."

And idiot that she was, she blushed. "As long as I get to corner you in the shower afterward."

"Oh, sweetheart, I'm counting on it." He moved to the passenger door and opened it in an old-fashioned, courtly gesture. "In the meantime, your coach, Cinderella."

She grinned and reached out to touch his face briefly before she got in. "So what does that make you? Prince Charming?"

"Definitely not." His smile became feral, and he gave her finger a playful nip. "I'm the wolf who's going to eat you for breakfast."

She laughed. "Do you promise?"

"When we get home tonight, definitely." His smile faded a little, became more serious. "Thank you, Sunny," he said quietly.

Her heart, already aching in her chest, tightened even further. "What for?" Though really, she already knew.

"For coming tonight." His smile had gone completely, his expression fierce, intense. "You have no idea how much it means to me."

No, she did. She knew. Her throat closed up, a full, heavy emotion clogging it, and for some reason, she couldn't speak.

Then Levi reached into the back pocket of his black pants and took something out, handing it to her. It was a piece of paper, and when she unfolded it and looked down, the power of speech deserted her completely.

It was the title deed to Sugar Ink's building.

And it was in her name.

Chapter 17

Levi had never felt so good in all his goddamn life. As he pulled the Firebird up outside the Novak Enterprises building in downtown Detroit, where there were a red carpet and valets ready to go, and he opened the door to the beautiful woman getting out of his car, he knew he'd fucking made it.

This was his moment. This was what the last eight years had been leading up to.

And it was even better than he'd dreamed.

He had the car. He had the money. He had the business. He was going to make everything right.

Best of all, he had Rachel.

It was everything he'd ever wanted.

Other people were arriving—women in beautiful gowns and dripping jewelry; men in classy tuxedos, dripping wealth. Men he'd always wanted to be, and now he was. And he was doing it his way.

He had the classy tux, sure, but he also had the tattoos and the ring in his eyebrow. He wasn't hiding his past. He was who he was, and he was here despite it.

Maybe it was the Royal part of him that liked that. The blue-collar, anti-establishment guy.

The part of you that's like Gideon?

Levi shoved that thought away as Rachel put her hand in his and got out of the car.

He wasn't going to think about Gideon, not now. Most times Levi had gone to the garage to work on the car over the past week, Gideon hadn't been there, and the times he was, the only thing they'd talked about was what the Firebird needed.

Gideon hadn't talked to Levi about Novak or the development plans, not once, which was just as well since it wasn't anything they were going to agree on. If they wanted to keep things civil between them, then it was best just to avoid the subject entirely.

"This is . . . full on," Rachel murmured as Levi handed the Firebird's keys to a waiting valet. "I didn't realize it was going to be like this."

Levi laced his fingers through hers, holding on tight to her as they joined the crowd of beautifully dressed people going through the front doors. He'd gotten used to the bright, hard glitter of the Novak building with its acres of plate glass and soaring atrium, all sleek, architectural sophistication. It reeked of wealth, of privilege, of class, of a business on its way up.

It was a whole different world from Royal Road, so no wonder she was having difficulty taking it all in.

But she didn't need to worry. She looked like a princess in her beautiful, silky, floaty dress. A hard-edged princess, her skin a canvas for the delicate artwork she'd inked into it. She didn't need jewels. She wore her own in the shape of the roses on her shoulders and across her chest.

He tightened his fingers around hers as they entered the atrium. "Yeah, I know. It's a little much initially. But you get used to it." He halted in front of the massive sculpture that dominated the center of the atrium, an abstract lump of something in dull gold, all strange planes and angles, that he didn't care for himself, but he thought Rachel might find it interesting. "What do you think of that?"

As he'd hoped, she frowned and moved forward to look at it, examining it.

He watched her, unable to stop his gaze from following the lines of her body that the dress she wore highlighted so beautifully. She was gorgeous; she really was. She was everything he wanted, and the fact that she was here, sharing this with him, was the icing on the cake.

He was glad he'd finally given her the deed to the building. He'd been holding off on it, because he hadn't wanted to make the secret that she'd told him that day in her tattoo parlor feel like a business deal. Oh, she'd meant it as such when she'd demanded he promise the deed to her, but that didn't mean he had to treat it like that too.

Better to give the deed to her now, as a gift in return for her presence at something that was important to him, because it seemed only right that he give her something that was important to her.

Sure, he'd hoped to have apartments in that building, but if she wanted to turn it into an art gallery or whatever, he was fine with that. He had other buildings. He could afford to let her have hers.

Besides, the look on her face and the kiss she'd given him in response had been worth it. Okay, so she didn't want to go to art school, but if this was what she wanted instead, then he was fine with it.

It was all coming together; it really was.

"I don't like it," Rachel said, at last stepping back from the sculpture. "It's kind of pretentious."

Levi grinned and reached for her hand again. "They should have one of your murals in here instead."

"They so should." She took his hand and let him lead her from the sculpture and over to the bank of elevators. "Not sure spray paint is the look they're going for here though."

He shot her a glance as he hit the button for the top floor. "Wait till you see what I've got planned." He was looking forward to that, the moment when she'd see his vision for Royal that he'd spent the past couple of weeks working on. Novak had been totally on board with it, pulling in a couple of prestigious architects to draw up some concepts. The whole thing was looking incredible, exactly how Levi had always envisioned the neighborhood should look.

Rachel was going to love it, and Gideon would too. All of them would love it once they came around to the idea.

Levi and Rachel took the elevator up to the penthouse level, where there was a fabulous rooftop garden that Novak used for private functions. It was strung up with lights that were wound around potted trees and shrubs of all kinds, a glass parapet bounding the whole area, giving beautiful views over the city. Low couches and chairs were grouped in various configurations. The sound of running water from the water sculptures that led into a big koi pond in the center was a calming counterpoint to the string quartet playing something classical.

Waiters moved through the gathered crowd bearing trays of champagne and other cocktails, while other staff carried trays of expensive-looking canapés.

Christ, there were a lot of people here. Novak had really come through.

Snagging a couple of glasses of champagne from a passing tray, Levi handed one to Rachel, then he took her hand again. "Come on, let's go and find Novak. I'll introduce you."

He led her through the crowd, ignoring the heads turning in their wake, people no doubt wondering who the hell they were, since it was obvious they weren't exactly on the same social level as everyone else.

It didn't matter. He was the mastermind behind this thing, and Rachel was his muse. And if these people didn't like it, they could suck it.

Over by the corner of the koi pond, Novak stood talking to a bunch of important-looking men in suits. He glanced at Levi and Rachel as they approached and smiled, waving them over.

Levi felt the initial resistance in Rachel's grip as he started toward the other man, but he exerted a little more pressure and it soon faded, her hand relaxing in his.

"Mr. Rush," Novak greeted them smoothly. "Are you ready for your big moment?"

Levi grinned, enjoying the dubious looks from the other men as they took in his eyebrow ring and the glimpses of tattoos at his wrists. "Yeah, can't wait."

"I bet you can't." The older man's gaze shifted to Rachel, and Levi watched with a certain satisfaction as appreciation unfolded in Novak's eyes. "And this is your lovely date?"

Levi drew Rachel closer in a blatant show of possession, his arm curving around her hip. "Yeah. This is my girlfriend, Rachel Hamilton. Rachel, this is Oliver Novak, the man who's hosting this party and who is hopefully going to get me the support I need to get this project off the ground."

Novak smiled and reached out his hand. "Nice to meet you, Ms. Hamilton."

"Likewise, Mr. Novak." Her voice was neutral, the expression on her face giving nothing away.

Novak's gaze dropped briefly to the tattoos across her chest. "Beautiful artwork. Your own, I take it?"

Rachel flushed. "Uh, yeah. It is actually."

"I can tell." Novak glanced at Levi. "We have some examples in our plans."

Rachel's eyes widened. "What?"

But Novak only laughed, flashing Levi a conspiratorial glance. "You'll find out. Won't she, Mr. Rush?"

Levi's sense of well-being broadened. Oh yeah, she was going to find out. And she was going to love it.

Novak began to introduce them to the others standing around, high-powered business people with deep pockets looking for likely projects to sink all that hard cash into. They were interested in Levi's development and were full of questions that he was only too happy to answer. It gave him such a kick to see their expressions of distrust and suspicion at his appearance morph into interest and the hard, direct looks of businessmen wanting to close a deal.

But he was conscious of Rachel beside him, silently watching and listening. She didn't offer anything to the conversation, and he could tell by the tense way she stood that she wasn't particularly enjoying it.

However, after about ten minutes, a lovely older woman, who Novak introduced as his wife Kate, approached and a couple of moments later led Rachel away.

Rachel gave Levi a look he couldn't interpret as Kate led her off, a look that for some reason made something ache in his chest. But he didn't want anything to spoil the good buzz he had going, so he only smiled at her. "I'll come find you in a while," he called as she walked away.

But she didn't turn around, and, seconds later, she was gone in the crowd.

Something pulled at him, an unease he didn't want to feel, especially not now, not in his moment of triumph. But then Novak was asking him a question and so he ignored the feeling, turning instead to answer.

It would be fine. Soon Rachel would find out what he'd been working toward all this time, and everything would turn out the way he wanted it to.

He had nothing to worry about. Nothing at all.

* * *

Kate Novak was very nice, but Rachel didn't miss the way the other woman's gaze kept returning to the tattoos on Rachel's chest as if she couldn't look away.

Jesus. First she had Novak whose blatant appreciation had more to do with the fact that her breasts were right underneath the tattoos than the tattoos themselves. Then there was his wife who couldn't stop looking at the tattoos themselves, probably because she thought they were disgusting. That was supposition on Rachel's part, because Kate's face gave nothing away, but Rachel was pretty sure that was the case. It had been her experience that people either really liked them or they didn't, and there wasn't much in between.

Kate had chatted to her for a while, and it was clear the other woman was the consummate politician's wife. Her manner was charming, and the conversation felt effortless. But Rachel couldn't shake the feeling it was all just as fake as the other woman's tan. She was the date of Novak's current business interest and thus had to be kept entertained with empty conversation about things like fashion and whether or not she had kids, and what was living in Royal like, etcetera.

Rachel was being patronized, and she didn't like it.

Every so often she'd glance over at where Levi stood with the other men, simply because it was difficult *not* to look at him. He was taller than the rest and much broader, his presence like a force of nature. And they were all looking at him with interest sharp in their eyes, hanging on his every word.

He wasn't like them in any way, shape, or form, and yet his "don't give a shit" attitude was clearly very attractive to them.

It stood to reason. Wealthy business people liked that kind of thing.

Which maybe didn't make Levi so very different from them after all.

The thought was disturbing, and she looked away, uneasy.

"Are you okay?" Kate asked, spotting Rachel's discomfort and instantly solicitous.

Rachel summoned up an empty smile from somewhere. "I'm fine. But if you could point me in the direction of the ladies' room?"

All smiles, Kate gestured, and Rachel excused herself, threading her way through the well-heeled crowd. The champagne she'd drunk sat acidly in her gut, making the uneasy feeling worse.

As she moved, people glanced at her, some of the men openly salacious as they took in her ink, while disapproval flashed in some of the women's gazes. She didn't care about them, didn't care what they thought, but she was supposed to be here for Levi, and that was what caught at her.

That he was associating himself with people like these. That he wanted to be among people like these.

Was *this* what he'd truly wanted all these years? She'd thought initially that once he'd fully realized what that meant, he'd change his mind. But apparently not. He was standing there smiling, the center of attention for all these people, and quite happy about it from the look of things.

Perhaps this really *was* what he wanted.

The thought made her feel worse.

She slipped through the crowds, the silk of her gown floating after her as she moved inside the main part of the building and into a deserted corridor. She leaned against the wall a moment, enjoying the silence.

Then she let out a breath, a deep sense of disappointment settling like a large, heavy stone in her gut.

She'd promised to be here for him, because he was important to her. Because no matter what he thought about it, he mattered. Both to her and to everyone in Royal. But she didn't think she could do this. She didn't think she could stand by and let him do this to the neighborhood she loved.

You promised him.

The stone sat heavier. She had promised him. But she wasn't here because she felt she owed him anything anymore. She wasn't here because of her guilt.

She was here because he was her best friend and she loved him. She always had.

But if he thought what he was doing was right, that this development was what Royal needed, he was wrong. So wrong.

A footstep made her look up, and there he was, no mistaking his tall, broad figure or the long, easy, athletic lope of his stride as he came toward her. He was smiling as he came closer, and the stone became a massive boulder in her gut.

She loved that smile, and she didn't want to take it away, not his pleasure in this, not his pride.

But you're quite happy to sacrifice yours?

She swallowed. What the hell was that about? She wasn't sacrificing her pride, was she? After all, hadn't he given her the deed to her building, essentially guaranteeing her plans for her art gallery and the art classes she wanted to start?

He only gave that to you because he doesn't need that building anymore. Don't kid yourself that it's some kind of grand gesture.

"Hey." Levi's deep voice rumbled in the silence. "I wondered where you'd gotten to. Kate said you'd gone to the bathroom. Did you get lost?"

Her smile felt fixed, as if she'd tacked it there with nails and it was now starting to come away from her face. "No. Just needed a moment of quiet."

If he'd picked up on her mood, he didn't show it. Instead he held out his hand. "Come on. Novak's planning on the big reveal in half an hour, but I can't wait anymore. I want to show you what all this big deal is about now."

She couldn't refuse him; she just couldn't. He needed this, and, pride or not, she wanted to give it to him.

So she put out her hand and let him lace his fingers through hers, reveling in the warmth of his touch. "Okay. Show me."

He drew her down the silent corridor and through a doorway into some kind of meeting room. The classical music and the buzz of conversation from the party drifted in the air, but the atmosphere inside this room was all business.

There was a large boardroom table in the center of the room with a whole lot of expensive, white leather chairs grouped around it. Sitting on the table were big sheets of paper, all unrolled to reveal a set of beautifully colored drawings.

Levi led her over to the table, then dropped her hand, leaning over to push aside a couple of the sheets. "Here they are. One of the architects was going over the concepts with me earlier today. Novak's going to be doing a full-on PowerPoint presentation, but I thought I could show you these now."

A strange hesitancy held her still. She didn't want to look. She didn't want to stand at his side and study all these beautiful drawings that he was so proud of, the culmination of his years in prison. The years he was so desperate not to have wasted. Because she wasn't sure she could hide from him her reluctance about all of this. And she didn't want him to see that. Not right now, not when he was . . . happy.

But he was looking at her, and there was so much pride in his expression that she couldn't refuse him. So she took a step over to the table and looked down at the plans that were sitting on top of it. Sketches of familiar buildings that had been repaired and restored into sleeker, cleaner versions of themselves. Streets with all the grime removed and sidewalks with trees, and park benches for people to sit in. There were bright, clean stores and cafés, a playground instead of the parking lot next to the old general store. Even her own studio was there, with Sugar Ink's sign in the window.

"Here," Levi murmured. "I saved the best for last." He reached over and pushed another piece of paper toward her.

It was a plan for a public square right where Gino's bar was. Except instead of the bar there was a wide-open space with more trees and a fountain in the middle. And a wall with a mural on it. The same mural as the one in Sugar Ink.

"It's just a concept at the moment," Levi said quietly. "But I wanted your art in here somewhere. You could do some massive piece like that one in your studio. Or maybe something else."

"Something better, you mean?" The words came out before she could stop them, and as soon as they did, she wished she could take them back.

He stiffened beside her. "No, that's not what I mean. Why would you think that?"

She took a slow, silent breath, trying to ignore the stone in her gut and the boulder sitting on her chest, crushing her. Her instinct was to soothe him, to tell him that it was all okay, that she knew he didn't mean it.

But that would be a lie. He did mean it, deep down, and she knew he did because even now, even after she'd told him that *he* mattered, not what he did or didn't do, he was still trying to impress her. Still pushing these plans that were, admittedly, lovely, and yet weren't Royal. In fact they could have been concepts for any neighborhood anywhere.

She swallowed. He was still insisting on this vision of his. Insisting on his vision of Royal. Insisting on his vision of her.

His vision of what *their* life should be.

Because he didn't realize that he didn't need to have any vision at all.

He just needed to be who he was. The man she loved and always had.

She looked down at the drawings, her vision blurring with stupid, unexpected tears. Was there any point explaining? Could he even understand?

You promised him this. You promised. Doesn't he deserve it?
"I'm sorry," she said thickly. "I didn't mean to say that. The plans are fantastic, Levi. They're really great."

He knew immediately she was lying. Because he knew what she looked like when she was excited, when enthusiasm and passion lit up her face, and neither were there now. There was no light in her face at all. In fact he was certain he'd seen the gleam of what looked like tears in her eyes as she'd glanced down at the plans on the table.

And the pleasure and satisfaction and pride he'd been feeling all evening suddenly drained away.

He'd thought she'd be pleased with what he'd done. He'd thought she'd be surprised by how thoughtful and sensitive to the neighborhood and its issues he'd been. Sure, he'd gotten rid of Gino's, but that place was a shithole and no one went there but the drunks. And, Jesus, he'd put her art front and center, in the middle of the new square. Where everyone would come and sit to enjoy the new atmosphere of the place. Where no one would be afraid to walk for fear of getting shot or raped or murdered.

But no. Apparently she wasn't pleased. Apparently what he'd presented her with wasn't right at all.

Anger flooded through him, and he let it, because it was familiar and far easier to deal with than his pain at the look on her face. At the way she was so obviously trying to do what she'd promised and support him.

"You don't like it," he said flatly, ignoring the barbed wire that had wrapped suddenly around his heart. Not making it a question because he knew the answer already.

She kept her gaze on the drawings. "I mean, I think you're going for the right idea. I mean . . . the trees and things . . ." She trailed off, as if she couldn't think of anything more to say.

He couldn't stop himself. He reached out, gripping her chin in his hand and turning her so he could see her face, look into her eyes. "Don't lie to me, Rachel. Not now, not fucking now."

Her throat moved, her gaze flickering away. Everything was there in her face. Pain. Regret. Sympathy. And her fierce determination. "I'm trying," she said, her voice shaking a little. "I promised you I'd be here. I promised you that I'd support you because this was important to you. But I'm sorry, Levi. These plans look good, but they're not for Royal."

He knew it. He fucking knew it.

Disappointment sliced through him and all the good things he'd been feeling tonight, cutting them all away.

He released her chin and took a step back from her, the warmth of her skin lingering on his fingers and somehow making everything worse. "Jesus Christ, I thought I explained why I have to do this. Didn't you listen to anything I said?" He was being an asshole and he knew it, but he couldn't seem to shut himself up. "It's happening. As of tonight I've already got the last few backers I need. I don't need your fucking approval."

Her expression seemed to shatter in front of him, breaking apart into lines of hurt and anguish, before coming together again in sudden determination. "If you didn't want my approval, then why the hell are you so goddamn angry?"

His jaw tightened. "I wanted you to like them because you're my friend."

But the look in her eyes skewered that particular fiction. She'd always been able to see right through him. "I didn't say I didn't like them. I just said they're not right for Royal. I mean, why don't you take them back and discuss them with—"

"Why the fuck should I do that?" His anger simmered, and it was so easy to grasp it, to use it. "I'm not starting all over again, Rachel. No goddamn way."

"But I'm not saying you should start again. All I'm saying—"

"I put your fucking art in there. Jesus, what more do you want from me? I mean, how much more Royal could you—"

"Let me finish!" Her voice roared over the top of his, silencing him. "You're so goddamn angry, it's making you blind, Levi. Blind to what's right in front of your stupid, gorgeous face." Her dark eyes were suddenly full of a fury to match his own, blazing. "We love you. *I* love you. And you don't need to do this. You don't need to be this. We want you for who you are, not for what you can do for us or what you can fix." And now here it was, the passion in her and the fire, lighting her up like a Roman candle in the night. "So you spent eight years in jail, eight years you'll never get back? So goddamn what? I whored myself out, and, yeah, I had a lot of trouble dealing with that, but I moved on. I made a life for myself, and, no, it wasn't perfect, but it was mine." Her voice was shaking now. "It was *my* choice, Levi. It was *my* vision. And what I really do not need is you coming back and telling me what that life should *really* look like."

"I'm not trying—"

"Yes, you are!" She closed the gap between them, getting in his face, the heat and scent of her swamping him, turning all the anger inside him into fierce, hot need. "You have to stop being so angry! You have to open your goddamn eyes and see."

But what was there to see? The same shitty neighborhood. The same shitty future he'd always feared. Where all his hopes and his dreams, the positivity that had gotten him through the first time around, were nothing but ashes at his feet. Where he couldn't fix anything or make anything better. Where nothing he did made any difference at all.

Where he'd killed someone.

"See what?" He kept his voice harsh and cold. "That Royal is just as shitty as it was when I left? That your life is better without me than it ever was when I was there? That there's nothing left there for me, nothing left there at all?"

Behind the anger in her eyes, pain glittered bright and sharp.

"Of course there's something there for you—me. Or am I not good enough for you now? Am I too low-rent?" Her gown tightened across her chest as she heaved in a breath. "I'm just an ex-slut, the owner of a crappy tattoo parlor, nothing like you expected, right?"

The look in her face, the edges in all those terrible words cut him like knives. Forcing him to acknowledge a truth that he didn't otherwise have the guts to acknowledge, a truth that yawned deep and wide inside him.

We love you. I love you.

That was Rachel, loyal to the bitter end. Here because of a promise she'd made to him, not because she'd actually wanted to come.

And all he'd done was trap her. Take away her choice, scorn the life she'd created for herself. Something he was doing even here, even now.

Christ, he'd thought that giving her the studio had been so supremely unselfish of him, such a grand fucking gesture. But it wasn't. Not when all he'd been thinking was that it didn't matter in the grand scheme of things. That he could easily spare one building for her little art gallery or "whatever."

No, that hadn't been unselfish of him. It had been the opposite.

And now he had to acknowledge that terrible truth, had to find the courage to face it.

It wasn't that she wasn't good enough for him.

It was the other way around.

He was a selfish, angry ex-con.

He was a murderer.

There was no scenario in which he'd be good enough for Rachel.

No universe in which he would ever deserve her.

His anger curdled inside him, seeping away, and there was nothing to replace it this time. Leaving him with the knowledge that without anger filling him up, he was nothing but a hollow shell.

"No," he said, his voice sounding weird and empty. "You don't understand. You were never any of those things to me. And I'm not blind. I can see. I know what I am." He took a step away from her, putting some distance between them. "And that's why I have to do this."

The ferocity was dying out of her eyes now, as if she'd sensed the change in him. "Levi. Please. Let's talk about this."

He shook his head. "I'm done talking, Sunny. I'm sorry, but this is all I have left."

She reached for him, putting a hand on his arm, her touch making everything inside him ache. "But I told you it's not. You have me."

He stared at her a long moment, the emptiness settling right down into his soul.

She was right; she had to choose her own life, her way. Which meant it was best that he not be part of it. Best that she forget all about him.

Best that she turn around and walk out of his life forever.

Unfortunately, he suspected that there was only one way to make her do that and that was to cut her loose.

So he moved his arm away, letting her hand slide free. "I'm sorry," he said, hard and cold. "But maybe you're right. Maybe you're not enough for me anymore."

He made himself watch her expression crack. Made himself watch the pain in her dark eyes shatter into a thousand glittering shards.

And he stood there and made himself watch as she turned her back on him and walked out of the boardroom without a word.

Leaving him alone with his plans.

Chapter 18

Rachel caught a cab straight home. It seemed pointless hanging around at a party with the broken pieces of her heart knocking around inside her chest, cutting her with every step she took.

Maybe you're not enough for me anymore.

He didn't think that about her. He didn't.

She leaned her head against the window of the cab, watching the city go past in a blur of neon.

No, he couldn't. She'd flung those words at him because she was angry, because he refused to see what was right in front of his face. That she was here for him and so were Gideon and the others, and they didn't need him to be anyone other than who he was. Neither did she.

Those plans of his . . . She didn't think they were really what he wanted for Royal or for himself. Because if he did, he would have talked to people in the neighborhood before he'd developed them, talked to Gideon, to her. And he would have listened to what everyone had to say.

But he didn't, and he hadn't. He'd carried on, letting anger drive him, blind him.

Her eyes filled with tears.

She'd hoped at the end that confronting him with her past would have made him see, but it hadn't. She'd had to watch helplessly as his anger drained away, to be replaced by a cold kind of nothingness that had made her chest hurt.

So no, she hadn't believed it when he'd told her she wasn't enough, especially not after he'd helped her deal with all those horrible, painful memories. What broke her, what had cracked her all the way through, was the fact that he'd lied. That he'd said those deliberately hurtful words so that she'd walk away from him.

And she had. Not because he'd been needlessly cruel, but because he'd been so deliberate about it. Because he'd chosen blindness and anger over clear vision and love.

Yeah, that was the bit that hurt especially. That he'd turned away from the fact that she loved him.

You could have stayed. You could have fought.

She could have, but then she'd told him already that he didn't have to do this. That he didn't need to be anything more than what he was. What more could she have said? What else could she have done?

The next step had to be his, and he hadn't taken it.

He'd turned away instead.

She'd made her choice, and so had he. Pity it hadn't been the one she'd wanted him to make.

By the time she got back to the apartment, her chest was aching and sore, and her cheeks were shiny with tears. But beneath her pain was a new kind of purpose.

So her friendship and then her abortive relationship with Levi were over and done with permanently. They'd tried it, and it hadn't worked, both of them too damaged by their pasts to make it work. In a way it was a relief, wasn't it?

It meant she could move on. Put him behind her. Start again from scratch.

She'd never feel the same way about another man, but that didn't mean her life was over. There was still plenty more living to do.

She kept telling herself that as she walked into the apartment, trying not to look at the evidence of their fledgling life together all around her. Instead she made straight for the bedroom, tearing off the dress she'd put on with such hope, then dressing in her favorite jeans and top. Then she flung open the drawers of the dresser and began filling her suitcase with clothes and the few things she wanted to take with her.

It didn't take her long to pack.

On her way out the door, she paused briefly in the main room, looking at the little knickknacks of hers that Levi had gathered and displayed so beautifully for her. But no, those pieces were part of the past, and she had a future in front of her.

A future without him in it.

She swallowed and turned away, heading toward the door. She wasn't going to take them. It was better they stayed in the past with him.

Rachel didn't look back as she headed out of the apartment, and, fifteen minutes later, dragging her suitcase behind her and feeling as if she'd been kicked very hard in the stomach, she arrived at another familiar door.

She knocked, hoping like hell either Gideon or Zoe was there, relief filling her when she heard a footstep and the door opened a crack.

"Rach?" Zoe jerked the chain off the door and pulled it open, her eyes widening as she took in the suitcase by Rachel's side. "Oh no. Was the party that lame?"

At another point in her life, Rachel would have laughed.

Instead she burst into tears.

The apartment was dark and silent when Levi finally got home at some Godforsaken hour of the morning. He was drunk, having tried to fill up the empty space inside him in the time-honored Rush tradition—meaning he'd had too many shots of Grey Goose to count. And hell, he was doing better than his old man; at least the vodka had been top-shelf and not the shit his father used to drink.

But no matter how many shots had gone down, Levi could not seem to fill that empty space in his soul. It was still there, beneath the alcohol and the slaps on the back from the business-men at Novak's function. Beneath the money they'd promised him and the enthusiasm they'd shown.

His development project for Royal Road had been a hit.

And he'd never felt so fucking awful in all his life. Not even when he'd stared at the guy he'd just pulled off Rachel and punched, the one who'd fallen on the pavement and hit his head. Who'd just lain there, unmoving, making Levi's stomach drop away and dread curl in his heart.

No, this was worse than that.

It felt as if his heart wasn't there at all, swallowed by all that emptiness.

But he'd done the right thing, that's what he had to keep telling himself. He'd let Rachel go, and that was the most im-portant part of it. He'd set her free. Free from the anger he couldn't seem to shake. Free from him.

Slamming the door of the apartment behind him, Levi chucked his keys onto the console table nearby and stumbled into the main room. He didn't want to go to the bedroom. Didn't want to face the potential emptiness of the room, the certainty that Rachel wasn't there, that she'd gone. Which made the couch the best bet, at least in his current condition.

But as he lurched into the room, he caught a glimpse of a shape sitting in Rachel's gran's chair, and his heart suddenly in-flated and shot up and out of his chest like a balloon.

"Sunny?" he said hoarsely, desperately. "Is that you?"

"No." The voice was male and deep and undeniably Gideon's.

Levi's heart plummeted back into the empty shell of his body and broke into pieces as it landed

You dumb fuck. As if she'd ever come back to you after you turned her away.

"What the hell are you doing here?" Levi demanded, bitter disappointment curdling in his gut.

"Sit down." Gideon said, his tone neutral.

Levi wanted to argue, but he couldn't be fucked. So he did as he was told, collapsing on the couch opposite where Gideon was sitting. "How the hell did you get in?"

Gideon ignored him. "You're drunk."

"Yeah, and?"

"You're never drunk."

"First time for everything." Levi leaned back against the couch and flung an arm over his face. The room was spinning around him, and he was spinning with it.

There was a terrible silence, and Levi wished Gideon would go the hell away and leave him in peace.

Sadly Gideon showed no signs of doing so.

"Rachel told me what happened," Gideon said at last.

Great. Fucking wonderful.

"Before you give me a damn lecture," Levi said, "I let her go. She's free of me. I won't touch her; I won't come near her ever again."

Another hideous silence.

"Why?" Gideon asked.

Levi took his arm away, squinting in the dark, trying to make out the other man's form. "What do you mean why? Wasn't that what you wanted from the beginning?"

Gideon sighed. "What I wanted was for you not to hurt her. For you to see what's right in front of your fucking face."

"Oh Christ, spare me. Rachel's already given me that fucking sermon—"

"You love her, Levi."

What a goddamned stupid thing to say. "Well, of course I love her. She's my friend."

"No, dipshit. You're *in* love with her."

It didn't feel like a revelation. In fact, his broken heart ached with the truth of that particular statement, the pain of it like the pain of his father's dismissal, knowing he'd been abandoned for a bottle of alcoholic fucking liquid. "Yeah, and?"

Gideon shifted in the chair, the springs creaking. "You're being particularly dumb today, Levi. If you love her, why the hell did you let her go?"

Beneath the protecting blanket of alcohol, Levi's anger stirred. "Christ, why the hell do you think? I've done nothing but hurt her since day one. All I wanted to do was help, to fix our entire fucking lives, but in the end I just forced her into doing things she didn't want." He gave a bitter laugh. "I was selfish. I was patronizing. I was angry. And she doesn't deserve that."

"No, she doesn't." Gideon's voice was quiet. "And neither do you."

Christ, his chest hurt. Nothing about this was good. He needed more vodka. Or maybe he just needed to close his eyes and sleep and pretend this day had never happened. "What the hell are you talking about now?"

"You've had it shit, Levi; no one can argue with that. But you've paid your dues. You don't need to punish yourself anymore. So don't you think it's time to stop thinking about the shit, and start thinking about the good?"

"I'm not punishing myself, and there's no good."

"Bullshit. Sure, your actions killed some motherfucking, drug-dealing scum. You can keep beating yourself up about that if you really want. But Rachel's the good, and you know it."

You have me.

His chest ached like a bastard, and nothing he did seemed to make it better. "Yeah, and she's too good for me," he said roughly, unable to keep the frayed edges of his voice together. "And I've got nothing to give her anyway."

Gideon let out another sigh. "That's bullshit too. You've got plenty to give her."

"What? Anger? Some fucking plans she didn't want?"

"You, Levi. You have you."

Levi wanted to laugh at the simplicity of it. The stupid simplicity of it. "Jesus Christ, you don't understand. Didn't you hear me when I said she was too—"

"You're not a coward, Levi Rush." Gideon cut him off with quiet authority. "Don't be one now."

A coward? But he wasn't being a coward. He was only accepting the truth. That no amount of fixing or helping or being positive ever changed anything.

He wasn't enough, and he never would be.

"I'm not a coward," Levi echoed, the words sounding pathetic and weak in the darkness of the room.

"Then if you're not, if you're any kind of man, you'd get up and go to her and you'd beg her forgiveness. Then you'd lay your heart at her feet." The springs creaked again, and Gideon's dark figure got up from the chair. "Just my two cents. For what it's worth."

Then he walked out the door without another word.

Levi sat there in the dark, staring at nothing. Then he shifted, and something rustled in his pocket. He frowned and put down a hand, drawing out a crumpled packet. Fucking Pixy Stix.

Rachel's the good, and you know it.

He stared at the packet of candy.

She used to buy him packets of the stuff to cheer him up, to make him feel better, the only thing she could afford.

She'd been his sunshine, right from the very first day he'd

seen her open the door of her gran's apartment, when she'd given him a shy smile. He hadn't known how rare those smiles were then. He only knew it had lit something inside him, something that was burning there still.

You have you.

Pathetic. Why would she even want that? After all his anger and all his demands, his refusal to listen to her, his refusal to see.

You're not a coward, Levi Rush . . .

No, of course he wasn't. After all, what would he be afraid of?

Levi blinked as something began to coalesce inside him. A realization and, more than that, a certainty.

Holy shit. He *was* afraid. Afraid of that pain of rejection, that pain of loss. He couldn't remember the number of times he'd cleaned up after his father or taken him to the emergency department for detoxing, or dragged him home from whatever bar he'd passed out in, and Levi had never gotten anything in the way of thanks from the old man. He'd told himself—shit, he'd told Rachel—that it was love that made him do it, and that was enough.

But it wasn't enough. He wanted more. He wanted to know he made a difference. He wanted to know he mattered.

No. You want to be loved.

His heart gave one heavy, hard beat inside his chest, the raw pieces of it rubbing together like the sharp edges of a bone in a broken leg. The realization hurt. It hurt like fuck. But it was true.

You fucking idiot. She was right. It was there right in front of your face this whole time. What you truly wanted. And you just threw it back in her face.

He went still, a shadow in the dark of the living room.

Gideon had told him to go to her and beg her forgiveness, but he couldn't go now, not reeking of vodka and more pathetic than his father ever had been. And Levi had no problem with begging, but he'd always been more comfortable with action. Now that he thought of it, he had the perfect way of asking her forgiveness. The gesture he should have made the moment he'd gotten out of prison. Made without anger blinding him or the past clouding his vision.

Because he loved her.

Because she was his sunshine and, without her, all he'd ever be was a pathetic, drunken asshole, sitting all alone in the dark.

Rachel got rid of the last client, locking the door of Sugar Ink behind her and turning back to clear up the last of the gear. Xavier had gone off to the local club, Anonymous, and had tried to drag her with him, but she'd refused. She hadn't told him about her and Levi, and, considering Xavier's distrust of Levi, she'd thought it best not to broach the topic until maybe Xavier asked.

Which she hoped wouldn't be anytime soon.

She went over to her station, tidying various things, keeping her thoughts very firmly on nothing in particular and not on the prickly, dry feeling behind her eyes or the dull ache in the place her heart used to be.

It was difficult, but thinking about her plans for the art gallery helped, as did thinking about the impending meeting she had with the Royal Road Outreach Center, to discuss the possibility of art classes for the kids there.

She was just getting her inks in order when there was a loud battering at the door.

Probably just another drunken asshole desperate to get a tat while the mood took him. Luckily she knew just how to deal with those.

Except as she approached the door, it wasn't just another drunken asshole.

It was Levi.

She stopped dead, staring at him, her mouth going utterly dry. And considering she only had pieces where her heart should be, it was ridiculous how the stupid thing suddenly started beating, hard and fast, as if it were running a race it was desperate to win.

He'd stopped knocking, the fierce intensity of his gaze holding her fast.

She wasn't going to open the door, because why should she? He'd made his choice. A choice that wasn't her.

Yet, she moved to the door all the same, unlocking it, then opening it.

And suddenly he was there, moving toward her, pulling the door shut behind him before reaching for her, gathering her up in his arms, sliding his hands into her hair, and tipping her head back, covering her mouth.

She didn't want to return the kiss, wanted to push him away, because she had no idea what this was or what it meant, and she couldn't bear it. But her head was falling back all the same, and her mouth was opening under his, letting him in, the kiss so sweet and hot and so painfully tender it brought tears to her eyes.

She didn't want to move. She wanted to stay here like this forever.

But he was lifting his head and letting her go, putting her from him and standing back.

"Levi . . ." She couldn't finish. Didn't want to hear yet another rejection from him.

"I need to give you something," he said, and he reached around and took something from his back pocket. More paper like the title deed he'd given her before, except this looked like a whole stack of them.

"What are they? And why are you here? What—"

"Look at them, Sunny. Then I'll explain."

Reluctantly she took the papers from him and glanced down at them. They were indeed title deeds, to a whole lot of buildings, including the apartment building he owned.

And then she saw the name of the owner.

Rachel Hamilton.

She looked up at him in shock. "What the hell is this?"

There was tension in his expression, an uncertainty she'd never seen there before. "What it looks like. The deeds to all my buildings. Or should I say your buildings now. They're yours to do whatever you want with them."

The shock deepened. "But . . . What about your development plans? I thought that was what you wanted?"

"No." His gaze never wavered from hers. "What I wanted was you. It's what I've always wanted, from the moment I first saw you. The moment you smiled at me. It's just taken me fucking years to realize it."

She blinked at him, not quite understanding. "But all those plans . . . You said they were all you had left."

"I *did* think that was all I had left. But you're right; I was blind. I couldn't see what was in front of me, because I was too angry and too afraid." He didn't move, and yet she could feel the sudden, leashed intensity of him getting stronger, more powerful. As if he wanted desperately to touch her and yet wasn't letting himself. "But I see now, Sunny. I really see. And what I see is you."

It was too much to hope for, wasn't it?

"I thought I wasn't enough." Because she couldn't help herself, couldn't stop from asking.

He didn't look away. "That was bullshit. I hope you know that. I was just afraid. Dad never wanted anything but the bottle, and he hated me for taking that away from him. And nothing I did seemed to fix him; nothing I did helped. And nothing I did helped you either." His hands were in fists at his sides. "You've built a life for yourself, Sunny. And after what you went through . . . Jesus, you don't know how much I respect your strength and your independence. But this life of yours and this business you built . . . You did it without me." He took a breath. "You don't need me. I'm just the son of a drunk. A fucking idiot who killed a man. What do I have to offer that you can't do yourself?"

Her throat closed up, the broken pieces of her heart all jamming together, trying to make themselves whole again.

"Yeah, you are a fucking idiot." Her voice was hoarse. "Why do you think this business is here? Why do you think I built the goddamned life I have now? It's because of you, Levi Rush. Because you believed I could do whatever I wanted. Because you taught me the power of dreams. Which makes this . . . *All* of this is because of you."

The look of shock on his face somehow broke her paralysis, and she took a step toward him, bridging the gap between them. The gap that was, even after all this time, not so very great after all.

And then she was right up close, and it was she who put her arms around him, she who drew him closer. "After you'd gone, I used to hear your voice at night, telling me what I could do. Showing me that there was more to life than what I'd ever imagined. And I couldn't let myself just waste away and do nothing. So I found a way, Levi. You were my inspiration. You're the reason this place is here, so don't you tell me you did nothing. Don't tell me you never helped."

His hands rose, cupping her face between his palms. "Christ, Sunny." His voice sounded as hoarse as hers was. "I love you."

And all the broken pieces of her heart slipped back together, easily and naturally and without any pain at all.

Just like that.

She rose up on her toes, pressing her mouth to his, kissing him sweetly and lightly. "And I love you. I always did, Levi. Always."

He stroked her cheekbones with his thumbs, sending waves of heat through her. "You don't know how long I've wanted to hear you say that. And I meant what I said about these deeds. They're yours to do whatever you want with them. I don't care about those plans; as long as I have you, nothing else matters."

"Well, those can wait for now." She turned her cheek into his touch. "What changed? What made you suddenly decide to come here?"

His smile turned rueful. "Gideon came over in the middle of the night and called me a dipshit."

"Oh, hell. I'm sorry. I went over there last night because I didn't know what else to do."

"I'm not sorry. He told me what I needed to hear. Even if the person I should have been listening to was you all along."

"Damn straight you should have." She stepped closer, sliding her arms around his waist and clasping her hands in the small of his back. "Now, since you've come to my tattoo parlor, that technically means you have to get a tattoo."

He smiled, his beautiful mouth curling in the way it used to all those years ago, when he was her friend. Her hot, sexy friend who used to make her weak at the knees and whom she used to dream about at night. "I'm okay with that. I know exactly what I want."

"Oh, yes, that's right. A sun?"

"How did you know?"

She shifted her hips against his. "And the placement?"

He lifted a hand, placed it over his heart. "Here."

She bent, placing her mouth directly over the spot, kissing him. "I think I can do that."

"I'm afraid I can't pay you." There was a wicked gleam in his eye. "I left my wallet at home."

Rachel grinned. "Then how about you get in that tattoo chair and show me what else you have?"

So he did.

Turned out it was enough to last them both a lifetime.

Epilogue

Levi rolled over sleepily, reaching out for the warm body that was usually there. And came up empty-handed.

Dammit.

Opening his eyes, he frowned when he saw the empty pillow beside him. Then he checked the clock. It was six A.M. Where the hell was Rachel? She wasn't the world's earliest riser, and, normally at this time of the morning, she'd still be fast asleep.

Briefly he debated going back to sleep since being up at this hour wasn't his favorite thing either, but then he shoved back the sheet and got out of bed instead. Just to make sure she hadn't slipped in the shower, banged her head, and now was lying unconscious somewhere.

He was heading toward the bathroom when he saw a movement through the double doors of their bedroom. In the room that he'd once thought would make a great studio for her.

It was still empty.

Because at nights, when she was doing business-type stuff for Sugar Ink, she joined him in the main room, her laptop on her knee. Or they'd be over at Gideon's, discussing the development plans for Royal, the ones they were all doing together, with Zee and Zoe and Tamara too.

It was all coming together, slowly but surely. Rachel and Gideon and the others had been liaising with the neighborhood, while Levi dealt with the money side of things. With any luck the investments he'd plugged some of his cash into would start paying out soon, and then he could get started doing serious stock market speculation. Seemed he had a talent when it came to making money. Fucking shame to waste it.

His latest task, though, had been to find an architect to do some concepts for them, and finally he thought he'd found the perfect one. He was going to meet with her today and sound her out.

Yeah, they'd been busy. No time to think about the one empty room in their apartment.

He wandered over to the doors and looked in. And sure enough Rachel was standing in the middle of the empty room, staring up at the skylight, a frown on her face.

For a second he just stood there, watching her. Because she was naked and beautiful and always had the ability to make his heart stop dead in his chest.

Not to mention making his dick go from zero to one hundred in seconds flat.

"Sunny?" he said after a moment. "You okay?"

She stared up at the skylight a moment longer, then turned to glance at him. "We'll have to do something about that skylight."

"Yeah? What?"

"Get a blind for it or something."

He wandered over to her, pulling her into his arms, relishing the heat of her skin against his. "Why? And why are you standing here, at six o'clock in the morning, talking about fucking blinds for the skylight?"

The smile she gave him was like the slow rise of the sun, a dawning of warmth and excitement over her face.

His Sunny. Fuck, he loved her.

"I just thought of what we could use this room for."

"Oh?"

She leaned against him, sliding her palms up his chest and over his shoulders, linking her fingers around the back of his neck. "I want a family, Levi."

He got it. Instantly. And a shock of intense, electric sensation went through him. "You want this to be a nursery, don't you?"

Her eyes were dark and wide, and he would have given her anything and everything in that moment. The sun, the moon, and all the stars in the sky. "I know we've got the others; I know that. But you and I, we've never had anything that's ours. Never had a family of our own. And I think we deserve one." The look on her face became hesitant, a little uncertain. "So, yeah, I'd like this to be a nursery. That is . . . if you want it to be too."

His throat closed up, his heart drawing in tight, and he couldn't find his voice to speak. So he gave her the only answer he could.

He bent, pressed his mouth to hers, giving her the kind of kiss that promised the world, holding her as tightly as the sensation crowding for room inside him.

And then, when he finally found his voice again to speak, he whispered against her mouth:

"I do."

Acknowledgments

I'd like to thank Martin Biro for his wonderful editing. Helen Breitwieser for her wonderful agenting. Maisey Yates for her endless support. And to Nicole Helm for reading and loving even when I didn't.

If you enjoyed *Wrong for Me,* be sure not
to miss the next book in Jackie Ashenden's
scorching Motor City Royals series

SIN FOR ME

Read on for a special sneak peek.

A Kensington trade paperback and e-book
on sale April 2017!

Chapter 1

Zoe sat on one of the coveted corner couches in the darkest part of Anonymous, sipping her frozen blackberry margarita and nodding her head up and down in time to the hard thumping bass that vibrated through the nightclub.

Anonymous had only been going a year, but its gritty, industrial atmosphere—the huge vaulting space used to be some kind of factory that had been abandoned along with seemingly half the buildings in Detroit—was a major draw for the young, cool, and often tragically hip.

It was Saturday night, which meant the place was packed with miles of tattoos, more piercings than a death-metal concert, and so many beards and man buns she might as well have been in Portland. Not that she minded any of those things.

In fact, it was the whole reason she was here in the first place. By herself. Without anyone cramping her style.

Anyone being Gideon Black.

She sat back on the couch, surveying the heaving crowd on the dance floor in the middle of the club, then checking out the long metal length of the bar on the other side of it, just to be sure a familiar tall and hulking figure wasn't lurking around.

But no, seemed he'd believed her when she'd told him she was joining Tamara and Rachel for a girls' night at Rachel's place.

Excellent.

Zoe picked up her margarita and took another hefty sip, scanning around for any likely looking dudes.

There were lots of guys, obviously, and more than a few were her kind of tall, dark, and handsome. Lots to choose from, in other words. But she wanted her first one-night stand—her first anything, really—to be with someone she kind of liked.

What does it matter? It's only one night.

True. She wasn't there to pick someone to have a relationship with. She only wanted someone hot who could make her forget her stupid, goddamn unrequited love for Gideon. A love that wouldn't ever be returned, at least not in the way she wanted it to be. Because he pretty much saw her as a little sister and nothing more.

Well, you are *his little sister.*

Not technically. She was his little *foster* sister. And she'd only been that for a year when she was seven and they'd lived in the same foster family. Then he'd turned seventeen and aged out of the system. So really it didn't count.

It still pissed her off that he refused to see her as anything different, though.

No, scratch *pissed.* She was fucking furious. Furious at him, somewhat unfairly, but mainly with herself. Because she'd felt that way about him for ten years, and nothing had changed.

Oh no, wait. Something had changed. He'd told her a couple of weeks ago to stop following him around all the time. As if she were some kind of stupid, eager puppy.

You are *a stupid eager puppy.*

Zoe swallowed half her margarita, balefully looking at the crowd around her.

Ever since she and Gideon had first come to Detroit from Chicago, she'd been at his side, living in their apartment above the garage while he'd protected her, looked out for her, made a family for her with Rachel and Zee and Levi. And she'd been happy. Safe, protected. Being near Gideon, knowing he was there, had been all she'd wanted.

But lately she'd started to find that safety and stability a little too stifling. A little bit too much like a cage. She'd started to think about what she wanted to do with her life, about the direction she was headed. And after watching Zee find Tamara, and Rachel and Levi find each other again, she'd begun to think about her own love life—which was nonexistent.

Currently you are headed to Nowheresville via Virginforever Town.

Zoe glowered.

The leash Gideon kept her on was short and feeling shorter by the day, especially in the past month or so. And his getting pissed off at her, for following him around and daring to ask questions about her future, hurt.

Something needed to change.

Hell, she hadn't been a rebellious teenager, not with Gideon's being a very strict big-brother stand-in, so maybe she was due a little rebellion time. Like now.

Attention-seeking much?

Zoe sniffed and drained her margarita, putting the glass back down on the low metal table in front of her with a click.

She wasn't seeking attention; she was just trying to do what any twenty-five-year-old woman would. Have a normal damn life, and part of that normal damn life included going out to a nightclub, getting drunk, then getting laid.

Not necessarily in that order.

Across the dance floor, over by the bar, her attention snagged on a tall guy with broad shoulders and dark hair. Pretty hot looking. No tats, but then you couldn't have everything. He made eye contact with her, and she found herself blushing and looking away, which was super annoying.

Her experience with men amounted to checking out hot dudes on Tumblr and talking to her friends in a few of the online forums she frequented. Though really, who knew what sex *they* were? She was assuming they were guys, but on the Internet it was never safe to assume anything.

Whatever. Her experience with actual men in real life was nil. If you didn't count Zee and Levi, which she didn't.

Maybe she should have brought Rachel and Tamara along with her as wing women. Then again, they probably wouldn't approve of what Zoe was doing, and she'd prefer to keep it on the down-low anyway.

It was bad enough *everyone* knew about her stupid Gideon crush. Having other people witness her general man-ineptness would be a blow to her pride she didn't think she could take.

She glanced back at the bar again to see what the guy who'd looked at her was doing, steeling herself to not look away this time. And her heart gave a small hop inside her chest.

Because he was coming toward her.

Holy shit.

She reached out for her margarita glass, but sadly there was no more left, so she had to fiddle awkwardly with it as the guy came closer and she tried not to blush or grin at him like a lunatic.

Man, he was pretty nice looking. Didn't have Gideon's air of gentle but firm authority or his compelling charisma, but there was something about this guy that she liked anyway. He was certainly approachable. At least, he was approaching her.

He wasn't a local—that was for sure—since locals knew who she was and who was protecting her and liked their balls to remain in place. So obviously this guy had to be from somewhere else. Which was fine. In fact, better than fine. It suited her purposes nicely.

She swallowed as he came up to the table, suddenly aware that she was pushing herself back in her seat. Stupid. She needed to chill the hell out.

"Hey," the guy said, giving her a very direct smile. "Looks like you're all out of . . . whatever was in that glass of yours."

"Blackberry f-frozen margarita," she said, the words coming out in a helpless, stammery rush. "And . . . uh . . . yeah, I am."

"Can I get you another?" His eyes were blue, and they roamed over her with disconcerting frankness, as if he was sizing her up.

Okay, this is your moment of glory. Do it.

Zoe gave him what she hoped was a natural-looking smile and not a fixed rictus, which was what it probably was. "Um, sure. That would be great."

Gideon was not happy. Anonymous was the last place on earth he wanted to be at one A.M. on a Saturday morning, but, unfortunately, since Zoe had not in fact gone to Rachel's for a girls' night like she'd told him, he was going to have to brave the revoltingly hipster crowds in order to check it out.

It wasn't that he didn't like nightclubs. He just didn't like them with Zoe in them. On her own.

Normally he was a chilled-out guy; never let his temper rule him. Was calm and considered and patient. But right now he didn't feel very fucking calm. Or considered or patient.

Right now, he felt fucking pissed.

The queue outside the door to the club was insane, and the bouncer was new, which meant he didn't know Gideon and didn't realize that Gideon basically ruled Royal Road—a fact that should have granted him automatic entry without any dicking around.

Sadly for both Gideon's temper and the new bouncer's reputation, there was dicking around.

Eventually, after a tense five-minute standoff, Gideon cowed the bouncer into submission with a promise to report him to Jimmy, the guy who owned Anonymous, before banging open the doors and stalking into the club.

The noise and the heat of well over a hundred people all dancing, drinking, and doing various other, probably illegal things hit him like the front of a particularly violent thunderstorm, fraying the already tenuous grip he had on his temper.

He didn't know if she was here or not, but he was hoping for her sake that she was, because he was coming to the end of his considerable patience.

The past few months had been a real fucking trial, what with Zee and his goddamn father threatening them all, and then Levi's getting out of jail and having a few issues adjusting. Which in turn had unfortunately attracted the attention of the very last person on earth Gideon wanted attention from. The person Gideon had been protecting Zoe from for the last ten years.

It hadn't been Levi's fault. Levi didn't know Zoe's or Gideon's background, or what had gone down with Zoe's mother. But still. Oliver fucking Novak was now sniffing around Royal because of Levi's development plans, which meant Gideon didn't want Zoe going AWOL, and certainly not at night.

Yeah, she better be here. He didn't know what had gotten into her, whether it was some kind of late puberty/rebellion thing or what, but that shit was getting old, and she didn't understand the danger she was in.

Which means you have to tell her.

Gideon glowered at the crowds on the dance floor, scanning around for a small, delicately built young woman with black curls, big golden eyes, and glasses.

He had his reasons for not telling her, the main one being

that he hadn't wanted her living her life in fear. Then again, if she was going to pull this kind of shit, then clearly they were going to have to have a discussion. Novak hadn't taken an interest in Levi's plans purely to shine up a down-and-out neighborhood for his senatorial bid. He'd chosen Royal for a reason, and maybe that reason was Zoe.

Gideon moved around the perimeter dance floor, trying to spot her. It didn't look like she was there, though it was a little difficult to tell, what with all the writhing bodies. Lights were flashing, sparkling off sequins and sliding over glistening skin. A woman ran a hand along his arm on her way toward the dancers, giving him a suggestive look.

He shook his head and, ignoring her pout of disappointment, shifted his attention over to the long, metal, industrial-looking bar. No sign of Zoe there either.

Last place to look was the seating area at the back of the massive space, and, if she wasn't there, he was going to have to figure out just where the hell else she might be, because there weren't many other places in Royal she would have gone to.

Worry began to thread through his anger, and he had to fight the very real urge to start picking people up and flinging them out of his way.

He'd protected Zoe ever since she'd been a kid, and he'd be damned if he was going to fail in that duty now just because she was having a teenage tantrum.

The seating area in Anonymous was composed of black leather sectional couches and small metal coffee tables. The lighting consisted of exposed, old-fashioned filament bulbs and glass shades. There was graffiti on the brick walls, some of it put there by clubbers, all adding to the gritty, industrial vibe of the place.

He checked out the huddled groups around the tables, and then, his anger beginning to flex like a body builder on steroids, the pairs entwined in the darker areas toward the back.

Not that it should matter to him either way whether Zoe was with anyone or not, but still. He didn't like the thought of it. She was too young for that kind of stuff, too innocent. Jesus, if some fucking asshole had picked her up, there was going to be hell to pay.

But Zoe wasn't one of any of the entwined couples, which made him feel relieved and yet even more worried. Because if she wasn't here, then where the fuck was she?

Connect with U s

Visit us online at
KensingtonBooks.com
to read more from your favorite authors, see books
by series, view reading group guides, and more.

for sneak peeks, chances to win books and prize packs,
and to share your thoughts with other readers.

facebook.com/kensingtonpublishing
twitter.com/kensingtonbooks

Tell us what you think!

To share your thoughts, submit a review,
or sign up for our eNewsletters, please visit:
KensingtonBooks.com/TellUs.